Sushi and Sourdough

SUSHI *and* SOURDOUGH

A NOVEL

Tooru J. Kanazawa

UNIVERSITY OF WASHINGTON PRESS

Seattle & London

To the dauntless Issei
whose "blood, sweat and tears,"
against impossible odds
helped build America strong

Copyright © 1989 by Tooru J. Kanazawa
Printed in the United States of America
Composition, printing, and binding by Edwards Brothers, Ann Arbor
Design by Audrey Meyer

Library of Congress Cataloging-in-Publication Data

Kanazawa, Tooru J.
    Sushi and sourdough: a novel/Tooru J. Kanazawa.
        p.   cm.
    ISBN 0-295-96713-7
    I. Title
    PS3561.A458S8 1989   89-35376
    813'.54—dc20   CIP

The paper used in this publication meets the minimum requirements of
American National Standard for Information Sciences — Permanence of Paper for Printed Library Materials, ANSI Z39.48-1984.

∞

Contents

AUTHOR'S NOTE

THIS IS AN ACCOUNT OF THE ADVENTURES of the Issei and Nisei in the Territory of Alaska during the gold rush days at the turn of the century. Its purpose is to fill some blank pages in the history of Japanese immigrants to the United States. Much of it is based on my own experience of being a Nisei growing up in the frontier gold-mining town of Juneau. Although single males were scattered throughout what was then the Territory of Alaska, it was in the towns, especially in the "Panhandle" of Southeastern Alaska, that families established what might be described as nuclei of communities. Juneau had a representative mix of married families and the more numerous single males.

Although I was born in Spokane, Washington, on November 12, 1906, our family moved to Douglas in 1912, and about two years later across Gastineau Channel to Juneau, where my father was a barber. My observations and interactions with the Issei, in particular with the itinerant salmon-cannery workers, planted within me the seed of a desire to tell the story of our Alaskan immigrant fathers and mothers as interpreted through my eyes and heart.

What took so long? Well, we Kanazawas are slow to mature. Sometimes as long as eighty years.

Our destinies can be greatly influenced by the period in which we are born. When I graduated from the University of Washington with a B.A. in journalism in 1931, I entered the marketplace in the heart of the depression. In 1932, I covered the Olympic Games for the Los Angeles *Rafu Shimpo*. After several years of driving a truck for W. H. Fukuyama's Juneau Laundry, on the basis of sales to the *Christian Science Monitor* and *Thrilling Sports* I moved to New York in October of 1940. I thereby escaped the evacuation of 110,000 Japanese Americans from the Pacific Coast in 1942.

My older brother, who was evacuated with other Japanese from Juneau, died in the Lordsburg, New Mexico, alien detention camp. My widowed mother and two sisters, with four and three children, respectively, were detained at Poston Relocation Center I in Arizona.

In 1943, at the age of thirty-six, I volunteered for the 442nd Regimental Combat Team. I was awarded a Bronze Star for meritorious service as a radio operator assigned to rifle companies and as a citations writer. The years since were spent in working and raising a family of three children.

To round out the sagas of Jujiro Wada, Frank Yasuda, and other Alaskan sourdoughs, I have relied on source material from Pierre Berton's *The Klondike Fever*, William R. Hunt's *North of 53°*, and Kazuo Ito's orally recorded *Issei*. In periodicals, Frank Cotter's three-part article on Wada in the *Japanese American Courier* and articles by Irving McK. Reed on Yasuda and Robert N. DeArmond on Wada in *Alaska Magazine* were informative. Mr. DeArmond, a historian, was particularly cooperative in providing details about Juneau personalities.

Nora Marks Dauenhauer and Richard Dauenhauer, authors of *Haa Shuká, Our Ancestors: Tlingit Oral Narratives*, were especially helpful. Mr. Dauenhauer's long paper on "Conflicting Visions in Alaskan Education" was singularly edifying.

I am also indebted to Naomi Pascal, Editor-in-Chief of the University of Washington Press, for her belief in the significance of the story and her patience and valuable editorial guidance in helping to organize the material that resulted in the creation of this book. Julidta Tarver, Managing Editor, Audrey Meyer, Art Director, and their colleagues at the University of Washington Press, and Lane Morgan, copyeditor, were most supportive in the final preparation of the manuscript.

I am deeply indebted to bilingual David Matsushita, who checked the Japanese for accuracy and contributed some of the philosophical sayings of the early immigrants among whom he grew up. I thank Bill Hosokawa for his comments and suggestions made after reading an early draft of this work.

Thanks to my wife Masako Mae for her patience over these many long years.

Tooru J. Kanazawa
New York City

Sushi and Sourdough

I

Money Grows on Trees

IN JULY 1897, a week before the S.S. *Portland* docked with a ton of gold from the Klondike, a barber named Matajiro Fuse arrived in Seattle. Rumors of a gold strike had run like a tantalizing vein through the dark days of the previous winter, days made sinister by a prolonged depression. In his San Francisco shop, Fuse had listened to this seductive call.

He packed up his barber tools, took the ferry to Oakland, and caught a train to Seattle. He carried a box of sushi and— his concession to American life—instead of sake a bottle of Rainier beer. His meager fare for the trip did not faze him. In his wanderings up and down the West Coast he had accustomed himself to privation.

Fuse stepped off the train into a big sigh of steam. Adjusting the backpack and bedroll, his only possessions, he walked through the dim, echoing cavern of the King Street Station. He emerged into an invigorating sunlit morning and breathed deeply, like a man walking into a new world. A cool, humid breeze came up from Puget Sound and nudged his back as he headed east.

The high sunlight of summer revealed a handsome face. His eyes were level and his left, arched eyebrow was heavier than his right, giving him a slightly quizzical expression. His mustache was thick and turned up alertly at the ends as if to challenge the world. Black hair sprouted through his battered gray felt hat like devil's horns, an unkempt touch in an otherwise tidy costume.

His beige corduroy pants contrasted with the denim overalls so many of the itinerant workers wore, and the pants and his brown plaid lumber jacket were neat and clean.

This was Fuse at thirty-four, or as the Japanese count, Meiji *sanjyu nen* (thirty). When the Emperor mounted Japan's throne in 1868 (Fuse was born four years earlier), he called his reign Meiji, the Era of Enlightenment. The Japanese counted the years from that date, like the Christian A.D. The Issei, first-generation immigrants, brought with them this tradition of counting their ages in Meiji years.

Fuse walked briskly up Jackson Street, where he felt the heartbeat of the Japanese community, toward a restaurant he remembered. He was buoyed by a hunch that he was close on the heels of a hope and a promise—of gold to be found in Alaska, or was it Canada, he wasn't too sure. He had visions of *hito hata*, raising the flag of success above the family home. Would this be the third year, the end of his *san nen ganbatte kaeru*? (Endure hardships for three years and return successful. This was a saying popular among Japanese immigrants to the United States.)

From a booth facing the restaurant's door he glanced up at the flyspecked menu on the wall and decided on T-bone steak with trimmings, twenty-five cents.

"First, black coffee," he said in Japanese, not paying any attention to the waiter. "Do you have a newspaper?"

"Ah, Fuse-san. We meet again. How are you?"

"Hah! Jiro-san." Fuse recognized the small, stockily built waiter as the teenage immigrant with whom he had piled lumber at the Port Blakely sawmill two summers back, before he left for California.

Jiro Masuda had large round eyes and mobile features that revealed his emotions. A clear skin and plump cheeks tinted like Jonathan apples gave him a baby-like appearance.

"Anything new?" Fuse asked.

Masuda swept his hand across the white apron he was wearing. "This is better than breaking your bones at the sawmill." He gave Fuse's order to the cook. "Plenty of sautéed onions," he said, remembering Fuse's preference. He reached across the counter and brought back a Japanese language newspaper. "Biggest news—about gold discovery in Canada."

"In San Francisco I heard rumors."

"That why you came back?"

Fuse sat back reflectively. "I didn't give it conscious thought. But maybe that was the real reason. Seattle seemed as good a place as any."

"Imademo branke katsugi ka!" Masuda laughed. "Still the blanket roll carrier!" (Like a bindle stiff, or migratory worker carrying his bundle of clothing and blanket. This was a popular expression of the day, in Masuda's jest meaning a wanderer.)

The call bell rang impatiently in the kitchen. Masuda returned with a steak, its fat sizzling from the frying pan.

"Um, that smells good." Fuse's mustache twitched.

As Fuse ate he turned to a headline that said a ship was arriving with the first gold from the new discovery in Canada's Yukon Territory, just across the eastern boundary of Alaska. At some hitherto unknown place that had been given the name of Klondike. In creeks where gold nuggets instead of pebbles lay for the picking.

Would it be a repeat of the disillusionment he had felt after he arrived in America two years ago? A few labor contractors had ventured into the mountain fastnesses of Yamagata Prefecture in the Tohoku Region of northern Japan. They talked of money that grew on trees in the United States, just as Europeans were led to believe that the streets were paved with gold, and the Chinese were told of gold mountains. Fuse had not been convinced enough to sign a contract, but he borrowed two hundred yen (for travel expenses) and took ship for Seattle.

He sat back over a second mug of coffee and rolled a cigarette using tobacco from a bag of Bull Durham and wheatstraw paper. He pulled the yellow drawstring with his teeth. With a touch of complacency he idly observed his fellow diners, who ate with one eye on the minute hand of the wall clock. The regimentation of a steady job was not his style. He smiled, his quizzical expression more pronounced, at fond memories, of his peregrinations as far south as Mexico, all over California, back to Seattle, and now perhaps to Alaska. He was a free spirit unencumbered by family or social obligations.

What was he thinking of! He was losing sight of what he had always said was his primary goal: to make enough money to rejoin his family. But then, what would he do with his money, with his life? It surprised him that he had not projected his life to a profession, back in Japan.

Or, and this was a thought that occurred more and more frequently, should he bring his family to the United States? Then what? Yes, then what?

He looked ruefully over the landscape where he had left his footprints. He was not much better off than when he first set foot on American soil.

Unless he struck it rich!

He thought of his wife, Yaso, so little, less than five feet tall. Her patience, her endurance. He thought of his son, Kennosuke, and his daughter, Miyoshi. How they must have grown! His mind became nostalgic, his heart sentimental. He grunted, drawing a startled glance from Jiro. He shunted this train of thought. This was no time for that. First things first.

His order of business was to find lodging, to dispatch a money order to his wife, and then to luxuriate in a Japanese bath. He had no difficulty finding accommodations, as the itinerant workers who hibernated in Seattle over the winter had long since departed for Alaskan canneries, farms and orchards, sawmills and logging camps and railroads.

He registered for a bunk at twenty-five cents (forty-five cents with meals included) at the Maynard Rooms, one of a dozen hotels and rooming houses in the Japanese community near King Street and Union Depots.

Fuse turned over the mattress and examined the bed-springs for pests. This was a losing battle, for at night the bed-bugs seemed to come out of the walls. They did not bite Fuse because of some chemical makeup of his body, but when they crawled over his skin by the dozen they would awaken him.

Fuse extracted a wrinkled but clean blue flannel shirt, a change of socks, and a two-piece suit of long underwear from his pack. He preferred two-piece underwear for he had learned from experience that when his legs got wet in forest underbrush or wading streams he could make a change to dry clothing without stripping. He packed his selection in his shirt, tucked the roll under his arm, and headed for the bank where he bought a money order to send home. The immigrant's favorite method of sending money home was to entrust it to a close friend from the same town or village, but such was not always available.

Waiting for the bathhouse to open, he strolled around the Japanese business district, which was bounded on the north by Yesler Way and on the south by Dearborn Street, and concentrated in the area from Fourth up to Seventh avenues. Actually this was four blocks long as there was a Maynard Avenue, named after one of Seattle's pioneers, between Sixth and Seventh.

Fuse was surprised at the growth of the community over two years. Besides the rooming houses—some immigrants, often from the same prefecture, rented and shared a house—there were restaurants and noodle shops, Japanese grocery and fish stores, dry goods shops, employment agencies, baggage and express companies, barbershops, laundries—all the businesses that would serve newly arrived immigrants.

Fuse's stroll ended in front of a bathhouse on Sixth Avenue. The *furo* was as much an institution as the community vernacular weekly. It was said that the editor took a bath every evening to keep up with the news. His wife gleaned juicy morsels of gossip in the women's section.

Fuse's boots clattered down the brass-edged steps to the basement of the hotel. He was immersed in the humid air of the bathhouse. On his left as he entered was a counter stacked alternately with a cotton print *tenugui*, or wash cloth, and a bath towel. The proprietor was ironing a shirt. At his back were shelves bearing brown-paper bundles, each package neatly identified with a laundry slip. Fuse paid fifteen cents, picked up his two towels, and entered the bathhouse proper through a screen door backed by a curtain that blocked the eyes of the curious. A spring slammed the light door behind him.

To the right of the entrance were shelves where Fuse placed his boots. He stepped up on the linoleum-covered platform and padded toward a row of wooden lockers ranged against the wall. Beyond these was an alcove with a table and chairs where bathers could relax after their bath and order soft drinks through a window. Hair tonic, bath powder, and several folding fans were set on a shelf. Fuse passed his soiled clothing through the window to be laundered. Shirts cost fifteen or twenty cents, a set of underwear twenty cents, socks ten cents.

From the raised edge of the platform the cement floor sloped down to a drainage hole. On the left was a shower that was no more than a head faucet sticking out of the wall. On the right was the concrete *furo*, about eight inches thick and eight by twelve feet, set against two walls in the corner. One wall was a strong wooden partition open about a foot at the top, over which a mischievous boy or two could peep, drawing squeals from the girls on the other side.

The bath was not sunk into the floor as in Japan or in some of the other community bathhouses. It rose waist high with a concrete ledge along its two exposed sides on which bathers could sit while they washed themselves. Lined in neat rows this early in the day were small, U-shaped wooden stools, a few small wooden tubs and tin wash basins.

Fuse tested the water and found it hot, but bearable below the surface. He picked up a tin basin and moved the water around until it was of uniform temperature. He scooped the water over his body and used the *tenugui* to scrub himself with soap and water until his skin glowed. Rinsing himself of soap, he stepped gingerly into the hot water, slowly immersing his feet, legs, body, until he was submerged up to his chin. He sat down with a sigh on the ledge that ran around the inside of the bath and soaked until the sweat was pouring down his face. He felt fatigue drain from his body.

"Ah, kimochi ii," he thought. "It feels so good."

He had come early to be alone. He stared unseeing at the wall, giving himself over to reflection and meditation. There was nothing he cherished as much as solitude, a possession that made him feel at home wherever he roamed. Meditation, which he had learned from a yogi in Los Angeles, had become part of his daily routine.

The clatter of footsteps roused him from his reverie. Feeling slightly miffed because he had been disturbed, he stepped out of the bath, took a cold shower, wrapped his bath towel around his loins, and walked to the alcove where he ordered an orange soda.

The entry of a boisterous group of youths, loud-voiced and exuberant, charged the air with energy. With quiet amusement he watched their horseplay as they stripped and headed for the bath, which could have held a dozen of them. From their language he gathered that they were young immigrants who had just come from a judo club. They soon departed for a Japanese-owned Chinese restaurant on Main Street.

Fuse sighed. All that electrifying activity had left him limp. Twelve years ago he had been like one of them, he mused. How time had flown. He went to his locker and got his cigarette makings. As an afterthought he called through the opening, "Matsu-san, cigar arimasuka?"

"Iie, arimasen," Matsu said. "No, I don't have any."

Fuse rolled his cigarette, struck a match on the underside of the tabletop, and lit up. Hearing the murmur of voices, the slam of the door that led into the women's bath, he looked up as two men entered the men's section. He recognized them as old acquaintances.

Eitaro Suzuki, the tailor, was a heavyset, fleshy-faced man with thick lips. His gold-filled spectacles were pushed up on his head. Ben Murakami, the drayman, was short but sturdily built, with a square-cut face and thin eyebrows barely visible against his persimmon-red skin.

"Oi, Fuse," Suzuki said. "When did you get back?"

"This morning," Fuse said.

"How are things in California?" Murakami asked. He grunted as he bent to untie his shoes.

"Fukeiki da. Everybody is saying fukeiki, fukeiki," Fuse said. "Depression. Depression. The farmers always have something to eat, but in the cities—" Fuse shook his head. "The Japanese American associations are having a hard time taking care of the destitute. How are things here?"

"Bad," Suzuki said. "Who is buying suits when stomachs are empty? Murakami here, at least, has the immigrants' baggage business. Look at his round stomach."

Fuse smiled as his friends squatted on wooden stools to clean themselves. "How about work?"

Suzuki shook his head. "Maybe waiter, maybe busboy, maybe—if things get any worse that is what I will be doing. Me, a tailor, a professional."

"As long as you have rice you won't starve," Murakami laughed. "You know I refer immigrants to you."

"For what?" Suzuki asked sourly. "Overalls?"

More footsteps announced the arrival of a newcomer. The man who stepped through the spring door was tall and slender, with stooped shoulders and a leaning-forward posture. Sadao Suda had a divot of hair above his brow surrounded by bare scalp and a thin rim of rough hair around his head. His face was long and thin, with hollow checks. Because of his appearance he was called Shin-san or Mr. China Man. His laugh resembled a gargle.

Fuse was pleased to see Suda, for he had been to Alaska. It was as if fortune or opportunity had smiled. Fuse wanted information to feed the purpose in his mind.

"Matsu-san," he called through the small aperture as the three men, having completed their baths, joined him at the table. "May we have another chair?" He also ordered sodas for his friends.

"Suda-san, have you been to this place called Klondike?" he asked, coming to the point. He saw Suzuki and Murakami glance at each other and knew they were thinking: Fuse is planning to chase fireflies again. But he didn't care, though he knew the news would be all over the community as fast as tongues could waggle. Normally he would have talked to Suda in private, but he was too impatient to wait.

"No," Suda said. "I went down the Yukon to a place called Fortymile, where gold had been found, so I must have passed the mouth of this newly discovered river. Just think about it. But you never know where gold is."

He looked quizzically at Fuse. "You plan to go prospecting?"

"Well," Fuse hedged. "Thinking about it."

"Fortymile," said Suzuki, with his usual curiosity. "What an unusual name."

"It was called that because it is forty miles down the Yukon from a place called Fort Reliance. That was a point from which distances were measured." Suda was enjoying his role as an encyclopedia.

"But how do you get to this Klondike?"

Suda turned serious. "Going to Alaska must be given deep consideration. It is not like going to view the cherry blossoms or the red maple. It is a life and death matter."

"But what is the best way?" Fuse persisted.

"There is no best way. No easy way. Men have reached the first mountain barrier, lost courage, and returned home. The shortest way is across the Chilkoot Pass near Skagway. Thirty miles, maybe more, just to cross the mountains. And you can't—how do they say it—siwash it. Siwash means live off the land. You have to take your food and supplies with you. No stores or villages, or if there are trading posts the prices are much higher than here."

Fuse's resolve weakened as he listened. "How much food would you need?"

"For one year, about fifteen hundred pounds of food and supplies."

Suda's estimate was five hundred pounds less than the minimum set by the North West Mounted Police in the winter of 1898–99 to prevent a second starvation winter in Dawson.

"First of all I would not go alone. Next, you would need a dog team or horses. One horse at least, to pull a sled loaded with your supplies. If you don't have either you have to pull a sled yourself. They have a harness that fits over your head and shoulders. They say heading it. If you don't have a sled, or if there is no snow, you have to carry your food and supplies."

Murakami, with professional interest, was doing some figuring on a piece of paper. "You say if you don't have animals to pull a sled, you have to carry fifteen hundred pounds thirty miles."

Suda nodded. "Over a mountain pass."

"Impossible! Sometimes I have to carry a hundred-pound sack of rice four or five floors. Carry it thirty miles? Baka na hanashi da," he said. "That is fool's talk."

"Crazy," Suda agreed. "But if that's the only way then this is how it is done: The average man can carry fifty to seventy pounds any distance, say a mile. You go back for the next load, and the next until you have moved your supplies one mile. You move ahead in relays in this way."

The three men looked on with interest as Murakami wrote down: 1500 ÷ 50 pounds = 30 trips. At 1 hour per roundtrip = 30 hours.

Say roughly four 8-hour days to move all the supplies one mile.

Four days times 30 miles = 120 days.

"One hundred twenty days!" Fuse said. "That is four months!"

"And no Sundays off," Suda laughed.

"Baka na hanashi da," Murakami repeated himself.

"You are crazy when you get gold fever," Suda said. "But that is only half the story. After you reach the top of the mountains and pass through Canadian customs, you have to carry everything down to Lake Bennett, where you build a boat."

"A boat?" Fuse said.

Suda nodded. "From the lake you have to float five hundred miles down the Yukon River to this place called Klondike. There are several dangerous places where you can capsize and lose everything, even your life. But to build a boat you need a big saw, hammer and nails, pitch and caulking, a tent and sleeping bag, a dog sled—all that is part of your fifteen hundred pounds."

"It must have been cruelly trying," Suzuki said sympathetically.

Suda agreed. "I was fortunate. I was cook for a party of strong, helpful white men who had dogs and sleds." He turned to Fuse. "I am not trying to discourage you, but you have to face hard facts. It is better to do that now than to be sorry up there."

"Kangae monda," Fuse said. "It is something to think about."

"What is there to think about?" Murakami said bluntly. "Just forget it."

Suda saw stubbornness in Fuse's expression. "To avoid all that work you could take a ship to St. Michael—that's at the mouth of the Yukon River—and then a riverboat up the river, a further seventeen hundred miles to the Klondike."

Murakami sniffed. "And what would that take? A year? Some choice. By that time all the gold will be gone." He looked at Fuse and softened his tone. "I am a practical man."

Suda studied Fuse's eyes. "Still thinking about it, aren't you? Well, it's your funeral. And it could be your funeral," he said grimly. "But if you are determined to go, then I would go by sea. And if there is as much gold on the ship coming here as they say, go now. There is going to be the biggest gold rush in history."

Fuse mused, unaware of the others. Half-formed ideas floated around his mind. He rarely thought things through to a logical conclusion. When reasoning reached an impasse he would dismiss the problem with a view to tackling it when he reached it. In this instance, he was thinking, he would reach Alaska by some means, and then decide upon his course of action. But he had a further thought.

"Seems it would take a lot of money?" he said to Suda.

"It would, especially if you bought a horse or dogs, besides your supplies."

"I sent much of my money to my wife," Fuse said.

"Instead of going on some wild goose chase, you should have your wife join you." Suzuki said.

"Be practical, man, for once," Murakami said. "If you wait until you are rich, you will never see her."

"I am struggling," Suzuki said, "but with my wife at my side, I am happy."

Outside the bathhouse Fuse greeted the wives of his friends. Suda was a bachelor. Mrs. Toyo Suzuki was a diminutive woman, active in church and welfare work. She was famous for her *makizushi,* a round of vinegared rice, with a center of seasoned vegetables, encircled by a rim of *nori* (dried seaweed), as well as her *inarizushi,* sweet fried *tofu* bags stuffed with vine-gared rice and toothpick-size pieces of cooked carrots and *konbu* (kelp).

Mrs. Naoko Murakami shared her husband's taste for good food and like him was rotund, but unlike him had a cheerful disposition. An exception among the Japanese women, she liked to bake, and her cakes and pies were snapped up at church benefits.

Her husband's complaint was that he never had a slice for himself. She would pat his stomach and wave a forefinger in front of his mouth. The two wives, knowing the men wanted to be alone and weary from past experience of their man talk, left for the Japanese Baptist Church.

The restaurant to which the four men went for Chinese *shu mai* dumplings was on King Street, a couple of blocks from the bathhouse. The stuffed dumplings came three to a plate. Each plate cost ten cents, so when it came time to pay up, the waiter just counted the empty plates. Besides the *shu mai* the men ordered steamed buns called *bao,* filled with *char shu* (roast pork), shrimp, or beef. This they washed down with Chinese tea.

"When your wife comes from Japan," Suzuki said, "she would feel perfectly at home with our wives. It can be lonely without friends. Don't deprive her of the happiness of being with you and sharing your hardships. Think about it seriously."

Suzuki's considerate words almost resolved the conflict within Fuse. After they parted he walked aimlessly around the Japanese district and the new section of Seattle around University and Pike streets. He spent some time on the Jackson Street aqueduct above the railroad yards, looking down at the locomotives shunting freight cars back and forth, building up the trains that would leave for the East or down the coast. The steel rails had always fascinated him. They led off over the horizon to promised lands and fairy kingdoms. In his travels he had heard their lone and mournful whistles in the night, calling him from his warm blankets.

Night had fallen when fatigue drew him to his cheerless bunk, but sleep eluded him. As he remembered Suzuki's words he could almost feel his wife nestled in his arms. He felt tears in his eyes. What was wrong with him? Why didn't he do the obvious? As he turned on his side he heard, almost symbolically, the whistle of a train. He lay on his back and closed his eyes against the darkness. Pain tore him inside. There was no peace, not even oblivion, to comfort him. He awoke sweating from a nightmare he could not recall. Somewhere in the darkness a man was grinding his teeth.

After eating a breakfast he did not taste, he followed his feet toward the docks. Neither purpose nor motivation guided his steps. He paused in front of the S.S. *Yukon*. It was high tide and the ship's prow loomed over his head like a building. He looked again at the name. *Yukon*. Impulsively, he boarded the ship. The first man he met was the purser, Fred Ostrak.

There are times when a man appears at the right place at the right time. Destiny may take a liking to him. This happened in Fuse's case. Ostrak was in need of a cabin boy and he liked what he saw in Fuse, who was to remember this encounter for the rest of his life.

"You sign for the round trip?" Ostrak asked.

"Yes," Fuse said, hardly believing his good fortune. He forgot the conflict of the previous night. Any thought of joining his wife vanished. "I sign for the return."

"Return?" Ostrak's frown was a shadow in his blue eyes. Then his brow unpleated. "Oh, you mean round trip. Okay, go get your duffle."

"Duffle?"

"Your clothes."

"Yes, I do."

Fuse was so entranced by his luck that his thought was only of his immediate future. When he returned with the backpack and bedroll, Ostrak looked at them suspiciously. "Is that all you have?"

"I travel all over California this way."

"You're not planning to jump ship?"

"Jump ship?"

"You know what I mean. Some of your countrymen do that."

"No, I promise."

Ostrak studied Fuse's ingenuous face. "You promise as a samurai?" he asked in jest.

"I promise as a Fuse."

They shook hands and so a promise was sealed.

Fuse determined then that he could not break his word. He might not disembark in Alaska, but at least he would visit this legendary land. Ostrak told him that the *Yukon* was scheduled to sail straight across the Gulf of Alaska to St. Michael. Come what might he would not lose face with this man who trusted his word and whom he liked. Otherwise it would be a betrayal.

2

A Promise Broken

RUMORS OF THE GOLD carried by the *Portland* had spread from the saloons and brothels of Skid Road to the executive suites of big business. They were verified by *The Seattle Post-Intelligencer*, which sent reporters to meet the ship off Cape Flattery.

Seattleites crowded the pier as the *Portland* docked with sixty-eight men and about $700,000 in gold. Sourdoughs walked down the gangplank bearing leather pokes, tins, and chests of gold. Onlookers gaped as armed Wells Fargo security guards escorted the men to the banks. Here was proof that the Yukon discovery was for real.

The nation was stagnant in a depression, and people were ripe for any hope of riches. Erastus Brainard, an energetic public relations man with the Seattle Chamber of Commerce, inundated the nation and the world with a masterly campaign of publicity. Dreams grew into a fever on the food of his handouts. The fever begot sheer lunacy.

Fuse and the rest of the crew of the *Yukon* escaped the infection, but Captain David Bell got a foretaste of coming events. On the morning after the *Portland* arrived he was called to a conference of the ship's owners. He was ordered to build twenty stalls for horses and kennels for forty dogs, and to make room for five more tons of cargo.

Captain Bell leaped to his feet and leaned over the back

of his chair, his knuckles white, his round face flushed with anger. "Am I to believe my ears?" he asked. "Are you out of your minds? We're loaded down to the plimsoll line. And may I ask, where is all this stuff going?"

"To Dyea."

"Now I know you're batty. You know damned well there are no wharves there nor warehouses. Where do you expect me to unload the stuff?"

"On the beach."

"And the animals?"

"Push them overboard and let them swim."

"Like hell!"

"Might I remind you," said Adam Barrows, the smallest man in the room and president of the Barrows Shipping Company, "that your job is to get the cargo there. I will assume full responsibility. Is that understood?"

Captain Bell wheeled on his heels and stalked out of the room. "Crazy as loons," he said.

Fuse looked on with interest and then with dismay as makeshift stalls in which the horses could hardly move and kennels for dogs were built on deck, and cargo distributed into every available nook until the deck was only a few feet above water.

As Fuse brought coffee up to the bridge he heard Captain Bell tell Ostrak, "I don't like it. The owners are mad, just like those gold-crazed men." He waved at the crowded wharf. "God help us if we run into a storm."

"Anything to make a dollar." Ostrak's thin, triangular face warped cynically. "I had the fever once but thank God I recovered."

"There's a limit," Captain Bell said. As he opened the door the hoof beats of frightened horses and the howling of desperate dogs disturbed the cabin air. To Ostrak he said, "Get the ship ready. The sooner we leave this madhouse the better." To the first mate, who was standing near the wheel, "Mr. Parsons, we sail at dawn."

As Fuse, a tray of empty coffee cups in hand, followed Bell down the steps headed for the galley, some men on the wharf shouted, "What's that Jap doing on the ship? Give a white man his job."

Captain Bell walked to the railing, his red face only a few yards from the men on the dock. "He's a member of the crew and not likely to jump ship like the lot of you. That's the only reason you want the job." He stared the men down. As they shuffled their feet and looked down, he laughed. "I know you."

"Thank you, Captain," Fuse said as they proceeded down the deck.

"For what? Nobody's telling me how to run my ship."

Bell gave him a quizzical look, then stepped into the salon.

The captain had been loyal to him, Fuse thought. I can be no less loyal to him. Alaska would have to wait unless fate decreed otherwise.

In the morning as the *Yukon* pulled away from her berth, it seemed to Fuse that every available dock space along the entire Seattle waterfront was occupied by craft, some hardly ships, that had been resurrected from maritime boneyards. He was seeing only the beginning of a harebrained madness.

If the Klondike was the lodestone, Seattle was the magnet that drew men and women like iron filings from across the seven seas. They arrived on foot, bicycles, horseback and wagon, crowded trains and overloaded ships. This great headless horde was accompanied by camp followers: prostitutes, con men, swindlers, and outright thieves. Seattle was described by some as worse than their native Hell's Kitchen, a den of iniquity, a modern Sodom and Gomorrah.

With bicycles and balloons becoming the vogue at the time, some brought bicycles with the idea of skimming for hundreds of miles down the frozen surface of the Yukon. During the Nome stampede of 1899, one bicyclist traveled from Dawson over the Yukon River ice until the intense cold congealed the oil on his wheels so they would not turn and froze rubber tires into fragile tubes. Taking advantage of warmer spells, he made it. Hot air balloonists cooked up schemes to fly over the mountains and land in Dawson. These came to naught. Every contraption that Yankee ingenuity could dream up was put on the market.

Hardly anyone was immune. Mayors of cities resigned without warning; bank tellers, bookkeepers and clerks walked off their jobs. Merchants sold their stores, lawyers took down their shingles, doctors put away their certificates, and dentists left their patients with cavities.

Fuse's chronicle was woven into this human tapestry, the history of one of the first Alaskan pioneers from Japan.

Fuse received an inkling of what the gold rush was all about when the *Yukon* reached Skagway, the gateway to Chilkoot Pass. Captain Bell anchored offshore until the tide was high. To the impatient and protesting gold rushers he said, "If I unload your supplies at full tide they will be beyond reach of the water and your animals won't have to swim so far."

When the tide rose he moved his ship as close to the beach as he dared. Barges lightered cargo ashore. Fuse was horrified when he saw men kick and beat trembling horses into the icy water and make them swim ashore. He turned away, sickened. "They are beasts," he said.

"You mean the men, eh," Ostrak said cynically. "Five of the horses and one of the dogs died en route. They were the fortunate ones."

Fuse noticed some of the crewmen going ashore on the lighters.

"I go, okay?" he asked Ostrak.

The purser looked at him from the corners of his eyes.

"I want to say I step on Alaska where you start for the Klondike," Fuse said. "I no jump ship. I make promise." To Bell, who was standing nearby. "You protect me in Seattle. I no jump ship."

Bell looked over Fuse's head at Ostrak, who nodded.

When Fuse jumped from the lighter and touched Alaskan soil the effect was electric, like a spark jumping a gap. The thrill was more moving than when he first set foot on a Seattle pier. He was entranced with a communion of first love for a great land. The Chilkat Mountains filled his eyes. His back straightened as he lifted his head and inhaled the primordial air. Ah! What possessed him!

Fuse walked along the beach in a state of levitation, past men who were scrambling around assembling their supplies in individual piles. The scene was chaotic. A sense of urgency seemed to possess every man, as if he could not wait another minute before he took off for the pass.

He passed the native village of Dyea, a collection of shacks surrounding a longhouse used for tribal meetings. He saw few Indians around, and women and girls seemed nonexistent. What he did not know was that the palefaces were regarded with suspicion. One Indian packer had been paid in worthless Confederate money and now they all demanded hard cash. Girls painted their faces in hideous masks to ward off predatory males.

At the Taiya River the trail turned to follow the river bank. Fuse walked beside men loaded down with gear, red-faced from their exertions, swearing as they stumbled over boulders and roots of trees. Fuse recalled the wisdom of Suda's warnings. Among the endless chain of men and animals were Chilkat packers who carried two hundred to three hundred pounds and walked with surefooted agility. What was once a path was turning into a muddy roadway under the hooves of overburdened horses and sleds pulled by dogs over bare, uneven ground.

Fuse, naturally tenderhearted and compassionate, was sickened and appalled at the callous treatment the animals received. He felt more sorry for the helpless animals than he did for the men, who had some say in the torture they were enduring.

He was spared the scenes that winter brought along the White Pass Trail, the alternate route over the mountains, where so many horses died or were shot when they broke their legs on the rocky ground that it was called Dead Horse Trail. Some horses were so mistreated that they committed suicide by walking over the edge of a cliff (or so men who were there testified).

On Chilkoot Pass the horses were useless after they reached the Scales because they could not negotiate what were called the "Golden Stairs," the last, forty-five-degree climb to the summit. Wandering around and nosing into tents seeking food and companionship, the abandoned animals were considered a nuisance and finally were killed indiscriminately.

The urge to reach the Klondike first turned otherwise normal men and women into beasts. Sick and dying men were passed by with hardly a glance. Men who survived have recorded their remorse and shame of memories they could never forget.

Fuse turned back where the Taiya River roared through a canyon on its way to the sea. He avoided the eyes of the sweating men and turned his head from the pitiful animals. He remembered anew Suda's warning and Murakami's calculations. How right they had been and what a fool he had been to embark on this voyage to nowhere.

"Baka," he said to himself. "Baka da nā."

As the barge brought him alongside the ship he felt Ostrak's sardonic gaze. "Mad. All mad," he said to the purser. "I no do to rat what they do to horses."

Ostrak was too perceptive to say, as he had to other returning crewmen, "Change your mind about jumping ship?" Instead he said, "That's what gold fever does to good, honest, God-fearing men."

Fuse threw himself on his berth, as depressed as he had ever been, and despairing of the human race. But when he awoke from a short nap his resilience reasserted itself. His great land was testing these men and finding them wanting. He was cheerful again as he climbed to the bridge with a fresh brew of coffee.

Several men approached Ostrak for passage back to Seattle, but when he told them the ship was heading further north, they left for other ships. Poor fools, Ostrak thought, yielding to an impulse of weakness.

Shortly before noon anchor was weighed and with a short blast of its whistle the *Yukon* headed south on Lynn Canal. To Fuse the men ashore looked like ants carrying loads larger than themselves. It seemed to him that the ship, relieved of its excess cargo, rode gaily and lightly over the sunlit waves as it crossed the halibut banks of Icy Strait and Cross Sound and nosed into the Gulf of Alaska.

Among the passengers was a Hawaiian Japanese who had a ukulele tied to the top of his pack. He said to Fuse when they first met:

"I come wit' two Hawaiians and one Japanee. When I see da mountains I say to my friends, 'Dat not for me. You want me maki!'" At Fuse's blank look he explained, "Maki mean die. Dey call me chicken shit, but dey pay me my share."

"I heard no easy way."

"Gotta be. Easier den dat." Sidney Toyama nodded his head back toward the saw-edged mountain range. "I change my ticket to St. Michael, den I take riverboat up Yukon."

Toyama was of slender build, his large eyes alert in a thin expressive face. Young as he was, possibly in his early twenties, he seemed to be aware of his limitations and inclinations. Free and easygoing in his attitude and mannerisms, he gave the impression, even when sitting, of contained, restless energy.

One thing puzzled Fuse. Toyama spoke two languages. During the voyage, as Fuse went about his duties, he heard Toyama's laughter as he raked in a pot at a poker table, or heard him singing Hawaiian songs to appreciative audiences. To haoles (whites) he spoke in what Fuse characterized as English English, though with a hint of the sound *d* for *th*. When talking to Fuse his speech was sprinkled liberally with "dese" and "wit'" and "dat kind."

One day as the *Yukon* neared the Aleutians, Fuse descended from the bridge bearing a tray of empty coffee cups. He saw Toyama at the railing looking over the sun-sprinkled sea.

"That way Hawaii," Fuse said. Still learning English and absorbing what he was exposed to, he almost said "dat." He had learned to pronounce the sound for *th*, which is not in the Japanese language, but it had taken some time until putting his tongue behind his upper teeth became a habit. "Dat" was easier and more natural, he thought, and maybe that was why Toyama used it. He seemed to be in a pensive mood, which was unusual for him, so Fuse did not disturb him further.

Landfall was made at Unimak Pass in a region referred to as the "cradle of storms." But good weather favored the ship, and it passed safely into the southern reaches of the Bering Sea.

The growing excitement among the argonauts reached a peak of expectancy a few days later when land was sighted again off the starboard bow, but crewmen dashed their hopes when they said they were passing Nunivak Island. The Yukon cruised through miles of silt-colored waters off the many-tentacled delta of the Yukon River before approaching St. Michael, the terminus of the three-thousand-mile voyage from Seattle. Its passengers were in the vanguard of those who tried the all-water route to Dawson in the fall of 1897.

St. Michael was a disappointment to Fuse. It was not much more than a trading post with a cluster of wooden buildings around it. A church, the trading post, and the remains of a blockhouse were symbols of the white man's invasion of a primitive people's land. As at Skagway, cargo was lightered ashore and dumped on the beach.

"Okay I take walk?" Fuse asked Ostrak.

The purser studied Fuse's eager face as if he were impressing upon him the promise he had made when signing on. "We sail at dawn," he said. "Remember."

"Come," Toyama said. "We look around. Maybe we have drink."

Fuse nodded. After days trodding an uneasy deck, the solid earth felt good to his feet. For some reason he could not explain this seemed the real Alaska, unlike the bustle and excitement of Skagway.

There wasn't much to see, and Toyama led Fuse into a saloon. The man behind the bar regarded them suspiciously. "You Eskimo?"

Toyama looked behind him to see if the saloonkeeper was addressing someone else. "What you t'ink. We Japanee."

Fuse noted that when Toyama was annoyed he lapsed from English English.

Fuse preferred *sake,* but it was nonexistent. He had never cared for the raw bite of whiskey, but he was to remember later that it was in Alaska that he developed a taste for the drink that was to consume and eventually destroy him. Toyama took his scotch mixed with water.

Fuse remembered the distant groan of winches, the sound

of Eskimo children's voices, the fuzzy feeling in his head and the effort he had to make forming sentences when he tried to talk.

He awoke to find that he was fully dressed, lying on a cot in a bedroom. Dawn was gray at the window. He bolted upright. The pain in his head made him groan, but instead of falling back on the pillow, he sat with his feet on the floor, holding his head in his hands.

He assayed a few steps, and then without a further glance at the snoring Toyama, bolted through the door and down the deserted street on unsteady legs. As he cleared the last houses and ran down to the beach he saw a puff of steam issue from the whistle on the *Yukon's* funnel and heard the sound a few seconds later. He stood at water's edge and waved his arms crazily in the air.

On the bridge Captain Bell surveyed the beach through a telescope.

"Fuse?" Ostrak asked.

Bell nodded.

"Can't we wait for him?"

Bell shook his head. "We've hauled anchor and we're underway." The iron plates under their feet were vibrating. "Maybe one of the passengers will want to work his way south."

"Aye, aye, Sir."

Ostrak watched until Fuse's figure became a dot. "Poor bugger," he said. He knew enough about Japanese culture to know that Fuse would be devastated. His heart went out to him.

Fuse's despair turned to anger. He was furious with Toyama, but even more so with himself. He had attained his goal, reached Alaska, but at the cost of his integrity. As he retraced his steps toward the room, he suddenly realized that all he owned was sailing from his life. He carried the memory of this bitter moment to his grave.

When Fuse returned to the room Toyama looked sharply at his expression. "Sorry," he said. "I got pilute" (Hawaiian for stinking drunk).

"I mad at you," Fuse said. "I mad at myself."

Toyama remained silent.

"I make promise. Return to Seattle."

Fuse found a piece of paper in the dresser drawer and, borrowing a stub of pencil from Toyama, laboriously composed a letter in English. Sometimes, at a loss for words, he would glance at Toyama lying with his hands folded behind his head and staring at the ceiling. Fuse tightened his mouth, thinking, he no care, and stubbornly returned to his task. He filled in an *e* and dotted it and crossed a *t* that he had overlooked.

"Now," he commanded. "You fix this letter. In English English, not Hawaiian English."

In a chastened mood, Toyama sat on the edge of the bed and read the letter. As he read he suppressed a smile.

My dere honorable the Captain Bell,

Please excuse for this my poor English. I beg to inform you I am not jump the your ship. I drink too much the whiskey. I much ashamed to do not keep the the most honorable promise I shall return.

I am deeply grateful, Sir, if your kindness of understanding in this matter.

In advance, I thanking you, Sir, from bottom of my heart I will respect and consideration.

I am, Sir,
your humble servent

MATAJIRO FUSE
P.S. Please kindly excuse for this my poor writing.

"This beautiful letter," Toyama said with his infectious smile.

"Uso tsuki," Fuse said. "Liar."

"Look," Toyama said. "I know you mad. I'm sorry. What you want I do?"

Fuse looked at Toyama's earnest, almost pleading face.

"Okay," Fuse relented. "But this not good English."

"But dat letter is you. Dat's why it beautiful. I write for you English English but den it not you."

"You fix up?" Fuse said, still not convinced.

"Okay. A few t'ings. Dere you spell dear. I still t'ink dere mo' betta for way you write."

"You copy for me? One Captain Bell. One Mr. Ostrak. Ostrak like my friend," Fuse said. "Tomodachi."

"No," Toyama said. "Da way you write, dat part of you."

They went to the trading post and bought a children's notebook, a few envelopes, and stamps. Laboriously, Fuse made two copies of his letter. They were addressed to Captain Bell and to Mr. Ostrak, S.S. *Yukon*, Barrows Shipping Company, Seattle, Wash. Fuse never learned whether his letters reached them but felt the satisfaction of having done what he considered his duty.

And the two officers did receive their letters. Ostrak was touched and wanted to reply, but there was no return address. He saved the letter as a treasured memento.

To Fuse, after his first violent reaction to the rape of his honor, came the realization that willy-nilly he had reached the Alaska of his dreams. His pleasure, however, was not unalloyed; it did not have a clean feel.

Tickets to Dawson were hard to come by, but Toyama managed to parlay his own valid ticket and his ingenuous charm into a passage for Fuse. The fare left Fuse nearly penniless.

"Got week to kill," Toyama said. "Wonder any gold 'round here?"

Down at the beach they met Jake Park, an Eskimo, who was tying the painter of his seiner to a boulder.

"You know where to find gold?" Toyama asked in jest.

Park threw back the hood of his parka, revealing a round, plump face beneath a bowl-cut mop of black hair. For a moment Fuse thought he was looking at another Japanese.

The Eskimo regarded them inquisitively. "What tribe you from?"

Even the quick-thinking Toyama was caught back on the heels of his mind. After a second's pause, "What ken you from?" he retorted.

"Ken! Ken?"

"You know. Prefecture."

Park's brow cleared. "Oh, you mean Japanese ken. I learned that from Japanese students when I lived in Seattle. Hai! Hai!"

"Tribe. Ken," Toyama said. "What's the difference?"

The three regarded each other solemnly, then burst into laughter.

"You look like my friend in Ewa," said Toyama, referring to his hometown.

"Yes, like Murakami," Fuse said. "My friend, Seattle."

"They say my people come from over there." Park waved vaguely toward Bering Strait and Asia.

"You even have Korean name."

"No, that come short from parka."

They laughed again.

"Come eat wit' us," Toyama said. "Maybe you tell us 'bout dis country."

Toyama mistook Park's apparent reluctance to accept his invitation. "You be our guest."

"Most white restaurants won't serve us," Park said.

"What you say? You mean dat?"

"That's first thing you learn about this country."

"Dat's crazy!" To avoid any incident that might embarrass Park, Toyama said, "You be Japanee while we eat. We be t'ree Japanee."

Although the waiter looked twice at the sealskin parka Park was wearing, they were served without incident. As they talked over their ham and eggs, Toyama gathered that Park had taken, with his English name, other paraphernalia of the white man's civilization. As one of his village who had anticipated the decline of the whaling industry, the life support of his people, he had saved his money and bought a seiner to fish during the sockeye season in Bristol Bay, the richest source of red salmon in Alaska.

"But what about gold? Your people must have run across it. It would help solve many of your problems."

"We can't stake claims. We're not considered U.S. citizens."

"But dis your native land!"

"You tell that to the white man." The genial lines of Park's features tightened. "We can't even homestead. The white people come in and take our land."

"You don't have to take dat. You got to fight for your rights."

"Our Tlingit brothers tried that at Sitka. Bows and arrows against guns, spears against big guns on warships. You see," Park said, "we're not considered civilized."

Even Fuse, who did not fully comprehend what Park was saying, felt the bitterness underlying his words.

As they emerged on the sandy roadway that might be considered a street, Park said, "I have to go get my supplies. Thanks for the grub."

Toyama took advantage of the geniality that had returned to Park's face. "We come to Alaska to find gold. You t'ink dere's any 'round here?"

"I think maybe west of my village. I live in Golovin, across Norton Sound from here."

"You take us dere?"

Park thought a minute, then nodded. "After I get my supplies."

"Good! We get our duffle and meet you at da trading post." The words "our duffle" gave Fuse a pang. "I got nothing," he said.

"Dat's right. I didn't t'ink 'bout dat. We get you new outfit."

Fuse demurred. "I not got that much money. Better I go back to Seattle."

"What's matta you! We in same boat." It was a favorite expression of Toyama's that Fuse was to hear often during the heartbreaking trials that lay ahead of them.

"You make me loan?" Fuse asked. His heart was not in his request. "I promise to pay back." Mentally he winced. The bright luster of promise had become tarnished when he betrayed Ostrak.

Toyama studied Fuse's determined expression. He shrugged.

"Okay. If dat way you feel."

They bought a .30 caliber Winchester rifle, four cases of

ammunition, a fur-lined sleeping bag ("dat most important"), a hunting knife, frying pan, pot, fork and spoon, cup, the bare essentials. For mining they bought two gold pans, a pick, shovel, hammer and nails, and mercury to assay gold.

"You rich," Fuse said.

Toyama flexed his slender, pliable fingers. "I got lucky at cards."

When Fuse and Toyama appeared at the post they were appalled at the quantity of food and supplies Park had bought.

"You buy out da store," Toyama said.

"We have store in Golovin but not everything. Running short. This for my family, relatives, and friends," Park said, grinning like a full moon. "Winter coming, you know."

It was still before noon as Park spun the pilot's wheel and pointed his boat across the sound. When darkness fell he was guided ashore by the lights of Golovin. As the three men unloaded the stores, men, women, and children disappeared into the night with supplies.

"That was fast," Toyama said.

"Thanks," Park said.

"Thank you," Fuse said. "we here now."

"Tomorrow I take you to the creeks."

"We camp here on beach," Toyama said. "Come, Fuse, we build fire here. You get some driftwood."

"Driftwood?"

"Wood. Lying on beach."

"New word," Fuse said. "Driftwood," he muttered, as he set about his task. "Ryuboku. Driftwood." He liked the sound of the word. As he drifted off to sleep he murmured "driftwood . . ."

The next afternoon Park put them ashore near the mouth of the Snake River near Cape Nome. He walked a ways with them along its bank. "Maybe you find color here," he said. "I come back in five days."

Fuse and Toyama surveyed their domain, an endless plain of sand dunes, dried grass, and anonymous bare bushes. It was an expanse as desolate and forbidding as any either of them had ever beheld, a complete contrast to the forests, snow-peaked mountains, fiords, and glaciers of Southeastern Alaska.

They pitched camp in the shelter of a bluff, a beach of riverbank as a front porch. Fuse itched to get to the sandy river, but Toyama started a fire to boil some water for coffee.

"If gold dere, it no run away," he said.

"You know how pan gold?" Fuse asked over his coffee cup.

"Yes," Toyama said. He had read how it was done. A sourdough at one of the poker sessions had given him some hints. "You scoop up sand and water in da pan, and whirl it 'round. Light stuff float off and heavier gold stay on bottom." To himself he thought, "If nuggets, no problem."

During the course of the next few days they explored the river and creeks. They reached Anvil Creek, a tributary, but after an afternoon of panning they gave up. Nothing, no hunch, no omen, urged them to persist.

In the fall of the following year "three lucky Swedes," John Byrnesen, Erik Lindbloom, and Jafet Lindeberg (a Norwegian) made the strike on Anvil Creek that led to Alaska's greatest gold rush.

Fuse and Toyama returned to the mouth of the Snake River and ventured toward Nome. They were unaware that flakes of gold clung to the hobnails of their boots.

The thousands who followed the "Lucky Swedes" staked claims on all the rivers and creeks that ran through the coastal tundra. It was not till by chance someone decided to try the sands of Nome that the electrifying discovery was made: There was gold in the sand underfoot!

Bedrock, where gold was concentrated, was not more than twenty inches below the surface, and at the edge of the tundra only about five feet deep. Here there was no permafrost, the solidly frozen earth that had to be loosened by steam or laboriously freed by successive fires built on the same spot, and then scooped up to be run through a rocker in the spring when water ran free.

On the beach of Nome, men and women, each allotted a width of land the length of a shovel, scooped sand into a rocker and retained the gold. About two million dollars worth of gold was recovered from that sand in 1899.

In the early fall of 1897, Fuse and Toyama looked up and down the miles of beach without hope.

"No gold here," Toyama said.

Fuse nodded. Nothing inspired them to test the sand.

Park picked them up as promised and headed across Norton Sound toward St. Michael. "Gold there some place," he said, nodding his head back toward Snake River.

"Gold is where you find it," Toyama quipped.

He had a struggle paying Park for their passage. Finally Toyama closed Park's hand over twenty-five dollars. "You take dis for your people. For what work you have to do for dem. I wish it more."

Park laughed, his round face aglow in the westering sun. "You hit me in weak spot."

Fuse shook Park's hand. "I always remember you."

Toyama nodded. "No matter where we be."

"Maybe our trails cross," Park said. "Alaska big land but small place."

Rivers were the most practical and natural thoroughfares in the Territory. Sourdoughs were forever running across each other in the most unexpected places, often on the way to the next gold strike.

Fuse and Toyama parted regretfully from Park and turned their faces toward the main street of St. Michael.

3

Stranded on the Yukon

S HOULDERING THEIR PACKS, Fuse and Toyama joined the passengers aboard the *Flora Belle,* for the trip upriver. As they assembled on the deck, Captain Sam Durkee addressed them from the bridge.

"You've bought passage to Dawson. If there's an early winter the river will be freezing up. I'll try my best to get you there but I will not guarantee it. If you don't want to chance it you can have your money back this minute."

"What if we get frozen in?" a voice asked.

"You will be on your own. Marooned in the middle of a snowy desert. You could starve, because sources of supply are limited."

Even as Durkee spoke he realized that his voice was lost in the passion of gold madness. He saw his passengers looking over the side at the crowd on shore. His words of caution were greeted by a chorus of noes. Having come this far they congratulated themselves as the lucky ones to have secured passage. One shouted "Dawson or bust."

As the crowd broke up into beehive buzzes of speculation, Fuse looked out over the tent city that had been building during their brief absence. Ships had been disgorging gold seekers. Those who had managed to buy through tickets to Dawson made connections within a few days. The rest were dumped unceremoniously ashore to fend for themselves. Among these were a few who sized up the situation and, like those at

Skagway, booked immediate return passage. They had the satisfaction, if that is the word, of later saying to friends and relatives that they had been to Alaska.

The gold fever of Chilkoot Pass infected St. Michael. A resourceful number paid for passage on a barge to be pushed one thousand, seven hundred miles up the Yukon by tugboat. Jerry-built shelters had been erected on the barge to accommodate these die-hard gold rushers. Two boats were completed in three weeks, an indication of their quality and seaworthiness.

In the bliss of their ignorance, the argonauts were oblivious to the vagaries and dangers of the Yukon River. The Yukon can be a benevolent thoroughfare in the summer months, and navigable almost to its headwaters. But from late October to early June it can be an implacable river of ice.

North America's fourth longest river (exceeded only by the Missouri, the Mackenzie of Canada, and the Mississippi) has its source in the southern part of the Yukon Territory about fifteen miles from tidewater. Instead of taking a logical course to the sea, it flows northward in a great arc through Alaska's heartland for 2,979 miles. It widens to two miles along its lower reaches and empties into Norton Sound through a delta network sixty-five miles wide.

Lt. Frederick Schwatka and a detail of seven U.S. Army soldiers were the first men to explore the Yukon from its source to its mouth, making the trip in the summer of 1883. Schwatka's reports of gold in the sandbars were not lost on the prospectors, who found his maps of special value.

To the impatient stampeders aboard the *Flora Belle,* the most exasperating delays were the two hours spent every day loading on about thirty cords of wood used to fire the boilers. The stations were maintained by woodcutters who had given up the chase for gold in favor of steady work and relative security. As the ship crawled upriver with the speed of a snail, or so it seemed to the passengers, the morning nip in the air turned to a bone-chilling cold. Ice began forming outward from the banks of the river and floes started drifting downriver. At Rampart, the mining town established in 1893 as the result of a gold strike, Captain Durkee tied up for the night to assess his position. They were only about half way to Dawson.

What surprised and disheartened many of the gold rushers was the number of boats of all descriptions, as many as a hundred in one day, running with the river. The men in them reported that there were no jobs, no gold, and little food.

The North West Mounted Police had practically ordered all those without enough food for the winter to flee from Dawson. Stocks of food were also low at Fort Yukon and Circle, the nearest supply points. In a week or so, those stranded at Rampart would not be able to leave except by dogsled.

Some two thousand people were stranded along the Yukon. Anxious passengers crowded around Captain Durkee. "What are we going to do?"

Durkee did not mention the warning he had given or the choice he had offered. "Stay put," he said. "We're about halfway to Dawson. We can't go ahead. By the time you return to St. Michael—if you make it—Norton Sound will be frozen over and you will find no ships."

In the silence Toyama asked, "When ice break up?"

"About May, June. Depends."

"What are we going to do?" It was the man who had said "Dawson or bust." The question was pregnant in the chill air.

"Get ready to hole up for the winter."

"You've got to feed us and put us up for the number of days it would have taken us to reach Dawson," a voice said.

"Fair enough. I have sufficient provisions for that." Durkee looked at the purser and chief steward standing nearby. "We'll be careful and stretch our food as far as possible. And no complaints. I'm trying to be fair. But after that you will have to fend for yourselves."

"And we get to stay on the boat?"

Durkee nodded. "About two to three weeks. After, we will have to play it by ear."

Toyama drew Fuse aside. "Dis be serious. Come."

He led the way into the lounge and sat at a table. He drew a sheet of wrinkled, frayed paper from his breast pocket and spread it out.

"Dis be list of food one man need to live for one year in

Alaska. Old-timer in Skagway give me dis. Look. Haoles eat too much."

Fuse pointed to one item. "Thirty-five pound rice."

"Crazy, huh! And see dat. Four hundred pounds flour. Who need dat much flour?" Toyama shook his head. "We Japanee. We switch around. But first we figure out what we need. We live and eat on ship till about end of October. Dat leave November through May, seven months food we need. By June riverboats bring food up dis way. Dis sourdough list for one year. We cut down to seven-twelfths of everything."

"Divide by half, make six months. More easy. Maybe Jake's people 'round here sell us meat and fish. Make up extra month."

"Good idea. Good t'inking." He looked at Fuse as if he were reevaluating him. "Long we got rice, we no starve. Okay, we get to work. First, we figure by year, same as sourdough. Den divide by two for six months. Instead of flour we make four hundred pounds rice."

"Flour, maybe one hundred pounds."

They continued down the sourdough's list. They crossed off cornmeal as neither one cared for it. They deliberated over the suggested amounts of evaporated onions and potatoes (fifty pounds each), and evaporated apples, peaches, and apricots (twenty-five pounds each).

"Dat to prevent scurvy. Scurvy! What dat in Japanee! When not eat fruit your teeth fall out and your legs get rotten so you have to cut 'em off."

"Oh, scurby. Wakari mashita."

"So you understand."

"No meat," Fuse said, pointing to the list.

"It spoil. But we get bacon. You t'ink we need two hundred pounds?"

Fuse shook his head. "No, we use for ajitsuke."

"Yes, for taste. Maybe four slabs. Dat enough."

Fuse wondered how much a slab was but trusted Toyama's judgment.

Toyama decided on a minimum of baking powder and yeast cakes. Once they had a starter for sourdough they could do without. They rounded out their list with salt and pepper, coffee, tea, jam, condensed milk, laundry soap, and a good supply of candles and matches.

When they had completed their list Toyama wrote it down in the notebook they had bought back in St. Michael.

Item	Sugg. Amt. 1 yr	Divided by 2	1/2 yr food
Rice	35 lbs.		400 lbs. (for Japanee)
Flour	400 lbs.		100 lbs.
Cornmeal	50 lbs.		0 lbs. (we no like)
Oatmeal	50 lbs.	2	25 lbs.
Beans	100 lbs.	2	50 lbs.
Evaporated apples	25 lbs.	2	12 lbs. (13 bad luck)
Evaporated peaches	25 lbs.	2	12 lbs.
Evaporated apricots	25 lbs.	2	12 lbs.
Evaporated onions	50 lbs.	2	25 lbs
Evaporated potatoes	50 lbs.	2	25 lbs.
Bacon	200 lbs		4 slabs (for taste)
Sugar	100 lbs	2	50 lbs.

"T'ing like sugar maybe too much. But we can trade."

"Good idea. Maybe Jake's people trade for meat."

"We buy some dried or canned meat and fish. Now we—"

"Uh oh," Fuse said. "We not thinking."

"What you mean?"

"'cept for rice that list for one people."

Toyama slapped the side of his head. "Of course." He shook his head in disbelief. "We got to double everyt'ing."

"Food for one year for one be enough for two people for six months."

To their dismay, rice was in short supply.

"I can only let you have three hundred pounds," Mc-Donald said. "Got to think of the others."

Toyama doubled their flour quota and bartered for rice. Alarmed, Fuse viewed bare spaces on the shelves, a portent of rationing.

"We just in time," Toyama said.

"Where we stay?"

"We stay on boat and look 'round."

The next day when they discovered the cost of lots and small houses, Toyama said, "Pay rent for six months! We need dat money for Dawson."

They walked to the woods about two miles away where men were chopping down trees and floating the logs down the narrowing channel of the river to town.

"Dat too much work," Toyama said, nodding at the toiling men. "If tree no come to town, we come to trees. We build cabin in da woods. We can walk into town anytime."

"You build cabin before?"

"I cabinet maker back in da Islands. We watch how dey do. We need two axes and big crosscut saw. No need build big cabin."

Over the ensuing weeks they cut trees and notched the ends for dovetail construction. They built the conventional four walls of logs. They remembered to leave an opening for a door at one end and an opening at the other end for a fireplace, which they built of stones from the riverbank.

They chinked the holes with mud until Toyama thought the chimney was airtight. But when they built their first fire smoke poured out of unsuspected crevices and filled the cabin. Crying and gasping for air, they finally plugged every hole until the chimney drew the smoke perfectly.

"Ah, said Fuse, holding his hands to the blaze.

"Feel good, eh."

As no snow had fallen they dragged their sled full of provisions over the ice along the riverbank. With their food stored away they felt prepared for any eventuality. The days were growing short and the sun was making smaller arcs above the horizon each day.

Early one afternoon, as they rested on a fallen log smoking their cigarettes they saw a canoe come racing down the narrow path of open water, pursued by an ice floe.

Toyama threw away his cigarette, grabbed Fuse's arm. "Come. Trouble." The floe rammed into the stern of the canoe and shoved it on top of the ice. Two of the four men fell into the current that would have tugged them under the ice to their deaths. Toyama grabbed one man and Fuse the other. Straining and grunting, they managed to draw the men half out of the water. The force of the current that had been a danger now pushed their legs out onto the ice. For a few minutes their panting disturbed the crystalline silence.

"Come," Toyama said, getting to his feet. "You freeze here. Come to cabin. Run if you can."

He built a pyramid of kindling above a log along which blue flames were flickering. He hung a kettle from an iron tripod over the fire. He made the two shivering men undress to their all-wool longjohns, threw blankets over their shoulders, and sat them in front of the fireplace. When the water started to steam he made six mugs of strong coffee. For a few minutes each man was silent with his thoughts.

Almost like a wake, Fuse thought. Except the god of fortune had smiled on them. He watched Toyama light a kerosene lamp and hang it from a beam. Finally the smaller of the men they had rescued shook the blanket from his head, exposing brown crewcut hair and sunken cheeks in a small, bony face.

"Thanks, chappies," he said, lifting his cup to Toyama and then to Fuse. "I was thinking this was like a wake for us. It could have been."

He spoke with a Cockney accent Fuse found difficult to follow. He wondered how many English Englishes there were.

"Glad we were there," Toyama said.

"I saw you running across the ice. That was quick thinking. I'm John. This is Pierre," indicating a black-haired man with a triangular face ending in what had been a Van Dyke beard now grown to weed. And this is Eric the Red, the Big Swede with the strong back and—"

"Go ahead, say it," the red-haired giant said, laughing. "And a weak mind."

"Don't let him fool you," John said. "He carried two hundred pounds up the Scales. That takes more than brawn. "And this is Beanie, because he looks like a beanpole."

"This is Mat," Toyama said, grinning.

Fuse looked around to see who Mat was, then realized his friend had shortened Matajiro.

"And I'm Sidney."

They shook hands all around, an odd assortment who could have exemplified all the gold rushers in Alaska.

"I'll cook up some grub," Toyama said.

John held up his hand. "You've done enough for us. Let Pierre. Wait till you taste his stew."

"Pot au feu," Pierre corrected. "But what I cook with?" Pierre began rummaging among the bags and tins that Toyama had neatly identified. "Good selection but not for French cooking."

"Never mind the fancy touches," John said. "We know you can cook. Anything will taste good. We're starved."

Over their meal the newcomers told their hosts of conditions upriver: of riots and near riots at the trading posts that had started to ration their dwindling stocks of food, of hunters returning without game, of desperate men scrounging for any means of transportation to escape. Most of them had given up their quest for gold and were intent only on returning home. Starvation was their immediate enemy.

"Seems like we jumped from the frying pan into the fire," John said. "The Sound will be frozen over before we get to St. Michael."

In the darkness relieved by the ghostly shine of the ice, the men walked back to the river to salvage what they could. Fortunately, the canoe was intact. Toyama offered them the use of the cabin.

When dawn was a grayness in the east the four men decided their canoe was seaworthy enough to carry two of them down to Rampart. In the morning cold the narrow channel was free of floes that could threaten their passage. John and Pierre, the smaller ones, set off, while Eric and Beanie shouldered into packs containing the rest of their possessions and with a wave of their hands started down the riverbank.

"Hope they find jobs," Fuse said.

"Not to worry. That John, he resourceful."

Influenced by what John had said, the two men reconsidered their goal. Gold was here at their doorstep in a manner of speaking. But they had come so far, why turn back? The men fleeing are the weaklings, Toyama said. *Gabatte, ne*. We must persevere.

Fuse and Toyama settled down to wait out the siege of winter. Wisely, they went their separate ways—Toyama to find a poker game in town, Fuse to explore the countryside. At different claims, marked by the smoke of fires, Fuse saw men burning away the permafrost and burrowing into the ground, heaping up mounds of earth they planned to wash for gold when the streams ran freely in the spring. Fuse busied himself cutting and chopping cordwood to last through the winter. He even found a market for his surplus.

For the thousands of men eager to reach Dawson but stranded along the Yukon, the winter was a time of frustration. Cabin fever dissolved more than one partnership. Even the best of friends got on each other's nerves. Half-demented men would slice a slab of bacon in two parts and squabble over which was the bigger half, cut a bag of flour in halves, even saw a sled into two parts that were of no use to either one.

On New Year's Eve of '98, after they had eaten their dinner of moose steak and rice, they built up the fire and spent the night in song and drink, with ukulele accompaniment.

Toyama had an untrained but natural tenor voice. Fuse was a baritone, also untrained, but he had a repertoire of *nagauta* (long songs), excerpts of which he taught his friend. From the latter he learned Hawaiian melodies. As the night wore on and the whiskey went to their heads they became nostalgic and maudlin.

Fuse contributed Japanese lullabies and Toyama turned

from laments of the Islands to Irish and Scotch heart jerkers. Teary-eyed, they finished off one of the most enjoyable evenings they had ever spent together with a rendition of *Auld Lang Syne*.

4

The Klondike

WHEN THE ICE BROKE ON THE YUKON in late May, Fuse and Toyama packed their remaining supplies on their sled and with a last regretful look at their winter home, turned their faces toward the dock at Rampart. They gave no thought to turning back.

Aboard the *Flora Belle* Captain Durkee had what he called two half-assed choices:

He was close to midway up the Yukon. He had fed his passengers for an agreed number of days. They had subsisted in one way or another. He felt morally committed to deliver his passengers to Dawson, but his stock of food was low. He could go back to St. Michael instead to replenish his supplies and put on more cargo.

The decisive factor in his choice was that he had barrels upon barrels of whiskey on board. In the North whiskey was the panacea for every ill of man, excluding possibly famine, and his cargo would be greeted by cheering throngs.

He was able to get some provisions from the trading ships that arrived in a steady stream from St. Michael. So one sunny morning after his crew had chopped the imprisoning ice away from the hull of his ship, Captain Durkee, to the cheers of his passengers, steered into the ice-choked Yukon and headed upriver.

The *Flora Belle* arrived at Dawson two weeks after the devastating flood of May 28. The Yukon, blocked by ice jams farther down, had backed up and overflowed its banks and inundated the business district to the height of an average man. Entrepreneurs with rowboats ferried passengers along Front Street at fifty cents each. The flood subsided June 5 but left the streets a quagmire through which even horses could not navigate. This was the scene that greeted Fuse and Toyama as they disembarked on the riverbank.

Fuse surveyed the muddy streets with dismay. It was enough to daunt the staunchest heart. He looked up and down the river, where boats of every shape and size were moored six deep for more than two miles. The armada that had waited for the breakup at Lake Bennett, the source of the Yukon, had arrived, and makeshift craft continued to float down the river all month. They brought with them an international assemblage from the thirty-two points of the compass. The river steamers from St. Michael disgorged several thousand more.

Strangely enough the can't-wait-a-minute urgency had disappeared, as if the magnetic lines along which the gold rushers had been drawn had suddenly vanished. The satisfaction of knowing that they had reached their destination by superhuman effort seemed to have become its own reward.

At its zenith Dawson was the largest city west of Winnipeg and north of San Francisco. Of those who stayed on, only a relative handful continued their hunt for gold. The rest had come prepared to set up businesses to cater to the needs of the miners and fellow adventurers.

The real dream of staking and fighting over claims had been staged on Bonanza and Eldorado creeks during the previous fall and winter. In the spring of 1898 a second rush started on what was to be called Cheechako Hill and the hills above the creeks. Old gold-bearing creek beds had been pushed up by upheavals of the earth's surface and deposits as rich as those on the present creeks seamed the hillsides. A few men who had reasoned out this possibility sank holes up on the hillsides to the derision of sourdoughs who "knew" that only cheechakos would be dumb enough to waste time digging up there. The experts were wrong to the tune of millions of dollars.

Fuse and Toyama reconnoitered the gold-producing area.

They found it staked to the last inch. They stood on a hill watching the miners below sluicing down the excavations of the past winter. Fuse felt a sense of hopelessness. He still was plagued by the thought of his broken promise, and his Alaskan adventure had begun to pall. He felt ready to return Outside.

Toyama was of a different mold. "We come dis far, we stay."

He got a job as a dealer at one of the gambling houses.

"You barber," he said. "We go find barber chair."

They searched along Wall Street and Broadway Avenue, which were like open air bazaars where practically everything under the sun was on sale, the discarded hopes of homeward-bound gold seekers. The enterprising Toyama found space in the front part of the gambling house, which was on the ground floor of a hotel. Before Fuse fully realized what was going on, he had a barbershop equipped with a real barber chair, a plate-glass mirror, and a marble counter complete with bay rum, cologne, and the tools of his trade. Toyama also had a wash basin installed.

"You wash hair and give massage. Charge double," Toyama said.

"How much for haircut?" Fuse said. "Three dollars?"

"You pupule," Toyama broke into Hawaiian. "You baka or something. You going to have private shaving mugs for every one of dose millionaires walking down Front Street. You charge ten dollar haircut complete. No shave and a haircut, six-bits. Come, we go buy up all shaving mugs. You going have high-tone shop."

A bewildered Fuse followed Toyama to the bazaar. From there they went to a printing shop where Toyama ordered a big sign, TOKYO BARBERSHOP, and a poster listing the prices of Fuse's services.

"Tokyo," Toyama said. "Everybody know Tokyo."

He was going to add "Tooth Pulled — $2" at the bottom of the poster, but Fuse put his foot down.

"No," he said. "I see dentist sign on Front Street."

"Okay. Okay."

In two days a flabbergasted Fuse opened his door to what proved to be a thriving business. So thriving that he had to set up an appointment book for the big shots, as Toyama called them. For the first few days Toyama acted as a sort of maitre d' for Fuse. To a big loser at his gambling table he would slip a personal ten-dollar gold piece and suggest a haircut at Tokyo's. "You feel like a new man."

For a while Fuse could not become accustomed to being called Tokyo by his patrons, who associated him with the name of his shop. His attempted explanation, "My name Fuse," fell on deaf ears. So throughout his stay in Dawson, he was Tokyo.

Fuse felt grateful to Toyama. His friend was under no obligation to help him out, and as far as Fuse could see he had no ulterior motive. During their year together he had found Toyama a friendly and generous soul who always acted in character. His mind was a fertile source of ideas upon which he acted positively without delay. Fuse, characteristically Japanese, hoped one day to repay his debt. He did not know that Toyama would have resented that.

Fuse was unaware of the generosity of Hawaiian people. It was a second nature that even Toyama would have difficulty in describing. If pressed he might say that it went back in history, beyond the kinship that the Japanese felt as landsmen in a strange land. Possibly back to the communal living of the Polynesians, when what is mine is yours and what is yours is mine. The immigrants seemed to have acquired this trait, almost as if by osmosis.

The fire that razed the heart of Dawson on Thanksgiving Day 1898 spared the hotel in which Fuse had his barbershop. But he was not so fortunate the night of April 26, 1899, when a fire destroyed more than a hundred buildings and caused more than a million dollars in damages.

With the temperature forty-five degrees below zero, the water from the Yukon froze in the hose and burst it. Buildings in front of the advancing flames were dynamited in an effort to form a firebreak. As charges were being laid to demolish the Arctic Hotel, Fuse felt a tug at his sleeve.

"Come! Your barber chair."

They dashed into the barbershop, where a kneeling man was about to light the end of a fuse.

"Hey! Where you damn fools going?"

Fuse and Toyama wrenched the barber chair free of the screws that held it to the floor. As they escaped through smoke and flames, bearing their burden between them, someone shouted, "Attaboy, Tokyo! That's the spirit!"

Dawnlight revealed the heart of Dawson smoldering in ruins. The Dawson that had grown up in three years, the Dawson as the sourdoughs and even the cheechakos knew it, was gone. Businesses reopened in tents until new buildings were constructed. Joe Ladue's sawmill worked overtime, the shrill scream of the great saws echoing across the flats. A city of lumber instead of logs, of macadam roads and raised sidewalks instead of mud, grew out of the ashes.

About this time rumors began to filter in that gold had been discovered in the sands of Nome. As reports took on more substance Toyama looked at Fuse.

"You mean we were standing on gold!" Toyama said. "Jake Park was right."

"We go?" Fuse asked, almost hopeful that his friend would agree.

"No, we stay. We be too late."

From his own feeling of disappointment Fuse sensed that Toyama's reluctance to return to Nome was the knowledge that they had stood on wealth, that they could have realized their dreams a few weeks after they arrived in Alaska. It was enough to take the heart out of a lion.

Uneasily Fuse watched men start trickling out of town. The trickle turned into a stream as sourdoughs felt the itch to be on the hunt again, which actually was the end-all of their lives, until in August as many as eight thousand men and women left in one week. The stampede was on. Fuse, feeling the old wanderlust, was vaguely annoyed by Toyama's decision that they stay put.

During Fuse's stay in Dawson there were about thirty Japanese in the mining district. No accurate count was possible as they were constantly arriving or leaving, working as cooks in outlying districts, or spending their time in the bush prospecting.

Fuse was surprised to meet two landsmen from his own Yamagata Prefecture. Immigrants from northern Japan were few compared to the number from southern Honshu and Kyushu. Fujitani and Tanaka were natives of the northern part of the prefecture, from the mountains of Zao. At nostalgic bull sessions with these two Fuse felt, more than at any other time, the spell of homesickness.

A frustration felt by anyone attempting to identify and reconstruct the lives of these early pioneers lies in the confusion inherent in their surnames. Until 1868 only the nobility, samurai, and a few artists and artisans were authorized to have family names. Two years after the advent of the Meiji Period a family could adopt a surname. This was made compulsory in 1875. Family names were chosen without any system or organization, leading to chaos. Intensifying the confusion was that a *kanji* (Chinese ideograph) could be used with its Chinese or Japanese reading, or part of the first name might be written together with the surname. In short, variations were limitless.

Among Fuse's compatriots and among Japanese in general, mainly surnames were used, with possibly an initial. A man hesitated to give his real surname and first or personal name because he had a superstition, found also in other countries, that anyone who knew this had power over him. As a means of localizing an origin, a ken might be given. Fuse always remembered his "kens-men" as Fujitani or Tanaka from Yamagata. Anyone who asked him what their first names were drew a blank.

On November 3, 1899, as elsewhere on earth wherever there were Japanese, the Dawson immigrants celebrated *tenchō-setsu*, the birthday of their Emperor Mutsuhito, in song and home-brewed sake. Their cheers of "Tenno-heika, banzai!" rent the Arctic night and no doubt startled the more sedate citizens.

In April 1900, a year after the second Dawson fire, Toyama joined a private game after the gaming tables were closed. He had a pile of two thousand dollars in gold chips in front of him. After watching a few desultory hands, Fuse was about to turn away when Toyama said "I raise you a thousand." There were about four thousand dollars in the pot.

His remaining opponent was "White Water" Bates, a thin,

sallow-faced man with tight lips. "How many you draw?" Bates asked.

"Two, same as you."

Bates looked at Toyama's expressionless face. He squeezed his cards. "I'll see you and raise you another thousand."

Toyama fingered his chips. "I see you."

"All right. What you got?"

Toyama turned over four sevens.

Bates flung down four sixes and started to rise.

Fuse drew a long breath. His legs felt weak. *Yūki da,* he thought. What courage.

"Wait," said Toyama, raking in the pot. "I hear you heading for Nome. We cut for high cards." He stacked two thousand dollars in chips. "This against your claim on Dominion Creek."

"You're nuts, Toyama," a bystander said. "Everybody's leaving for Nome."

"You shut up," Bates said. Then his lips tightened and he stared at Toyama. "What do you know I don't know?"

"I think there's still gold in them thar hills," Toyama mimicked in his best Western drawl.

He flung the cards face down on the table. "You mix them up, Fred," he said to the dealer. "Mix 'em up good." He looked at Bates. "Well?"

Bates licked his lips. "Okay." His voice came out in a croak so he repeated, "Okay."

"You go."

"No, I want a new deck of cards."

Fred broke out a new pack and fanned the cards face down around the table. Bates looked at his partner standing at his side. The latter had an adjoining claim.

"Ace is high," Toyama said.

Bates turned over the ten of hearts. All eyes were on Toyama's hand. Fuse's hand tightened over the back of a chair. His friend was *baka.* No one heard the sound of a piano in the background.

Toyama turned over the jack of spades. "Seven, eleven," he said. "Lucky tonight."

To Bate's partner he said, "I buy your claim for two thousand. Give you grubstake."

As the gambling house owner made out the bills of sale, Toyama glanced up at Fuse. "Two claims better dan one," he winked. He stood up and shouted to the bartender, "Drinks on me."

"I need a drink," Fuse said as they sat at the bar. He drew a long breath as if savoring the pleasure he felt at his friend's good fortune. "You baka or something."

"I feel lucky tonight."

Fuse shook his head. He fell into Toyama's Hawaiian patois, "You mo' betta dan me."

Toyama laughed. He shook his head. "I hear t'ings at table. Hear rumor big dredging company planning to buy up all claims."

"That take time. What you do now?"

"We come dig for gold. We dig. We come dis far, no dig?"

The use of the plural pronoun was not lost on Fuse. "You always say we. Claims belong you."

"We," Toyama said, emphasizing the we. "We in same boat."

Although Toyama had showed surprising skill in building the log cabin at Rampart, he had not struck Fuse as one who liked to toil with his hands. They were more adept at shuffling and dealing cards, a skill he could always fall back on. Perhaps, Fuse thought, that had been at the back of his mind when he risked a fortune on a turn of the cards.

As Fuse closed the door of his barbershop the next morning, he saw Bates and his partner race by on a sled pulled by eight huskies. The dogs' tails were high and eager and the men seemed to be in a good mood. They waved as Fuse shouted, "Good luck."

The sky was blue and the temperature about ten degrees below zero. Good traveling weather if it held true, but seventeen hundred miles lay ahead of them.

This would be an exploratory trip, Toyama said, as he and Fuse carried picks and shovels out to their claims. Only a withered leaf here and there clung to the shattered trees. But even the shambles along the trail did not prepare them for the devastation ahead. What had been virgin land three short years ago appeared to have been pulled up by its roots and tumbled upside down. The valley looked like an exhausted battlefield of shellholes, trenches, and dugouts.

"This never happen in Japan," Fuse said.

"Not in Hawaii," said Toyama. "We live in Paradise. Why for we come here?"

The answer came in the sound of the *puck, puck, puck* of picks and the sound of iron striking stones. It came with the sight of many smokes rising in the still air like pipes of peace, floating together and raising a canopy of blue haze.

They spent the next few days cleaning up the cabin Bates and his partner had shared. They had left their buckets and windlasses as though they had planned to return.

The luck Toyama had at the gambling table did not follow them to the claims on the hillside above Dominion Creek. They followed the usual method of building a fire, scraping the earth that melted, building another fire, *ad infinitum*. It was hard, dirty, muscle-hurting work at the bottom of the shaft.

The earth they piled up hardly looked to contain gold, and nuggets were nonexistent. As a respite they explored the thousand feet of the two claims, seeking seams of grayish gravel that might have been an old creek bed. Failing in this they had to sink hole after hole, living only on hope and blind chance.

One spring morning they sat eating lunch on the hillside. The brooks and creeks were chattering away and gurgling up at the benign sun. On the banks the miners were sluicing their winter harvest by the shovelful in their wooden rockers.

Toyama waved his hand over the mounds of earth they had excavated during the spring. "Wonder if dey worth washing."

"We got to finish job," Fuse said.

"You right. Bates had gold dust. Gotta come out of here."

Toyama held up his hands. They were curled like claws. Fuse's hands were in no better shape.

"Dis make monkeys of us," Toyama said. Ruefully he examined the palms and backs of his hands. He flexed his fingers to see if they were pliable enough to shuffle cards. "After we wash up the dirt we got to t'ink what we do."

The sluicing produced more gold than they had expected, more than enough to cover the cost of their supplies for the winter past, but not enough to raise their expectations of getting rich.

"I t'ink we keep claims but go back to Dawson."

"You do better poker," Fuse agreed. Then he was struck by an idea. "You go Dawson. You make money, I work claim."

"I no wish dis slavery on worst enemy. Together okay. But not alone."

Fuse hefted their leather pouch of gold dust. "We partners. You go do what you do best. I want dig. You take this poke—that what they call it?—and play poker. I got gold fever."

Toyama regarded him doubtfully. "You know w'at I t'ink 'bout dis. But dis," he pointed at pick and shovel, "not for me."

"You do what you like, I do what I want." Fuse emphasized want. "Gold here."

Toyama reluctantly agreed. "Summer not so bad, except for mosquitos. Come winter you open your barbershop."

So it was agreed, each man to what he wanted to do. At the back of his mind Fuse was thinking that if he could come up with more gold he could pay back what Toyama had advanced in their partnership.

Their stubbornness and tenacity took them through the uneventful winter of 1901–2, but these wore thin as the next summer waned. Early in September they decided to leave Dawson—before the freeze.

"What you do?" Fuse asked, as they left the bank where they had signed quit-claim deeds over to a dredging company syndicate, relinquishing their hold on a dream of riches that had died. They had also bought bank drafts and sent money to their banks in Seattle.

"I t'ink I go back to Hawaii," Toyama said. "Maybe stop Californi'."

"I take boat down Yukon," Fuse said. It was one of the more difficult decisions he had to make: to part from his friend.

Toyama looked suspiciously at Fuse. "I know you pa'aikiki

head, but you not t'inking try some more?"

At Fuse's blank look, "Hard head," Toyama said. "Stubborn."

"You mean ishi atama," Fuse laughed. "Stone head. No, no, I no do."

"Maybe hai, hai."

"Fuyu wa hidoi!" Fuse lapsed into Japanese when he had strong emotions to express. "Winter too cruel! Like last winter. Forty below for one week. Enough ganbaru! But summer hard to beat. This country suki da," he said, "I love this country."

This did not allay Toyama's suspicions. "How old you?"

Fuse paused. Whenever he was asked this question he hesitated. Like most Issei he thought of his age in Meiji years. The year 1902 was Meiji thirty-five. But he was born four years before Meiji 1. With his forefinger he wrote thirty-five invisibly on the palm of his hand and added four which gave him thirty-nine.

"Thirty-nine years old," he said.

"Why, you old man. Time you come wit' me."

"You come with me?" Fuse asked wistfully.

"No, I take boat and White Pass railroad to Skagway. I want see where my friends go."

On this note they parted. Each knew the other could not be moved. Fuse looked into Toyama's eyes, so clear and so young, and saw the affection reflecting the five years they had endured together. He felt a poignant sense of loneliness as their partnership was sundered. The next morning they shook hands at the pier.

"Kiotsukete," Fuse said. "Be careful."

Toyama handed Fuse a slip of paper. "Dis my home address. Back in Hawaii. Aloha, Fuse. Good luck."

Toyama turned quickly and walked up the gangplank. He bumped into the door jamb as he entered the salon without a backward look.

Fuse felt infinitely alone as he stood on the riverbank long after the ship bore Toyama out of sight. Would their trails ever cross again?

5
Wada Ju

FUSE STEPPED OFF A STEAMER AT FAIRBANKS, carrying nothing but his pack and bedroll. It occurred to him that his appearance and possessions were the same as seven years ago when he got on the train leaving Seattle for California. The thought amused him and a small smile lurked at the corner of his mouth as he shed his baggage in front of the Tokyo Restaurant.

The name struck him as an oddity in the heart of a wilderness until he recalled his own Tokyo Barber in Dawson. The front window framed a dark interior. He rolled a cigarette and was patting his breast pocket for a match when a stranger leaned forward, a lighted pipe in his mouth. The man puffed and the tobacco gleamed red. Fuse was below average height, but he had to lean down to light his cigarette in the proffered bowl. His eyes were inches from the other man's enigmatic look. Fuse was uncertain as to whether he should thank him in Japanese.

"Thank you," he said, adding with his quizzical smile, "Arigato."

"No need," the small man said. His engaging smile was a light on his large, rough-hewn features. "I am Wada Jujiro. Call me Wada Ju." He gave his surname first after the Japanese custom.

"Fuse Matajiro," responded Fuse.

So it was that Fuse met the man who was on the threshold of legend as a trailblazer of the Northland. He beheld a man about five feet tall, stockily built, with a resolute face that gave Fuse the impression of latent strength.

He invited Fuse inside for coffee. He pronounced coffee as an American would, not *ko-hi* as a Japanese might. Fuse watched with interest as Wada lighted two kerosene lamps, revealing a counter with stools on his right and small, square tables on his left.

"This is my restaurant," Wada said, setting two cups of steaming coffee between them.

Since Fuse had just stepped off the boat from Dawson, maybe he could tell Wada something about the Interior. Fuse expanded the account of his adventures to include his experiences down the Pacific Slope to Mexico. Wada listened intently, as though filing the information.

Wada interrupted Fuse when he had to wait on diners, always with a pleasant word and a cheerful face. He returned with a fresh cup of coffee.

"How very interesting," he said as Fuse finished.

Then, seeing the curiosity on Fuse's face, he told him the path that had brought him to a Fairbanks cafe.

Before the turn of the century he was one of several young men from wealthy families who crossed the Pacific Ocean to attend American colleges. One of them attended the U.S. Naval Academy, and Wada had been accepted at Yale.

In Japan and aboard ship they studied English zealously. Then in San Francisco Wada met a man who seemed to be refined and who told him of a professor who could teach him fluent English in three days. The naive Wada was delighted.

He was introduced to an unlikely looking *sensei* (teacher), a bartender in a saloon on the Embarcadero. Wada had a *hen na kimochi*, a strange feeling, but he had been exposed to so many odd things in America that he dismissed his uneasiness. Told that it was customary to seal an agreement with a drink, Wada, revealing all the money he had brought to pay for his first year's expenses at school, bought drinks for the other two. It was a strange liquor, he thought as he drank.

He regained consciousness on a ship's bunk. All his money was gone. He had been shanghaied onto a whaling ship headed for three years in the Bering Sea. His appeals to be put ashore were ignored.

He soon learned, though, that the captain was a considerate man in a tough job. He had to rule with an iron fist the dregs of the Barbary Coast who had been shanghaied to supplement his original crew. Wada learned to cook on board, and this became his calling for the rest of the voyage and thereafter when his situation required.

The captain maintained a well-stocked library where Wada spent his off-watch hours reading and learning to write English. He read every book and, with the captain's help, learned to keep the ship's log and accounts. By the time the whaler dropped him off at San Francisco, he had a fairly good education in English.

When he telegraphed home he learned that his family had given him up for dead and disinherited him. Cut off from his old life, he thought of the Eskimos he had met when the ship anchored along the Seward Peninsula. In his negotiations with them he discovered that many of their words were the same as Japanese. He learned enough of their language to converse, and he felt an ethnic rapport. It was his theory that Japanese fishermen, driven by storms, had been shipwrecked on this coast and had cast their lot with their rescuers. He decided not to return to Japan. The people of Alaska liked him, he said, and he liked them.

In 1901, according to one account, Wada shipped as a cook with Elbridge T. Barnette. Barnette had chartered the *Lavelle Young* and loaded her with provisions, supplies, and merchandise with the purpose of establishing a trading post on the Tanana River, the Yukon's greatest tributary.

A chance meeting with Felix Pedro (actually Pedroni, from Bologna, Italy), a coal miner turned prospector, determined the site of Fairbanks. Barnette had cruised up the Tanana until blocked by shallow waters, and then ventured up Chena Slough, a tributary. Here the boat's skipper, C. W. Adams, helped the party pitch tents and then left them stranded in the middle of nowhere. Pedro was seeking to replenish his supplies when he ran across Barnette and told him there was gold in the region.

When Fuse arrived, Fairbanks was in the throes of birth pains that gave rise to the "largest log-cabin town in the world." In one of them Wada, now thirty, had opened his Tokyo Restaurant.

"You could write a book about your life," said Fuse.

Wada shook his head. "I am not one to sit and reflect. I want action, I want to be on the move. These past two winters I learned how to drive and take care of a dog team. I am preparing for my great adventure."

As the two men talked they understood that they were kindred souls.

"I am sorry to see you going Outside," Wada said. "Your strike may be around the next bend."

"How many bends have I left behind me." Fuse was so moved he squatted on the floor and moved his hands back and forth as though he were rocking a gold pan. He resumed his seat. "How many footprints." His fingers walked across the polished wood.

Wada smiled. "You are a comic."

"Me! A comic." He shook his head. Of course, when he had too many flasks of sake he might come up with some good stuff.

"You have lunch on me," Wada said.

Fuse was about to *enryo,* a Japanese charade of holding back so as not to inconvenience a host, but he realized this was not the Alaskan way. Toyama had exorcised *enryo* from his psyche. He sat at the counter near the stove where Wada would be preparing orders.

An unshaven, unkempt man approached Wada, looking shamefaced, and spoke to him softly. After a sharp glance Wada pulled a coin from his pocket and slipped it to the man. Fuse caught the glint of gold. The man sat at the counter a few seats from Fuse. He ordered a hamburger steak and french fries and wolfed them down as though he had not eaten for days.

"Thanks, Wada Ju," the man said as he paid up with Wada's coin.

Wada nodded and gave him change. "You help someone when he has a problem. Okay."

"Will do, Wada Ju. I will remember you. Many times over." The man tipped his hand to the brim of his felt hat. His back was straight as he walked out the door.

"I am curious," Fuse said, as though he had not noticed the byplay. "You talk like a Tohoku man." (Tohoku is the part of Japan north of Tokyo.) "I am from Yamagata ken."

Wada laughed. "Many make that same mistake. No, I am from Ehime ken." This was a prefecture on Shikoku Island in central Japan, forming the eastern limits of the Inland Sea.

The blast of a steam whistle interrupted them.

"I must leave," Fuse said reluctantly.

"I am sorry to see you go," Wada said. "Your trail is south. Mine leads north. Next year I will have my grubstake. Nothing will stop me."

"I believe nothing will. Sayonara, Wada Ju."

Sayonara, Wada Ju. The words had a swing to them. Wada had impressed Fuse deeply. Despite the setbacks he had suffered, he exuded confidence. Fuse sensed he would leave his mark on the wilderness. Sayonara, Wada Ju. Someone could write a ballad around that title.

When he did leave Fairbanks, Wada Ju once again turned bad luck into opportunity. To create a market for his goods, Barnette had hired Wada to go to Dawson to spread word of a gold strike in the Fairbanks area. Wada did not have much to go on except what Fuse had told him, but, using the Yukon River as a guide, he eventually reached the site of the Klondike strike. His report of gold in the Tanana Valley sparked a stampede. The miners and entrepreneurs who had not already been drawn to Nome flocked to Fairbanks. Wada also returned to Fairbanks, to find disappointed and disgruntled miners who had expected to find placer gold in large quantities.

Some accounts say the stampeders' anger focused on Wada. In their view he had misled them. A miners' meeting, an extension of the town hall meeting of early America and the only law in some mining camps, was held to determine if Wada should be hanged. The only defense Wada could offer was that he had been sent by Barnette. The proceedings turned into a mock trial intended to scare the bejesus out of Wada. He was released with the solemn warning to get out of town, a form of banishment resorted to by many frontier towns. The miners realized that the trader was really to blame. Wada disclaimed this version. He said he had overextended his resources in buying town lots, so that he went broke and left Fairbanks. He said he never was threatened.

Wada decamped with forty mink furs claimed by Barnette. He may have taken them in payment for his services to the trader. Barnette, unlike pioneer predecessors such as Jack McQuestion, Arthur Harper, and Alfred Mayo, and unlike Wada's countryman Frank Yasuda, was tightfisted and opportunistic, an unsavory character. When he tried to raise the price of flour, the miners reacted so violently that he built a stockade around his trading post.

When Wada showed up in Nome he was promptly arrested. He jumped bail provided by friends. The marshal believed he took a ship for the Outside; others, that he lived awhile in Kotzebue, with Eskimos he had met during his whaling days. Apparently he appeased his friends and the law, for he reappeared in Nome.

Using what he had learned from Barnette, Wada went into business on behalf of the Eskimos. For the first time, they got a square deal for their furs and ivory. They were so impressed and appreciative that they made him a chief, possibly the first and only Japanese to hold such a position.

But Nome fur traders, disgruntled at no longer being able to trade with the Eskimos on their own terms, complained to the Bureau of Indian Affairs. The BIA resurrected an old law that stated that only a member of a tribe could be its chief. Wada thereby became the first Japanese to be deposed as chief of an American native tribe. But through Wada the Eskimos had learned to deal with the crafty fur traders.

Wada was not the Eskimos' only Japanese friend, nor the only legendary Japanese sourdough. Frank Yasuda, who was a member of the crew of the Coast Guard cutter *Bear* in 1898, left the Coast Guard to work for Charles Brower at his trading post at Barrow, the northernmost settlement in Alaska. Working as a fur trader, he traversed the Arctic Slope above the Brooks Range. He came to know this area as well as anyone. He learned to speak Inupiat (an Eskimo language), Athabascan (the language of the Indians of interior Alaska), and English. He married Nevelo, an Eskimo woman.

When overharvesting threatened the whaling industry, the Eskimos faced a bleak future. Yasuda was instrumental in leading his wife's people across the Endicott Mountains of the Brooks Range to the north bank of the Yukon. Instead of whalers they became hunters and fur trappers. They gave up dugout homes for log cabins and houses. Their diet changed from whale meat to caribou and reindeer.

When a road was started from the Yukon to the gold-mining camp of Caro, Yasuda chose the river terminus as the site of a village he named Beaver. His trading post there became a supply point for the Chandalar Gold district. Yasuda joined a pair of prospectors, Sam J. Marsh and Tom Carter, to explore the region.

Marsh and Carter had set out in 1901 from Port Clarence, northwest of Nome, on a thirty-five ton schooner provisioned for two years. They were determined to approach the headwaters of the Koyukuk River from the Arctic Ocean. The expedition, hounded by an Arctic storm, ended in disaster, but the two men survived. Another ship picked up the crewmen. For the rest of the decade, enduring incredible hardships, they and Yasuda explored the only gold-bearing regions discovered north of the Arctic Circle. Insects were a misery in the brief summer, and winter temperatures below minus 60 were not uncommon. The coldest temperature ever recorded in Alaska, 80 degrees below zero, was measured here at Prospect Creek Camp. At these temperatures a steel ax head that hits a rock or nail will shatter like glass.

Yasuda was more than an intrepid pioneer. He was generous to a degree that puzzled his daughter, Hana, for years. His home was open to strangers. When a man wanted to establish a store that would compete with his trading post, Yasuda helped him. He helped build a schoolhouse for the Eskimo children. He took care of mail and at times acted as a banker. He was a general factotum, an institution, trusted by all. During World War II, he was interned at an alien detention camp in New Mexico, but at war's end he returned to his beloved Alaska. He died in 1958.

Jiro Nitta, a Japanese novelist who died in 1980, wrote a romanticized account of Yasuda's life. *Arasuka Monogatari* became a best seller and was made into a popular motion picture. An English edition is planned.

Wada Ju also became a legend. In a land where physical endurance can mean the difference between life and death, where it measures a man's stature, the indoor marathon race was the most popular sporting event, especially during the winters. Big stakes exchanged hands on the outcome. One prostitute bet $5,000 on Jujiro Wada at odds that enabled her to return Outside to respectability.

An account of one such race, run in March 1907, was recorded by a newspaper for posterity: "Carrying an American flag in his hand for the last two laps, James Wada, the Japanese representative, won the big 50 mile race on Saturday last, in the fast time 7 hours, 49 minutes, 10 seconds."

This marathon was not for a mere twenty-five miles, but for fifty miles, a superhuman goal. It was held in the constricted confines of the Nome Eagles Hall, thirty-two laps to a mile. The runners reeled off lap after lap, spurred on by their backers. Exhortations became feverish over the last two hours.

James Wada, "the phantom prospector of the North," was Jujiro Wada. In various accounts he was given the names James, Jujuira, Jujira, and Jujiro (which would be correct in Japanese.) Among Japanese he was popularly known as Wada Ju.

One significance may be lost in the symbolism of the American flag. Wada believed he was an American citizen, an honor conferred on him by a governor of Alaska. In fact no Issei, not even veterans who fought in World War I and were promised U.S. citizenship, was ever granted this right until the Walter-McCarran Act of 1952.

Among the closest of Wada's friends and trail mates was Frank Cotter, later a news editor of the *Alaska Weekly*. Cotter met him for the first time in Fairbanks, where Wada planned to enter a marathon. It seemed doubtful if he could run, as he had a sprain and a wrenched muscle, but with liniment, a heating pad, and hot towels, Cotter was able to get him in shape.

In the winter of 1909–10, Wada was commissioned by the town of Seward, an ice-free port on the Kenai Peninsula, to stake out a route to Iditarod, site of the latest gold strike. Cotter ran into Wada at Flat, nine miles from Iditarod. Wada invited him to join him in his mapping expedition, a trek of about 500 miles.

It was forty below zero late in January when they and two other men with two teams of twenty-two dogs left Iditarod. The temperature soon dipped to sixty degrees below zero. The snow turned hard and gritty like sand, and the sled runners whined a song of protest audible a mile away. They mushed on into a black, eerie fog, a sign of dangerous weather. The gritty snow abraded the dogs' feet so that when they camped at night Wada made moccasins for the dogs, using a spare suit of woolen underwear.

The next noon when Cotter tried to chop wood for a fire to heat water for tea, his ax head shattered. On the night of the fifth day, Wada discovered that some of their dogs' legs were frozen up to the belly. When rapped by a gun barrel they sounded like marble.

Wada stood up from an examination of the dogs. "They will have to be shot," he said. "When the frost starts coming out of their legs, the pain will drive them mad and make them dangerous."

"They have earned a last good feed," he said, patting their heads.

After their meal Wada called the five dogs and they followed him down to the river. Cotter heard five muffled shots. Wada returned and went to his bedroll without a word.

The party crossed Rainy Pass and headed down to the Yentna River that runs into the Susitno River, which in turn empties into the head of Cook Inlet. Here they ran into a new danger: Wolves began following the party, skulking in the shadows beyond the light of the campfires.

The two men's pride was the leader of their team, a beautiful setter named Chief, the most friendly sled dog they had ever known. When he started limping, an examination revealed that his legs had begun to slough off, the dead skin parting from the living. He was cut from harness and allowed to follow as best he could.

Chief would come staggering into camp an hour late, but holding his tail high and wagging a greeting. They applied lard and bound his feet. They brought him into the warmth of the tent and Cotter used his warm, heavily-furred body for a pillow. In the morning Chief could hardly move but would stagger along, soon to be lost in the distance. They could not put Chief on the sled because the other dogs were so far gone.

One night Chief came in, his sides slashed. He had fought off the wolves and staggered along the trail into camp. The next morning as they broke camp, Chief stood up and struggled to follow. This was too much for Wada.

"It's a shame to let the wolves tear poor old Chief to pieces," he told Cotter. "He's going to die, but he deserves a kinder fate. Please, Mr. Cotter, take a gun and put him out of his misery before the wolves kill him."

"My God, Wada. Chief is my pal. I've slept with him, shared grub with him. I can't kill him. You do it, please."

Silently, Wada took his .45 and waved Cotter on. He sat down on the edge of the trail to wait for Chief. Cotter looked back, hoping to be out of sight before Chief appeared. He saw the flutter of the beautiful red silken neckerchief that Wada always wore on the trail. He had turned a bend in the river when he heard the crack of the .45. As Cotter thought of Chief back there slowly stiffening, tears were freezing on his cheeks.

At noon Cotter stopped the team to make tea. Wada looked different, and Cotter realized the red kerchief was gone.

"Where's the red hanky, Wada?" he asked.

Wada's face was as sober as Cotter had ever seen it. "I left it with Chief," he said. "You see, he trusted me, and when I put the muzzle of the gun to his ear he looked at me with those big brown eyes and licked my hand. I couldn't let him see me kill him, so I took off my handkerchief and tied it around his head and shot. I did not even look back."

Wada went on to become a familiar figure at Alaskan stampedes. One of his most impressive feats was to drive a five-dog team along the Arctic Coast as far east as Winnipeg, 2,500 miles in the heart of winter. To the end he was prospecting for gold, and then for oil. Mushing phantom trails was his life.

This great musher, who wanted to live and die in Alaska, passed away in San Diego on March 5, 1937, at the age of sixty-five. He had fifty-three cents in his pocket.

Frank Cotter provided a eulogy that spoke for all Alaskans who knew him: "The best musher and the best man in snow-shoes that ever made a track in Alaska. He had a heart in him as big as a ham, a decent, kindly gentleman that it was a plea-sure and a privilege to have known. He was game to the core, resourceful and cheerful at all times."

His destitute end cannot be considered the end of his trail. Chief lives. Wada lives. The image that remains and should be remembered is of a great pioneer who extended the vast fron-tiers of Alaska and Canada and helped in their development and growth. Among his sourdough peers, of whom there were none hardier in all the world, he was considered one of the fabulous and giant trailblazers of the North. Sayonara, Wada Ju.

6

Metzgar

W HEN FUSE ARRIVED at St. Michael he was told there were no berths to be had.

"How about job? I be cabin boy before."

The agent shook his head. Fuse went outside and stood irresolutely on the sidewalk. He became aware of a tall, bearded stranger with blue eyes so intense Fuse looked a second time.

"Looks like we're in the same boat," the stranger said. His use of Toyama's favorite expression made Fuse do a double take. "Or out of a boat," the man said. He seemed relaxed and easy, a six-foot edition of Fuse's Hawaiian friend.

"Man say he can book us out of Nome," Fuse said, craning his neck to look up at his new companion.

"Let's try it." The agent sold them tickets and turned to his telegraph key.

As they emerged from the ticket office the big man looked across the dancing waves of Norton Sound. "How do we get there?"

"Maybe ask Eskimo."

They picked up their packs and walked along the beach, pausing before a man who was untying a painter from a boulder.

There was something familiar about the burly figure. As the man straightened Fuse said, "Jake Park! We meet before."

The Eskimo studied Fuse's face. Recognition widened his eyes. "I remember." He cocked an eyebrow. "Five years ago.

Took you and friend to Nome beach. Never find gold, but gold there."

"You take us Nome?"

Park shook his head. Waving a hand toward his boat he said, "Food, supplies, same like last time. Come to think about it, September, too. No, I go back to my village. Golovin."

"That's not too far from Nome," the red-bearded man said. "You take us to Golovin?"

"I go there." He nodded toward his boat.

"I'm Dan Metzgar." He extended his hand to Park, and then to Fuse.

"Me, Fuse. Fu-seh. Matajiro Fuse."

"Mata—. I'll call you Mat for short."

"Me short," Fuse laughed. He liked this Metz—this Dan, with the observant eyes; understanding eyes, too, it seemed to Fuse.

The sky, which had been clear, was hazing over, and an array of dark clouds was invading and overrunning Seward Peninsula. The low-lying land was a long shadow on the blackening sea waters. Whitecaps raised their banners and advanced against the puny craft daring to challenge their domain.

"Looks like a norther," Metzgar said, as the boat started to pitch and the air grew cold. He untied a parka from his roll and shrugged into it. Fuse followed suit and the two men crowded into the tiny cabin where Park was struggling with the wheel. He turned on the running lights.

The howling wind raised Fuse's apprehension. His anticipation of a pleasant cruise across the sound was turning into what could be a nightmare. His dread was reflected on Metzgar's face, but Park's expression remained stolid.

"Been in worse storms," Park said. He patted the wheel. "*Mary Ellen* strong boat. Always get me there."

He steered by compass and to some extent by instinct as the boat bucked like an untamed stallion raising hooves against the ten-foot waves. Park glanced occasionally at the faces of his passengers, pallid in the weak glow of the pilot light. As he saw their shoulders begin to heave, he said, "If you puke, you puke outside. But grab on to something."

Suddenly he was alone in the pilot house. He did not think of the comic aspect of their situation: that seasickness was more overpowering than the threat of drowning. Only those who have experienced the sickness caused by unruly seas can lend a sympathetic heart.

Park grunted as he saw a few scattered lights dead ahead. To port and starboard he saw waves tossing up manes of white as they broke on the beach. Continuing on course toward a relatively black expanse of water, he steered through the entrance into Golovin Bay, which was sheltered to some extent by the mountains behind the village. Fuse and Metzgar tottered ashore and collapsed on a boulder, oblivious to the villagers who suddenly appeared on the beach and began to unload the boat by the light of kerosene lamps.

Park brought the two men their packs. "Come. You come to my house."

The aroma of coffee greeted them as they entered the kitchen. Park's wife, Mary, a plump, kind-faced woman with a shy smile, poured their coffee and disappeared. Park, with a furtive look at the door through which his wife had left, took a flask of whiskey from a cupboard and spiked their coffee.

"Ah!" said Metzgar. "That hits the spot."

As he laid his cup down he was struck by the workmanship of the table. Its surface seemed to have been constructed from pieces of driftwood joined together, sanded and polished until they looked like one piece of wood. About three inches thick, the long edges of the table had been left with the original contours of the wood.

Metzgar regarded Park with respect. "Beautiful," he said. He ran his hand over the glass-like finish.

"I like it," Park said. "Took lot of work."

Everywhere about the two-room house was evidence of Park's handicraft, from the cupboard above the sink to the stone fireplace where flames licked at the logs. Fuse noticed white flakes at the lone window that looked out over the dark bay.

Park went to the door and looked out. "Be heavy snow," he said.

"We got to make tracks if we want to catch that boat," Metzgar said.

"You sleep here tonight," Park said. "Floor okay? Tomorrow you walk along beach to Nome. Don't matter how much it snow. I take you by boat but we have big talk here tomorrow. All villages in this district." At Metzgars's questioning look he added, "Whales disappearing. We got to do something else."

Metzgar thought of the millions in gold that had been shoveled out of the sands of Nome. It was wealth, if wisely directed, that could give all the Eskimos economic security. The possibilities were endless. He said as much to Park. "Why, with the right investments . . ."

Park recapitulated what he had told Toyama five years earlier. Like Toyama, Metzgar was incredulous and grew angry. "I don't believe it! You're telling me you don't have the rights of citizenship!" (It was not until 1924 that the Native Alaskans were granted citizenship.)

"We're treated like wards of the government. The Christian churches regard us as uncivilized heathen who must be converted. On their terms."

"I wish I could help."

"We need white friends. Friends we can trust."

Park's pointed words brought Metzgar up short. At a loss for words he jested, "You think you could trust me?"

Park studied Metzgar's resolute jaw, felt the heat in his voice, the fires in his eyes. "I would put my faith in you," Park said.

"Thanks," Metzgar said. "I appreciate that."

Park shook his proffered hand.

Metzgar sat back on his mental heels. He had never pictured himself as a knight on a white charger. Here he was offered a challenge. Until this moment he had been a journalist fresh out of an Ivy League college in search of adventure.

"I should put my poke where my mouth is," he said tentatively. "But you've planted a seed."

"One more white voice—there are so few—would help us. Here or Outside."

Logs made little noises settling in the fireplace and white

ash began to edge the embers. What followed was a little above Fuse's head. He had trouble stifling his yawns.

With a laugh Metzgar poked him. "Go to sleep, Mat. You stay with me, you'll catch on by and by."

Metzgar and Park became engrossed in talk of cooperatives, such as Father Duncan had established in Metlakatla, and the Territorial education system as a means of training future leaders. As they talked Park grew in Metzgar's estimation. He was talking to a cultured and well-read man.

"That educational system," Park said, "is out of joint with our culture and our needs. Let me explain."

Two men, Park said, charted the course of education among the Native Alaskans. First, early in the nineteenth century, there was father John Ivan Veniaminov, a priest of the Russian Orthodox Church, who established his first church at Unalaska. He was a big bear of a man with a heart as large. A measure of his charisma was that he was able to overcome the fear and anger of the Aleuts, a legacy of their brutal treatment at the hands of the first Russian traders.

He developed bilingual education as a means of converting the Aleuts to his church. "Isn't that the logical and practical way!" Park said. Veniaminov learned the Aleut language, with a bilingual Aleut worked out an alphabet, translated the Scriptures from Russian, and wrote textbooks with the two languages parallel on each page. A remarkable man, who rose from being a priest in Irkutsk, Siberia, to Metropolitan of Moscow, the highest post in his Church.

The other man was Sheldon Jackson, a Presbyterian minister originally from New York State, who established the current educational system after the United States bought Alaska from Russia in 1867. Blind to the culture of the Native Alaskans, he made it mandatory that English, and only English, be used in the school system. This was a losing battle because outside school and at home the children spoke what came naturally.

"Here you had two diametrically conflicting philosophies." Park paused, laughed. "I haven't used such big words in a long time." His expression became serious, as though firelight was dying on his face. "What Jackson was trying to do amounted to cultural genocide of a people."

Metzgar was aware of the genocidal atrocities committed over the course of two centuries on the Native Americans living in the Lower Forty-eight. The concept of cultural genocide was being brought to his attention for the first time.

In the morning Metzgar was torn between his desire to sit in on the big talk and the necessity to get to Nome if he and Fuse wanted to catch their ship for the Outside.

During the night a strong wind had piled the six inches of new snow into drifts. At breakfast Park announced that the big talk had been postponed. Over a third cup of coffee he offered to take his two guests to Nome.

Fuse and Metzgar went outside and looked across the bay. If its surface was lashed and tormented, what would it be like on the open sea? They looked at each other and hastily withdrew from the bite of the salt-laden wind.

"No, thanks," Metzgar said. "We'd rather walk, eh, Fuse."

"Sometime this last for days," Park said.

"We've got no choice. We don't want—at least I don't want to be stuck up here another winter."

Fuse nodded. "How long it take?"

"Maybe three days."

Fuse and Metzgar exchanged glances.

Park drew a map. "This Golovnin Lagoon. Cartographers spell it that way. Our village, we spell it Golovin. You reach Bluff first night. Near White Mountain. Next night, Solomon. Then Nome."

"Thank you, Jake. We'll make a stab at it."

"Let me see. You been in Alaska five years. You know country. Maybe okay." Park sounded doubtful. "Follow beach. Longer but easier. No need snowshoes." To Fuse, "No get lost."

For the first two days they followed Park's advice. With the wind at their backs, they made good progress and reached their destinations on schedule. Fuse's endurance, developed in years of rambling, helped him now, and he found himself leading the way.

On the third morning the two men awoke to find that the

wind had veered to the west and was approaching storm pro-
portions. They would have to fight for every step against wind
and snow. It was here they made a fateful decision, disregard-
ing Park's warning.

They decided to strike straight across land, avoiding the
indentations of the seacoast, but attempting to keep the ocean
in view on their left. In the first few miles they discovered that
ploughing through the deep snow, especially where it had piled
in drifts, taxed their strength. They veered to the coast, but the
tide was high and the coastline jagged with newly formed ice.

Metzgar, though a strong man, did not have the endurance of the wiry Fuse and had to stop from time to time to recover his breath and restore his energy. The early afternoon
darkness found them still short of their final destination. The
wind tore up the crusty snow and drove it like pellets into their
faces.

As they stopped for a breather in the shelter of a knoll,
Metzgar told Fuse, "You go ahead. I'll catch up."

"Only a little more," Fuse said, though he was feeling the
cumulative exhaustion of three days fighting the snow and now
a headwind. He pulled Metzgar to his feet and adjusted his pack.
"Come. We go."

They struggled on, Metzgar plodding in Fuse's footsteps.
Once, as they stopped to rest, Fuse became aware that the wind
was bearing in from his left. Had it shifted direction, or had it
driven him off his course as he tried to lessen its head-on im-
pact? He rose from his haunches, beckoned to Metzgar, and
headed directly into the wind. He felt uneasy, for he had heard
stories of lost hunters walking in circles. There were no trees,
no landmarks on the tundra. He began to feel that the tundra
was stalking them.

He decided to bear to the left where he felt the beach was.
He turned to tell Metzgar and was startled and frightened to see
no sign of him.

Bending low to discern his fading footprints, he retraced
his way. Possibly Metzgar had wandered off. The thought
alarmed him and recharged his energy. He had gone so far that
he was considering casting around the area off his trail when he

stumbled over what he thought was a snow-covered log. But he had not crossed any logs. There were no logs on the tundra.

He brushed snow off the form. It was Metzgar. *Ureshii,* he exulted. Happy, happy. He slapped Metzgar awake, oblivious to his "Let me be. I want to sleep."

Fuse knew that danger. It was one thing to sleep in a cave or sheltering cliff, in full control of one's faculties, but an entirely different thing to drift off on the tundra, to be discovered as a body when warm weather melted the snow.

"You. You break trail," Fuse said, hoping that the exertion would awaken Metzgar to the dangers of their ordeal. From behind he guided Metzgar straight into the wind.

For a while Metzgar threw off his fatigue. The wind died, the snow stopped, and stars appeared among the broken clouds. But a different danger emerged. An intense cold settled over the white plain. At first they felt relieved and exhilarated, but the cold proved an insidious drug. It penetrated to the marrow. It formed a crust on the snow that taxed their legs. Finally Metzgar set down his pack, rolled over on his back and closed his eyes to the North Star and Big Dipper overhead. Fuse sat down on his pack to catch forty winks.

He snapped awake when he fell off his pack. He had bumped his face against Metzgar's pack and felt no pain. He touched his nose. It was not there. He realized at once what had happened. He scooped up some snow and began to rub his nose with it. With his other hand he rubbed snow on Metzgar's nose. The pain of restored circulation aroused Metzgar, and Fuse roughed him to his feet.

"Get up! Get up!" Fuse screamed. Fear made him lose his composure. Arm in arm he made Metzgar half-run, half-stumble around in a circle. Metzgar was rubbing his nose now of his own volition.

Fuse laughed without sound. "Baka," he called himself. "Fool." Unencumbered, Fuse thought, he could make it alone to Nome. He looked toward where he thought the town lay. At first only a white expanse brightened by starshine was visible, but then he stiffened. He hoped the shape he saw was not a hallucination.

"Come," he said.

Dragging their packs, they stumbled forward. It was what he had hoped. A shed, or not much more than a shed. What it was doing in this isolated spot Fuse never questioned. He did not worry about the sagging roof, the door hanging by a hinge. It represented shelter.

As they staggered into the cabin the air felt warmer, but Fuse knew this was an illusion. By the dim light reflected from the snow outside he found some moss that had been used to chink a crack in the log wall. He made thin shavings from chips of wood on the earthen floor.

He nursed the flame until it was throwing their shadows against the walls, and then opened his parka and exposed his front and hands to the heat. He felt warmth coursing through his body. He felt his nose. It seemed to be all right, but to be safe he got some snow and the two men massaged their noses with it.

Fuse took a pan from his pack, went outside and scooped up snow, which he heated until it was boiling water. He stirred in a handful of ground coffee. As they drank and warmed their hands around their cups, Metzgar looked across the fire at Fuse.

"Thanks," he said quietly.

"We in same boat," Fuse said. The remark was becoming standard repartee, he thought. "We come out."

"Thanks to you." Metzgar stood up. "I feel like a new man. I'll make some mush." He looked at Fuse and smiled. "No, maybe rice?"

"No," Fuse said hastily. "I make rice." These barbarians didn't know the first thing about cooking rice. "You fry bacon."

"Okay," Metzgar smiled. He knew what Fuse was thinking. He took what was left of a slab of bacon and began to scrape off the mold. Bacon tasted all right as long as you got all the mold off.

The danger past, the two men fell asleep. They arose in the morning to a cloudless sky. The nightmare was behind and they looked confidently forward to what lay ahead. A sound sleep and a full stomach can work wonders.

They repacked and stepped outside. Fuse pointed toward a nearby knoll. Metzgar nodded. "We can see where we are."

As they topped the rise the men stood as if transfixed.

"Well, I'll be damned!" Metzgar stopped, at a loss for words. "Looks like."

About two miles away, behind a beach littered with broken and discarded machinery, stood a settlement of tents and houses that had to be Nome.

"You mean to say we were that close," Metzgar said, unable to believe that they had been the victims of such a grim jest.

"It true."

Imbued with a delight that lightened their steps, they walked into Nome in what seemed no time. They reconfirmed their reservations. Their ship, the S.S. *Baranoff,* would arrive the next day and sail the following morning. They found rooms for two nights at the Dawson Hotel.

After lunch the following day Fuse said to Metzgar, "I want to think. I take walk up beach."

Metzgar nodded. "I think I'll find me a poker game."

"Don't lose stake."

"Not to worry."

Fuse walked to the point where he and Toyama had stood five years ago. 1897. How time had flown. They had looked up the miles of beach as far as their eyes could see. The sandy surface had looked as bland and guileless as a poker face hiding a royal flush. The sand had contained millions of dollars in gold. Fuse could understand why Toyama had not wanted to come back this way. He felt heartsick.

Savagely and uncharacteristically, Fuse kicked the sand in exasperation. He kicked again as if the act gave him relief. It had been criminal, he thought, not to have panned the sands for gold. But who would have thought . . . If they had come up with the big strike, then their destinies . . . There was always that if, that big IF.

Fate was such an ironic jester, who could say what was written in his stars up there, or when the candle of his life in the sky would be blown out? Fuse squatted and let the ice-cold sand run through the hourglass of his hands.

His narrow escape from death had brought him up short. The experience caused him to review his life. His panning had produced little gold. His wanderings could be described as a search for greener pastures, but at no time or place had he felt the urge to put down his roots, to call for his family in Japan to join him. He knew he had a wanderlust that put wings on his boots. Now he was led to ask himself whether he was seeking or running away.

Was he avoiding his responsibility of raising a family? Or, and this was most important, was he afraid to face up to himself? If so, he could roam the world to tether's end and his problem would remain. He had only to look in a mirror and know the answer. It was there, in the dark and complex world of his mind. He had reached a crossroad, here on the sands of Nome, and the sign pointed to Japan.

As he seated himself on a rusting steel tray barrow, someone else's broken dream, he quarried another vein of his dilemma. He faced a choice, as hundreds and eventually thousands of other immigrants from Japan were to face: to return to his homeland or to earn a place in America. To choose between his Eastern culture and that of the West.

Two planets hung like lanterns in the darkened west and a million stars were rushing in to fill the heavens as Fuse plodded back to the lights of Nome. As far as he was concerned the oracle within had spoken. He was returning to Japan to bring his wife back to the United States. Once he reached this decision he felt free of a debilitating uncertainty.

He slept soundly but awoke early, all his senses alert. He had not eaten dinner and felt hungry, but he first shaved and brushed his teeth with cold water from a pitcher. By the light of the kerosene lamp he packed his duffle. Without knocking on Metzgar's door—it was too early to arouse him—he proceeded along the street to Ishii's Dawson Cafe. Ishii was stoking the stove, so Fuse threw his pack in a corner and walked out to the beach. Wistfully, he felt that a cup of hot coffee would have hit the spot.

Fuse had wrestled with his problem and to some extent laid it to rest. It still itched, though, like a healing injury; the mind draws no attention to itself when healthy.

Breathing deeply of the salty, humid air, he watched shooting stars silently scratch the black emery of the sky and the tinted panels of the northern lights shift and dissolve into each other like scenes from an ethereal ballet. His heart responded in pain to the beauty of the heavens at play.

He awoke from his reverie. His senses recalled him to the physical world about him. Tossing at anchor far off shore was the shadow of the ship that would bear him away. Riding lights beckoned through the quickening dawn. Some men with lanterns appeared at the lighter that was gradually taking shape on the beach. Because of the shallow waters fronting Nome, everything had to be transferred back and forth from ship by barges.

Head down against the weight of the rising wind, he trudged toward the lights of the restaurant. His boots thudded on the wooden sidewalk and he bumped into a burly figure. By a window's glow he saw small, bloodshot eyes above a reddish beard.

"Out of my way. Let a white man pass."

Fuse drew back. He did not fully comprehend the significance of the man's words but he felt their venom. The unexpectedness of the verbal attack left him with his mouth open. He watched the man enter the cafe.

"Ketō!" he said. "Dirty, hairy foreigner!" He had almost reached the door when the man reappeared, shouting over his shoulder, "I'm not eating in any Jap restaurant." He walked unsteadily into the dawn.

As Fuse entered the now warm air of the restaurant, he threw back the hood of his parka. The light of a kerosene lamp hanging from a beam showed that his mustache was in need of a trim. Fuse's normally kind expression was taut with anger.

"Chikushō!" he said, after the departing back.

"Ai, a beast. Like a wild animal," Ishii said.

"Atama ni kita," Fuse said. "Anger came to my head. That kind of white man leaves me speechless."

The cafe owner was square-faced and heavily jowled, with thick nose and heavy eyebrows that pressed down on his appraising eyes. His body was wide but lean, and his stomach was flat. He wore a short-sleeved white shirt and a chef's hat.

Ishii might be considered the earliest of Japanese restaurateurs in the west. He came to Seattle from California in 1881, was in Astoria, Oregon, the following year, and returned to Seattle in 1883 when the Japanese population numbered only a handful. In 1887 he opened a restaurant on Occidental Avenue in the Skid Road section. He established the Dawson Cafe in Nome during the 1899 gold rush. A wanderer like Fuse, he opened restaurants wherever he went, generously helped other Japanese open their own, sold his, and moved on. He left restaurants behind him like footprints in the sands of his time.

"Hotcake and coffee." Fuse rang a silver dollar on the counter. He could have the same meal in Seattle for fifteen cents, he thought.

"So, you are going back," Ishii said, as he ladled out the pancake batter.

Fuse saw regret, if not envy, in Ishii's eyes.

"Issho ni kaeritai na," Ishii said. "Together I would like to return. Name is Fuse, you said. Matajiro? Yamagata ken. Mezurashii. Unusual. I am from Ehime."

Precious few Japanese immigrants came from the northern part of Japan, and strangers from the same ken were landsmen. In the history of the Japanese in America, the *kenjinkai*, such as the Hiroshima Kenjinkai, or prefectural club, formed a social force of some importance.

"Business seems to be good," Fuse said, glancing around the crowded cafe.

"Food is too expensive. The boom is over. Money cannot be made."

Fuse accepted the other's comment as a Japanese understatement.

A shadow fell across his plate.

"Hi, Mat," a young voice said. It was Metzgar.

"Coffee, Ishii, black. Maybe I'll have a stack of hots, too." He patted Fuse on the shoulder. "And bacon and eggs for my lifesaver."

Fuse felt embarrassed. It had been nothing he had done,

he thought, deprecating his deed after the Japanese fashion. "Nothing I do."

"Don't kid yourself," Metzgar said. "Without you I'd been a dead duck."

"Dead duck?" Another of those crazy expressions.

"Dead duck. Yeah, like dead. Forget about the duck." Metzgar threw back his head and laughed.

"So we leave Alaska." Fuse looked slyly at Metzgar. "No more—what you call—research? No more experience?"

"You're a joker, aren't you," Metzgar laughed. "I could write a book on what I've been through since I left New York. Maybe I will. No, there's nothing more to keep me in this godforsaken land."

A ship's whistle sounded, distorted by the wind. Men in various parts of the restaurant shouldered into their packs.

"Kiotsukete," Ishii said. "Be careful. Sayonara."

Fuse carried the memory of that lonely, wistful figure with him to the beach. He was aware of the solitude of men in unknown places, of the strands of memory that bound them to the past.

The lighter, actually a scow, transferred the passengers over a sea chopped into whitecaps by the wind. It was a diverse crew that boarded the ship: a few defeated and broken, others like Fuse and Metzgar with pokes of gold in money belts, or in wooden boxes that took two men to carry. Mention a trade or profession and it would be represented. Among them were those who would return—river pilots, construction workers, prostitutes, and traders going Outside to replenish their goods.

Fuse's hobnailed boots rang on the steel steps as he descended into the indescribable aura common to all ships, the distillation of salt air, oil, grease, food, sweat. He flung his pack on an upper berth to avoid the wrangling he heard between two men vying for a lower in another part of the hold. What did it matter where he slept after the nights he had spent tossing on rocks and roots felt through his sleeping bag? He preferred staring at the steel beam overhead rather than the bulge of someone's hindquarters.

He heard the distant rumble of the ship's engines, steel

protesting as chain drew up anchor, and felt the vibration and swaying of the ship as she got underway with a last blast of her whistle. With the start of each voyage there was always this feeling of excitement and anticipation of new experiences beyond the tossing horizon.

He went up on deck for a farewell look at a vast land that had been his home for the past five years. As he opened the steerage door, black smoke from the ship's smokestack borne by a following wind poured down the companionway. He slammed the door shut on a flood of coughing and profanity that erupted out of the steerage quarters.

He chuckled, a faint smile on his face, and scurried to the shelter of the forward cabin. The wind had brought fat, wet snowflakes, blotting out sight of land on the eastern horizon.

The Great Land is well rid of me and I am well rid of it, Fuse thought. So he thought.

The *Baranoff* escaped the ice floes that were gathering like wolf packs in Norton Sound, passed through Unimak Pass, and headed eastward across the Gulf of Alaska. The air grew warmer as the ship entered the Japan Current, known as *Kuroshio* to the Japanese. The days lengthened perceptibly, and more seagulls scavenged the roiling water astern. One morning after breakfast Fuse saw the long gray cloud of Vancouver Island off the port bow. He unbuttoned his parka to the warming rays of the sun.

"It's always a thrill to make landfall," Metzgar's voice said at Fuse's shoulder. Fuse glanced up at his tall friend. The sunlight glinted on his auburn beard and intensified the blue of his deep-set eyes.

"Feel good." Fuse looked curiously at Metzgar. Fuse had watched him play cards day after day during the long voyage. "You win?"

"About broke even, I guess. I set aside two hundred dollars that I could afford to lose. Tried to make it last as long as I could. Just to kill time."

"You strong man. Me, I play till I lose everything. But this time I keep my stake—for my wife and children."

"Where you staying tonight?"

"Japanese hotel. Jackson Street."

"Mind if I tag along?"

"You come."

Their ship nosed into Juan de Fuca Strait, rode the placid waters of Puget Sound, and finally entered Elliott Bay. Curiously they examined the waterfront.

"What a difference from ninety-eight. That was a mob scene."

"Everybody crazy," Fuse agreed.

This time the waterfront scene was orderly and purposeful. Little tugs noisily nosed steamships into their berths, or pulled barges piled with lumber, sand, or coal stolidly up and down the Sound. Ships' horns bayed for rights of passage. Windjammers stood at anchor out in the placid bay. Ferries cut white-crested *V*s toward Vashon and Bainbridge islands.

"Looks like things are booming," Metzgar said.

As the *Baranoff* docked the two men shouldered their packs, walked through the Skid Road district and up Jackson Street. To their dismay they discovered the hotels and rooming houses were full. The seasonal workers had returned to their warrens.

Finally they entered a small lobby in a basement. Ahead of them a man, dressed like a laborer, reached the front desk, looked at the Japanese clerk, said "Goddam, Jap," and left. Behind him a better-dressed man asked, "Do you have a Mr. Brown staying here?"

As a bystander, Metzgar suddenly comprehended the significance of the scene. The first man had been frank about his hatred; the second was just being polite, having no intention of renting a room in a Japanese-run hotel.

Fuse looked at Metzgar. "You want stay here?"

"Why not."

As Fuse signed the register, the desk clerk kept looking at Metzgar. "Ii desu ka?" he asked. "Is it all right? Single or double room we do not have any left."

"Shikataganai," Fuse said. "It can't be helped. He has decided."

Shikataganai is a Japanese word philosophically accepting

a situation or condition that fate has decreed.

"Bedbug nai shindai kudasai." Fuse looked obliquely at Metzgar. "I ask him give us bunks no bedbugs."

"Hai. Kore wa kesa coal oil de yakimashita."

"He say this morning he burn bedspring with coal oil."

They went down a hall on the second floor to a large room that held six cots. "Like a flophouse," Metzgar thought. The common bathroom and toilet was down the narrow, ill-lit hall. Fuse would have preferred to luxuriate in a Japanese bathhouse, but he did not dare take his companion there. In all his experience he had never seen a white in a *furo*.

They went to the Jackson Cafe for dinner. They had left their packs because, as Metzgar said, there was nothing worth stealing. He looked up at the framed restaurant license with a dollar bill in the lower left hand corner and the age-brown menu. Ham and eggs 15 cents, pork chops 10 cents, T-bone steak 25 cents.

"Wonder if they have a porterhouse steak? That's like a T-bone but a better cut. And an extra order of fried potatoes."

Fuse recognized the waiter. "Ha! Jiro-san! Still working at the same place."

"You see me," Jiro said. "I am saving money to open my own restaurant."

"Good."

Jiro brought glasses of water, a plate of crusty French bread sprinkled with blue poppy seeds, and butter that didn't come out of a tin. "Coffee first?"

The men nodded. "Damn, this is good," Metzgar said, bulging his cheeks with thickly-buttered bread.

"Take easy," Fuse said. "No room for meat."

"I've dreamed about this minute for years. Fresh meat, fresh potatoes right out of the ground, apple pie made with apples just plucked off a tree, good coffee. Hot damn! This is good. Good as Delmonico's. That's a high-tone restaurant in New York."

Over their third cup of black coffee and smoke-plumed cigars Metzgar leaned back and said, "It was all worth it just for this minute. This is the reward. You've tested yourself against impossible odds and achieved something. You've become a man."

Fuse asked, "Achieved?"

Metzgar crossed his long legs, thought a moment and said, "Like climbing Mount Fuji."

Fuse smiled. "Ah! So desu ne." He beckoned to Jiro. "Brandy arimas' ka?"

Jiro glanced at Metzgar and at their reflections in the front window mirrored by the black night, as if looking for the law.

"Ii, tomodachi desu."

Jiro returned with brandy disguised in coffee cups.

"Tomodachi?"

"Friend."

"I'll drink to that."

"This is—what you say, barbaric—drinking brandy out of cups. Sorry, no brandy glasses."

"What's the diff. Tin cups would be okay."

They became aware of the fragrance of perfume. The woman who stood before their table was petite, her hair arranged in a Japanese-style pompadour. She was wearing a navy blue jacket over a pleated blouse and an ankle-length woolen skirt that revealed button shoes. To Metzgar her pretty face hardly required the heavy makeup she wore.

"Good evening," she said in Japanese. "Welcome back, Fuse-san. You are in good health?"

"Hai. How are you?"

Metzgar stood up. "Please have a seat."

"Oh, thank you." She glanced at the entrance. "Gomen na sai." She smiled at Metzgar. "Excuse me."

She left them to greet a white man who wore a homburg hat and a gold chain across the vest of his black suit. He wore pearl gray spats.

"Who is she?"

"Her name is Hana, flower. She is—we call them hakujin chō. White man's butterfly."

"A madam?"

Fuse nodded. "We in center red light district. You want girl you look for sign white only. Inside, white, black, Japanese girls. Pink house, anybody go in. Be careful Ohana-san. Your two hundred dollars go like that." Fuse snapped his fingers.

"Very interesting. Would make a good story. But Ohana-san. Why?"

"She say, why not? Wife of farmer, work like horse." Japanese came automatically to his lips. "Asakara ban made. I mean—morning to night. Have kids—four, six, maybe ten."

"Like the Old West. The white pioneers went through the same thing. Come to think of it, this is the West."

They watched Ohana-san leave with the man. Each was silent with his thoughts.

"What you do now?" Fuse asked. He felt regret that he might be parted from his friend.

"I'm thinking. I was going to take a train east tomorrow. See my folks. But what could be more interesting than here? Maybe I'll stick around a few days. Get the feel of the place."

"You make me feel good."

Metzgar nodded. "I would hate to part, too."

As Fuse dropped off to sleep that night, he heard someone mutter. "Koko ni ketō nani shitoru no ka?"

Fuse stared up into the darkness. *Ketō*, a derogatory term. A dislike, a distrust, if not a hatred, that had grown out of the harsh treatment so many of the Japanese immigrants had received when they arrived in America. Yes, what was a white man doing here?

Over a thick slab of ham, eggs, and home fries the next morning, they discussed their plans for the day: to see if their bank drafts had been deposited to their credit, Fuse to buy a money order to send his wife, to outfit themselves in city clothes. And for Metzgar to find sleeping quarters.

"What do you plan to do?"

"I take ship to Japan and bring back my family. But I worry. When we come back here, what we do?"

From Fuse's incomplete English, Metzgar gathered that he did not want to bring his wife back to a farm, sawmill, or railroad. He remembered Ohana-san's philosophy.

"Well," Metzgar said realistically. "If you start a business, you can't leave it to go and bring back your family. Get your family and then start a business."

They were interrupted by the entrance of a small Japanese in his late thirties. He had a pockmarked, ravaged face with shrewd, observant eyes. His expression was dour and cynical. When he spoke his voice was brusque and businesslike.

"That is Shiro Sato," Fuse said. "He own employment agency. Boy contractor. Maybe get news from him." Fuse stood up. "Sato-san, have coffee with us."

Fuse introduced Metzgar as Sato joined them. "How's business?" Fuse asked.

Sato shrugged his round shoulders and ran a hand through his prematurely gray, crewcut hair. "Alaska boys back from the canneries and most of them looking for jobs. I place some in sawmills and logging camps, but the rest . . ." He shrugged again.

"What kind of jobs? What do they pay?"

"Short-order cooks, maybe seventy dollars a month. Dishwashers, busboys, vegetable washers, silver polishers, porters—about forty to fifty a month. Work twelve to fourteen hours a day, seven days a week. No time for fun. So you can save money."

Fuse translated as Sato rattled on.

"Sawmills, too, about one dollar, maybe dollar-and-a-half for ten-hour day."

Sato pulled a dollar Ingersoll watch from a vest pocket of his gray suit. "I am late. Must open office."

"How about own business? Like barbershop?"

Fuse listened in dismay as Sato sniffed. "Too many already. Besides, having union trouble. Can't join white union so Japanese have own union. But Japanese crazy. They lower price and lower price."

"You mean price war," Metzgar said.

Sato nodded. "Too much competition."

"Cheerful little bugger," Metzgar said after Sato's retreating back.

"He always call—what you say—he call a spade a spade."

Metzgar laughed. "You're picking up English, Mat."

"I still worry."

"C'mon, let's take care of first things first."

Metzgar found a front room in a private home on Fifth Avenue, in the white district north of the Yesler Way cable. He had invited Fuse to join him in his search. Fuse had pointed to his own face. "They see this and you never get room."

Metzgar had frowned. Back East he had moved in the rarefied air of Ivy League circles. It had never occurred to him to question the nonexistence of blacks, except as domestics. He had met a few Negroes in the mining camps, but in Alaska, on the trail and in the camps, a man was accepted for what he was and not what he looked like.

Through his experiences with Fuse in the past few days he was beginning to see a ghetto presence within West Coast white society. He was aware of the prejudices that the Irish and Italian and Jewish immigrants faced, but he felt that the prejudice against Fuse and his countrymen was more insidious and unjust because it was based on race. It troubled his conscience.

Fuse turned his attention to the problem of what he should do when he brought his family from Japan. How was he to support them? Where would he find a roof to cover them? As he pondered this problem over breakfast it suddenly occurred to him that this was Sunday. His old friends would be at the Japanese bath according to their weekly ritual.

Suzuki and Murakami were there, and momentarily expecting Suda.

"Oi, Fuse," Suzuki said. The tailor's fleshy face was red from his bath. "When did you get back?"

"We had given you up for dead," Murakami said.

It seemed to Fuse that the drayman had grown even stouter and rounder than he remembered him.

"We hadn't heard from you for so long. And Suda-san had never run across you anywhere in Alaska."

"You mean. . . ." Fuse said.

Murakami's grin was so broad it reminded Fuse of Jake Park. So much alike, he thought.

"Remember that day when we were all here and he advised you not to go to Alaska? That it was too difficult and too dangerous?"

"Like yesterday," Fuse said. "He depressed me. But he was right. If I had known what it was like, I would have stayed here. It was everything he said. Only worse. I am lucky to be alive."

"Well! Remember Suda said he would never go again?" Murakami doubled up with a laugh and slapped his thick thigh. "When Suda heard about all that gold the *Portland* brought back, he went mad, mad as all of them. You know, I go down to the docks to meet the ships from Japan. I wasted good hours when I could have been making money, just watching the—the circus. It was a circus. And all the performers were madmen. You would not believe me if I told you."

"From what I heard," Suzuki said, "they tried to have the ships from Japan go to Alaska. Crazy! But Fuse-san, we're so happy to see you back."

"Yes. How did you do?"

"I never struck it rich, but I came back with enough to go after my family."

"I am happy," Suzuki said. Murakami nodded.

"Dōmo arigato." Fuse bowed his appreciation. "Thank you. But I am of two minds. Shall I send for my wife or should I go after her?"

"Depends," Murakami said. "If I had the money I would go."

"Murakami-san's wife had a terrible time," Suzuki said.

Fuse did not understand. As far as he knew, if one had steamship fare and show money, and passed a physical examination, what else could go wrong? If you didn't have hookworm, trachoma, or venereal disease, it should be simple.

"This doctor in Japan," Murakami explained, "claimed my wife had trachoma. She had several operations and that took a long time. In her last letter she wrote that she finally changed to another doctor who said that she did not have trachoma. This all happened before you went up to Alaska, as you know."

"She thinks that the first doctor told her lies so that he could make money from her. She had used up part of her passage money so I had to work and save to send her more money. Hidō katta," he said. "It was cruel."

"Warui koto surune!" Fuse said. "What bad things they do."

"There are evil Japanese who take advantage of the innocent. Can't you see them? Wearing that polite, considerate mask, with greed in their hearts. Koroshitai," Murakami said. "I would like to kill them. If I ever met the doctor who mistreated my wife I would mash him like a bedbug." He banged the table so the soda bottles danced a jig.

In Yokohama and Kobe, the two main ports of departure, innkeepers of what were known as emigrant houses, often working together with unethical doctors, milked emigrants of as much money as they could. The former might say that no passage was available, or the latter diagnose nonexistent diseases. Delays of days, even weeks, resulted while the innkeepers and doctors fattened on the lambs.

"It took two years," Murakami said grimly.

"Two years!" Fuse was aghast. "If that's the case I am going after my wife."

"I understand that if you come first class you do not have to pass a physical examination," Suzuki said.

Murakami shook his head. "Not always. I heard of this health officer in Honolulu who made the wife of a vice-consul to Hawaii strip and subjected her to indignities. Well, a protest was made by the Japanese consul to the United States Government and the dog was fired. That is the way to treat such men." Murakami doubled his hand into a fist. "Only I would beat them into mochi first."

Suzuki said to Fuse, "I do not want to alarm you without cause, but sometimes it takes days to be cleared right here in Seattle. You must be prepared to be patient."

"These hakujin think we are animals. They treat us like animals."

A clatter on the brass-edged steps announced the arrival of Suda. Fuse noticed that there was a touch of gray in his fringe of hair.

"Oi, Fuse," Suda said, with his gargle-like laugh. "You are back."

"You see me." Fuse smiled, lifting his black mustache at the corners. He felt a certain pride in himself because Suda would understand the hardships he had undergone.

"Let's see," Suda said, as if he were counting in his head. "You went up in ninety-seven. This is nineteen hundred and two. You were away five years. My, time goes by so fast. They told you I went up to Alaska again, I suppose. Crazy, ne?"

"We were all crazy."

"By the time I got to Skagway the North West Mounted Police said every man going across the Pass had to have at least one year's food and supplies because the previous winter the people of Dawson almost starved. Many who tried to escape died. I shipped back to Juneau and worked in the mill at the Treadwell mines to make a grubstake."

"Before the river froze, my friend Toyama and I got as far as Rampart," Fuse said. "Spent the winter there. But before that we stood on the sands of Nome."

"Huh!" His listeners grunted as one. The Nome stampede was still fresh in their minds. "On the land you actually stood!"

Although it made Toyama and him look like blind fools, the story of the role played by chance was too good to withhold.

"That is the story of gold strikes," Suda said with sympathetic understanding. "I finally got up to Dawson. I looked for you everywhere."

"Dawson was so crowded. Maybe more than thirty thousand people," Fuse told Suzuki and Murakami. "If you got separated you could not find each other." To Suda, "The last winter Toyama and I were out working our claims."

Suda nodded. "Much of the time I was cooking at different camps. In between I would go prospecting."

Murakami looked disappointed. "But where was the adventure, the hunting for gold?"

"For every prospector who hit gold, there must have been a hundred storekeepers and businessmen, dancehall girls and prostitutes, cooks, waiters, bartenders, professionals, everybody you will find in a city like Seattle," Suda said, looking at Fuse, who nodded.

Fuse added, "There were about twenty to thirty Japanese in Dawson."

"Who were they?"

Fuse mentioned several names. His friends shook their heads. "A good number of them were from Fukuoka. They had a Fukuoka House. In Nome I met Ishii Kentaro."

"Ah! Is that right! Most of us know him," Suzuki said. "He helped my friend Yorita start a restaurant."

"He has the Dawson Cafe in Nome. He was in good health. By the way," Fuse told his interested listeners, keen to hear what other Japanese were doing, "I met Wada-ju in Fairbanks. He told me that when he arrived in San Francisco he was shanghaied and spent three years aboard a whaler. He is a kindly and friendly man. He speaks good English that he studied aboard his ship." He also told his friends about the work Frank Yasuda was doing among the Eskimos.

"Eh! Hontō no kaitakusha da na," Suzuki said. "Real pioneers."

"Alaska is their true home," Fuse said. "Not for me. I am going to make this my home."

"Eh! So you have decided," Suzuki said, in his even-toned way. "That is good news."

"After what you have told me I am going back to Japan to bring my wife. But I must decide what I will do when we return. That is one reason why I came to talk to you. Maybe you can advise me."

His friends exchanged glances. Finally, Murakami, the realist, said, "There are so many barbershops here."

"Well," Suzuki said. "There's Tacoma. Or a lot of Japanese are settling in Yakima and Wapato. Then there is Spokane."

"Where is this Spokane?"

"In the east part of Washington," Suzuki said. "There is a railroad from here. Good farm land."

"I have a friend there," Suda said. "He has a farm. I can write—"

"Please send a telegram. I will pay. Ask him how the prospects are in this Spokane."

Suda agreed. His friend's telegram said that there were no Japanese barbers, none with a shop. Fuse could make a good start.

As Fuse parted from Metzgar, the fire of friendship kindled on the Nome tundra was aglow in their eyes. "This is my friend Suzuki's address," Fuse gave Metzgar a slip of paper. "Through him we will keep in touch in the future."

"Sayonara, Fuse-san."

A few days later Fuse was aboard the *Hikawa Maru* bound for Yokohama.

7
Roots

THE FAMILY GRAVEYARD was about a hundred yards from the road junction where the ancestral home of the Tanagis had stood. At this distance the six gnarled pines that marked the site looked like a grove of bonsai. The pines stood about fifty feet from the graveled road along which Matajiro "Mat" Fuse was directing his feet. He was followed by a family entourage.

His mind was busy with a kaleidoscope of thoughts. In the background was the euphoria of his achievements in Alaska. He had returned with enough money to impress his banker father-in-law. He glanced briefly back at his wife, Yaso, who followed behind him as was the Japanese custom. She had welcomed him back with a joy that transformed her. As her older sister, Nasu, who was walking beside Yaso, had said, "Yaso was born again."

If there had been reproach in his wife's eyes he had never detected it. She had accepted him with the love, patience, and wisdom of a Penelope greeting Ulysses so many centuries before. Happiness over his return had been paramount in the Fuse household.

Behind the two sisters walked their parents, Chotaro and Hisako Fuse. Expressions of pride and well-being brightened their faces; their family was together again, they hoped for good. When Matajiro had married Yaso, he had given up his surname of Tanagi and became an adopted son of the Fuse family to carry on its lineage. He had done fairly well in Alaska.

Matajiro looked beyond at his children, Kennosuke and Miyoshi. He had been delighted at their filial piety, conduct, and intelligence. He was indebted to the Fuses for their upbringing. He had beeen impressed by Tatsuo Kurita, who was escorting Miyoshi up the road. He was tall, curly-haired, and handsome, distinguished by a mole on his right cheekbone.

The women carried offerings of flowers, food, incense, and candles. Matajiro was to pay his respects to his ancestors.

Through broken clouds the noonday sun was struggling to remove the chill from the October air. The mountains of Yamagata, robed in red maple-colored patterns like paisley, ringed the valley of the Uesugi warlords who had ruled this land for four centuries. Reaching a point opposite the stand of pines, Matajiro struck off along a path that ran beside a water-filled ditch toward the yard of gravestones.

While the women placed their offerings at two small altars in the grove, Matajiro went from weathered stone to stone reading the inscriptions that marked the final resting places of Tanagis dating back to the sixteenth century. They had been retainers of the Uesugi court—one a treasurer, another in charge of the rice granary—holding positions of prominence down through the generations. He had stopped at the tombstone of his father, Keizo Tanagi, when his ancestral spirits expressed their displeasure.

Without warning the air beneath the trees turned to the darkness before a thunderstorm. An icy wind blew out the candles and scattered the incense and food like dry leaves. For a few minutes the members of the stricken party held their ground, expecting this eerie phenomenon to vanish as it had come. The paralyzing breath of winter persisted.

The women broke for the sunlit road, followed by the men. Matajiro retreated stubbornly, facing what seemed a threat. He was no more superstitious than most, but he felt shaken. He bumped into Yaso, who alone had stood her ground: all four feet ten inches of her. Fright had paled her face and her small eyes were wide in wonder. Matajiro felt the comforting strength of her hands as they gripped his arm. He sensed her trust and faith in him as her protector.

"Somebody over there," he said, "doesn't like me. Or what I am planning." He smiled down at her anxious face. "Not to worry."

"It was so sudden, so cold, so cruel," she said. "Samishi katta." So lonesome.

To admit that he had felt the same would reveal weakness.

"A warning," she said.

The tossing branches of the pines seemed to mock them. Like an *oni*, like a demon out of Japanese mythology, she thought.

It was a subdued group that assembled in the living room of the Fuse home. *Makizushi*, rice cakes, and green tea in colorful array adorned the coffee table for what was supposed to be a festive occasion.

"Your ancestors are angry," Fuse broke the silence. His long face was still pale from the ordeal.

"You were away so long," Mrs. Fuse said. She went around pouring tea. "Dōzo," she said, waving her hand over the food. To Matajiro, "Maybe they are angry at you for leaving your ancestral home for the land of the barbarians."

Or renouncing the family name, he thought. Family was such a strong tradition. His years of freedom had made him forget. He found Mrs. Fuse trying to evaluate the effect of her words, her bold eyes steady on his. He smiled. He liked her for being forthright and pragmatic. He remembered how happy she had been at the union of a samurai family to her merchant-class husband's lineage. It was leading them to status in the maturing Meiji era.

Matajiro was aware that the Fuses wanted him to settle down in Yonezawa. He looked at the gold watch chain his father-in-law sported across his vest. With his contacts it would be a simple matter to find a position for him. But as he reflected on his Alaskan experience he knew that America was indelibly in his heart.

"So," Mr. Fuse said, "you are still determined to return to America with my daughter. I pray that you are taking her back to a life worthy of her."

Matajiro looked into the future of a barber's wife in Spokane. He would have to have a heart-to-heart talk with her. Dare he tell the others of the hardships faced by Japanese immigrants in a new country? Without the passport of language? No friends? For Yaso, over a vast ocean into the unknown?

Normally inclined to procrastinate, he recognized this was a crisis of confrontation. He had to face up to the unpleasant and get it over with.

"I will have a barbershop in a place called Spokane," he said.

"A tokoya!" Fuse said. "A barber! No!" He rubbed his gold chain, like prayer beads, for strength and assurance.

Mrs. Fuse rose quickly and started to massage his shoulders. "Now you must not get excited," she said. Much less hysterical, she thought, heeding their physician's warning. She felt the tension lessen in his neck and shoulder muscles. Her mind was abroad in the town: what would their neighbors think!

Mr. Fuse had listened entranced to Matajiro's account of his experiences as a gold seeker. That was adventure. Even as a conservative banker he had been seduced by the lure of gold. He had to credit his son-in-law with courage and perseverance. But that was another world from that of a barber.

"You would be satisfied with that life?" he asked.

"From what small roots did you grow?" Matajiro asked.

Fuse recalled his early beginnings as one of the lowest caste, the merchants. Those had been meager and shameful years: the butt of coarse samurai insults, the disparaging remarks of farmers and peasants. What was wrong with earning a *koku* of rice a day? he had thought. Now look at me.

"Your brother was a plantation worker in Hawaii," Matajiro said. "He made seventy cents a day, maybe twenty dollars a month, working six days a week from dawn to dusk. Now he has a business of his own."

Fuse could not argue with success. He tried a new approach. He assumed the role of Lucifer tempting Christ on the mountain top. But his son-in-law could not be bought.

Fuse fired his final gun. "You are my adopted son. You stand to inherit everything." It was the oldest-son syndrome that had ruled the destinies of families throughout the history of Japan.

"You never give up, ne," Matajiro said. "Gambaru ne."

"You are as stubborn as a mule," Fuse said. "At least Kennosuke will stand by me."

"I am going, too," Kennosuke said.

Mr. Fuse felt betrayed. Kennosuke's statement was also news to his father, who had considered but dismissed the thought. His son was sixteen. Matajiro had met Japanese immigrant workers about that age who would have benefited from more education. He wanted Kennosuke to be better prepared when he came to the States.

It was now two against Ken. He had listened to his father fending off Mr. Fuse and he resorted to similar tactics.

"But I don't have that much money," Matajiro finally said.

"I have saved enough for passage and show money to pass immigration."

"Eh!" Fuse said. "Behind my back you saved money." He intercepted Kennosuke's glance toward Nasu. "Hm! So!" as if that explained everything.

His wife helped him to an easy chair. "Poor chi chi. Young birds must spread their wings," she said. "You have me."

He held her hand and looked gratefully up at her. "You have been my strength," he said. "And we still have Miyoshi and Tatsuo." He looked at them suspiciously. "I suppose you will be leaving our nest."

"Not now," Tatsuo Kurita said.

"Oi. Not now, you say." Miyoshi was two years Kennosuke's junior and too young to marry. Fuse would have the comfort of their companionship for at least another couple of years.

Before her daughter's departure for Yokohama, Mrs. Fuse drew her aside. "You are married to a descendant of samurai. You must be his sword. As strong, as durable." Tears were in her forceful eyes. "Why am I weak, to give you such strong talk. Shinu-made. Unto death, you must be as iron. Or like bamboo, sway with the storm. Ganbatte."

Yaso bowed to hide her tears. "I will endure," she said.

Matajiro had heeded the warnings of his Seattle friends to

beware of corrupt doctors and their innkeeper cohorts. Fuse, with his banking contacts, had directed them to an honest physician and an innkeeper who doubled as a travel agent. Once having accepted the inevitable, Fuse cooperated with every means in his power.

The generous *sembetsu* or farewell gifts had helped Matajiro decide to return to America in cabin class. His wife deserved this treat. Further, on arriving in Seattle they could hope to avoid the degradation and humiliation that steerage passengers were sometimes exposed to during their physicals.

The first test of Yaso's will was the ocean voyage. The *Hikawa Maru* pulled out of Yokohama harbor on a crystalline day. Fujiyama thrust into the October sky with not a cloud to mar its beautiful white cone. Yaso, like all the passengers, fell silent as though they were in the presence of a shrine. It was the parting glimpse of their homeland. It would draw many of them back at least once in their lifetime: a dream like the Holy Grail that would sustain them through their trials in the United States.

Fuse returned to Japan when tension was rising with Russia over the control of Korea. In the summer of 1903 the two nations began a protracted series of negotiations that ended when Japan declared war on Russia on February 10, 1904. Japan had an army of 200,000 well-trained men, with a reserve of equal size of older men. Fuse felt conscience- and duty-bound to remain at home while his country was at war. Following the Treaty of Portsmouth on September 5, 1905, he did what he could to help Mr. Fuse through the economic crisis that followed war's end.

Now aboard ship he thought regretfully of those years that he considered lost. Not entirely lost, for Yaso was pregnant and expecting in November. Another mouth to feed at the start of his second great adventure. He wanted to prepare her by pointing out the hardships they could expect to face. She had turned her wan face and misery-filled eyes to him and said, "What could be worse than seasickness?"

He literally sat back on his heels, his head level with hers on the lower berth. He put his hand on her brow cold with sweat. Her hand tightened on his.

"Ganbatte," he said.

She nodded and turned her face to the steel hull.

"You must get up and walk around," he said. "You will never get your sea legs."

"Tomorrow," she said.

"Now," he said. "We might see Kennosuke."

That brought her upright. He helped her, seemingly weak as a kitten, out on the deck. "We must walk. Gaman."

"Hai, gaman." Nobody, not even her mother, had mentioned seasickness.

From the deck below the bridge they saw steerage passengers doing calisthenics.

"Oh! There's Kennosuke!" The sight of their son revived her spirit. She waved down at him.

He walked aft until he was below them. "Happy to see you up, Mama. Feeling better?"

"Seeing you, yes. I hope your food has improved?"

He made a face. "Bearable." He did not tell her that they were served hard-to-swallow, second-class rice and a side dish of vegetables or fish so oily it was like eating lard. They sat in a circle on deck as they ate.

Kennosuke had refused his father's offer of a berth in cabin class. "I'm young. I want the experience." He laughed up at his mother. "I sure would like some of your home cooking. Be careful and take care." He waved and rejoined the exercise group.

Yaso was getting her sea legs when the *Hikawa Maru* entered the same latitude as San Francisco. She enjoyed the rest of the voyage and looked forward to her future.

8

North Yakima

I N SPOKANE Matajiro and Yaso rented a small house at 1105 East 3rd Street near Liberty Park. Here their first American-born son weighed in at 10 pounds 4 ounces. His certification of birth recorded his Christian name as Joe Toranosuke, which his Alaskan playmates were to shorten to a manageable Thor. His sex M, color Jap., legitimate—yes, born—alive. The date was November 12, 1906.

His mother's maiden name was given as Yaso ——?——, age 32 and color W. Number of child of this mother 3. Why she was described as White died with the recorder. She was confused at the time about Yaso's maiden name. If Yaso Fuse was her married name, as Matajiro insisted, then she had to have a different maiden name. If Mr. Fuse could not supply this then she would have to put a question mark after Yaso.

Matajiro made a brave effort, considering his language handicap, to enlighten the recorder. Yaso Fuse *was* his wife's maiden name. The same as his because—His face beamed with the light that had struck his brain cells. "I give you *my* maiden name. It Matajiro Tanagi.

"You mean in Japan a man takes his wife's name?"

"Sometime. For me, yes."

Doubtfully, with an eye on Matajiro's ingenuous face, she wrote in "Yaso." "For the sake of future argument I will put in a question mark."

"But that satisfy nobody," Matajiro said.

Whatever, it was so recorded for posterity.

Matajiro was recorded as 42, color Jap., and occupation barber. The birthplace of each was recorded as Japan.

Baby Joe Toranosuke was the first Nisei in his family. European immigrants considered their children born in the United States as the first generation of Americans. The Japanese immigrants regarded themselves as Issei or first generation, with the notion that they were the first to arrive in this country. They considered their offspring born in this second generation, Nisei.

In 1907 Kennosuke suggested they move to North Yakima. "This is a deadend place," he said. "There are not many Japanese."

His father nodded. "We are just making ends meet."

"This young man I met on the ship has found a job in a packing shed in North Yakima. He says there are many Japanese in the valley. That there are opportunities everywhere. With your permission I will go and look around.

"Genki da ne," his father said. "I like your spirit."

"But he is so young," his mother said.

"Mama, you always worry too much. We must explore all the possibilities."

"Kennosuke is right, Mama." To his son: "You have my permission. I have been thinking, too, that we should use the short form of our names. Like the Americans."

"That is good. You can use the name your hakujin friend gave you—Mat. I will be Ken. And Toranosuke will be Tora."

"Kiotsukete ne," his mother said. She made him take a bite of *umeboshi* for his safety. It was one of her little superstitions.

So it was that the Fuse family moved to North Yakima. For the then-large sum of twelve hundred and fifty dollars gold coin of the United States of America, Mat bought a business consisting of a cigar and confectionary stand, barber shop and pool room, and everything on the premises. The bill of sale was dated December 1, 1908.

"It will be a family business," Fuse said. "When Tora is older mama can take care of the baths and Ken can run the pool-room, and I will cut hair."

"If only we could buy the land and building." Ken said.

"Only citizens can do that. Or those eligible for citizenship. We are not eligible for citizenship."

"Why?"

"Because we are considered of the Mongoloid race."

"Haiseki desu," Ken said. "That's discrimination."

"We do not make the laws."

In order to put up the cash for the barber-poolroom business, Fuse had to borrow money from Ken's acquaintance. Then only four months later, the lender demanded return of his money as he was going to Montana to buy a restaurant business. Fuse had to take out a mortgage on March 31, 1909, "in the amount of two hundred and thirty dollars payable on the 30th day of June in the year A.D. 1909 with interest thereon of 12 per cent per annum."

Although Fuse was able to meet this obligation, he determined that he would never again join in partnership, however limited, with a second person. He impressed this on Ken and later on Tora.

The Fuse who had proved his courage and perseverance in the Alaskan frontier was lost in the wilderness of the marketplace. His years of wandering had ill-prepared him for business. The barbershop-poolroom was his one major effort, and after four years he gave it up and moved his family, now numbering seven, to Seattle. Three children had been born during their stay in North Yakima: George in 1908, Helen in 1910, and Peggy in 1912.

To add to their problems, Ken was stricken with appendicitis shortly after their arrival in Seattle. Tora looked on frightened as his brother doubled up on the sofa, writhed and screwed up his face in pain. He was rushed off to the hospital and recovered without complications, but the emergency further drained Fuse's resources.

During his convalescence, Ken came to his mother with a letter written in Japanese. A friend in Treadwell, Alaska, wrote that there were good jobs to be had and that Ken should join him.

As Yaso listened fear struck her. To her, Alaska was a place that had kept Papa away from her for many long years, years of loneliness that she had struggled with alone. If Kennosuke left her she would never see him again.

Ken reassured her. His friend said that working in the miners' boarding house as a waiter included board and room, so that he would be able to save most of his wages. Perhaps there would be opportunities up there for Papa and the family. He would write her every week, he promised.

"I would like to return to Alaska," Fuse said to Ken. "My experiences there were the richest of my life."

"You were doing what you wanted to do."

"Without much success," Fuse said. He did not want his son to know that he was starting to feel hemmed in. That he was being driven and not master of his future.

He felt the void left by his son's departure. He had no alternative but to resume his trade. He had always refused to work for anyone, so on August 20, 1912, he bought a barbershop located at 603 Main Street for fifty dollars. It contained three plate-glass mirrors and two chairs, with sink and hot water tank. The price reflected the low demand for barbershops. Mat Fuse had reached the end of his tether.

As he trimmed his friend Suzuki's hair—the tailor could have waited another week for a haircut—he felt warmed by his kindness. He smiled into the mirror where Suzuki was dozing, and saw behind him the snoring Murakami, whose crewcut hardly required a trim. His pride was not offended because it was in this manner that they let him know they were concerned.

He caught his own eyes in the mirror and frowned. He thought of his wife and four fledgling mouths to feed. For the first time he began to feel that his father-in-law had been right. In the banker's presence he would have been too proud to make such an admission, nor could he picture himself returning to Japan like a dog with his tail between his legs.

"No!" he said. He awoke Suzuki and Murakami.

Ken's letter inviting them north proved to be their salvation. He had an option to buy a barbershop in Douglas, he wrote.

"We will go," Mat said.

To him this was the point of no return. For the first time he gave up the hope of riches and success. From now on in his life endeavor was for the sake of the children. It was a decision reached by thousands of Issei like Matajiro Fuse. *Kodomo no tame ni.* For the sake of the children.

He gave his wife a shopping list for clothing and food. He asked Murakami to book them passage on the first ship to Douglas. He negotiated for the sale of his barbershop. He was making a clean break with the past.

Yaso packed with misgivings. Alaska was a land of ice and snow, not the kind of place in which she wanted her children to grow up. Mat, who rarely talked of his Alaskan experiences, was not very helpful. "They have good schools there," he assured his wife.

"What kind of schools? And the country. Hidoi kuni," she said, "A cruel country, from what I have heard."

"Now, Mama. Do not worry. It is a great country. It offers many opportunities." He tried to put into his voice a conviction he did not feel.

In the evening before the sailing their friends dropped in with *senbetsu*, parting gifts. Knowing little, they gave freely of advice, dispensing tidings of dire portent or of encouragement.

"It's so cold," Mrs. Toku Tanaka said, "you have to wear fur coats."

Mrs. Tanaka was the community gossip, a thin, wiry, tireless woman with small features over which her sallow skin was tautly drawn. Her eyes were restless brown beads. She made up for her small size, even smaller than Yaso's, with a big mouth and bigger ears tuned in to everything unpleasant that happened to her neighbors. She was like a quick, nervous bird, picking up crumbs of scandal and tragedy and flying away to broadcast from the treetops. She appeared at the door uninvited, avid for news.

"People live in ice houses," she said. "And no heat, not even hibachis. That's why you need fur clothes. You don't have any? How brave.

"Sore yori mo hidoi," she said. "Worse than that, you can't

get any Japanese food. No shoyu, no miso. And nappa or daikon! Forget it! What are you taking with you?"

"Rice," Yaso said weakly, overcome by the torrent of words.

"Rice," Suzuki repeated. As usual, his gold-filled spectacles were pushed up on his head. And as usual, he was always looking for them. He was a conservative bound by Japanese traditions and disapproved of Mrs. Tanaka's irresponsibility. Beside him sat his wife, Toyo.

Sitting next to them were Ben Murakami and his wife, Naoko.

"Rice?" repeated Suzuki. "They must have lots of rice up there."

"So de mo nai," Mrs. Tanaka said. "Not so. Ano sawado—"

"Sawado?"

"Ano Alaska no pioneer."

"Oh," Suzuki's brow unpleated. "You mean sourdough."

"Sawado, that is what I said. Ano sawado wa mame to furawa—"

"Eh, beans and flour," Suzuki said. Instead of hemming *uh* or *er*, he had a habit of hawing *eh*.

"Write it down," Mrs. Tanaka said. "So you won't forget."

Yaso got out Japanese stationery with vertical lines and wrote down *azuki* and *kuromame* in Japanese *katakana*. Red and black beans.

Mrs. Tanaka leaned across the plain yellow oilcloth. Her thin hair, tightly drawn back to a bun, glistened under the candlepower light. "No, no. Beans. Like Boston baked beans. Azuki and black beans are for festivals."

"I am also taking these," Yaso said firmly. "They are already packed away."

Mrs. Tanaka drew back, eyed her shrewdly. "If you want to do it that way. Shoyu and miso. Katsuobushi."

"Eh, dried bonito won't spoil," Suzuki agreed, "and it makes food tasty."

Trying to stem the gossip's verbal flood, he asked her, "You know why Japanese have brown eyes?"

Mrs. Tanaka paused in midflight. "Why?"

"Because they are full of misoshiru" (a popular brown soup).

Mrs. Tanaka slapped his arm. "Will you stop interrupting."

"I think I have everything," Yaso said. She looked across at Suzuki and smiled. "Including umeboshi."

To Yaso *umeboshi*, a red pickled plum, was better than aspirin for every kind of ache and pain. It had the power to ward off evil and danger. "I will check off my list again to see if I have forgotten anything." She pulled out a piece of paper.

Nori, she checked, dried seaweed. *Beni-shoga*, pickled ginger. *Kampyo*, dried gourd strips. *Konbu*, dried kelp. *Shiitake*, dried mushrooms. *Ocha*, green tea.

"No fresh fruit or vegetables," Mrs. Tanaka said. "No radishes or cabbage. Terrible, isn't it? You will get skabi and all your teeth will fall out."

Even Suzuki had problems with Mrs. Tanaka's pronunciation of English words. "Teeth will fall out" gave him a clue.

"Eh, you mean scurvy?"

"Skabi. That's what I said."

She asked Yaso for permission to use the phone. To the operator she said, "Ebagureen oh-ho-oh-āto."

The operator had a problem with *ho* and *āto*.

Mrs. Tanaka: "You no understand English. Ho like t'ree, ho. Ato. Like seben, āto, ninu."

After Mrs. Tanaka left the family felt the calm after a storm.

Suzuki said, "By tomorrow night everybody in town will know that the Fuse family has left for Alaska. In a year they will be back." Suzuki mimicked Mrs. Tanaka's thin, reedy voice. "Defeated."

He turned to Mat and Yaso. "Do not listen to her. She is the most depressing woman in the community. She is always the bearer of bad news with wings on her zori, and bitterly disappointed if she is not the first to break your heart.

"She must have been conceived in a typhoon and born in an earthquake—if she didn't bring on the earthquake while her mother was in labor. Forget this, what do the Americans call such a woman? Jane. Jane. Eh, yes, Calamity Jane. Forget this Japanese Calamity Jane.

"If things were as bad as she makes out, your good son would not have encouraged you to come. The worst thing I have heard about that part of Alaska is that it rains too much. Alaska is a huge country. I am sure the stories are true about the—the way up north, but Juneau is not much further north than Seattle. How can it be so cold when it rains so much? So deshō," he said to Papa. "Isn't that so? Eh?"

"I keep telling Mama," Mat said, "that even in a small country like Japan you have a Hokkaido and a Kyushu. Even in Yamagata we have heavy snows," he said to Yaso. "In Arctic Alaska where I lived the country is cruel and can be deadly." In order not to alarm her he had never told her that he had almost frozen to death on the tundra. "In Douglas we will be all right."

To the parting guests he said, "Thank you for coming. And thank you for the gifts."

As the visitors bowed their leave, Suzuki said to Yaso: "Fuse-san proved his courage. You, too, must have yūki. And gaman, ne. Patience and perseverance."

A kinder friend they never had. She bowed through her tears.

9
Alaska Bound

BEN MURAKAMI, who owned a transfer company under his own name and represented an Alaskan steamship company as well as several Japanese lines, had booked the Fuse family on the *City of Seattle*, a steamer with an unusual sounding steam whistle. Old sourdoughs will remember her. In the gray November dawn, he drove up to the house in his horse-drawn, closed panel wagon. His round face jolly for the moment and ruddy from the cold, he announced his arrival with a blast of an automobile horn which he had proudly mounted beside the seat.

As he loaded the baggage—two telescoping wicker trunks, the top fitting over the bottom, a footlocker full of Japanese food, and two suitcases—he said, "I can drive you all down to the pier if the children don't mind sitting in the back on the floor." He looked up the street. "Well, look who's coming."

"Eh," said Suzuki. "Cold, isn't it! Even the birds need fur coats. How subdued they are." He handed Yaso a basket of fruit and a bottle of sake for Mat. "I thought I would catch you before you left." He bowed to Yaso. "How pretty you look."

Yaso wore a flowered hat held in place by a pearl-headed hatpin that Murakami had given to her as a farewell gift. She was dressed in a simple, gray woolen coat and her hands were in an Astrakhan muff.

"Thank you," Yaso bowed, smiling. Suzuki's concerned

presence strengthened her resolve for the ordeal ahead. "Papa said I could buy a warm coat."

The wind snatched Mat's homburg hat and Tora ran to retrieve it. Mat wiped off the dust with the sleeve of his greatcoat. Tora and George wore gray frieze reefer jackets over thick wool sweaters, while Helen had on a cadet blue melton coat. Yaso held six-month-old Peggy, who was bundled up in pink blankets.

"We bought everything new here," Mat said. "They cost about three dollars each. We have mackinaws for the boys."

"Very wise," Suzuki said. "In Alaska I am sure they would cost much more."

"We must be going," Murakami said, picking up the reins. "You want to ride in back?" he asked.

"Eh! I will go."

When they reached the pier, Murakami unloaded and checked in their baggage. "Here are your baggage checks," he said to Mat. "Don't lose them. I can't be responsible for what happens at the other end." He bid them farewell with a shake of his whip and a blast of his auto horn.

Yaso led the way up the gangplank with Peggy in her arms and Tora clinging to her coat. Mat held on to his homburg with one hand while Helen clung to his other hand. Suzuki escorted George. In his other arm he carried the fruit and sake.

Suzuki looked at Yaso's face as they stepped on deck. "You don't look well," he said. "Are you all right?"

"I think I am going to be seasick," she said, her face pale.

"But the ship isn't moving. It's the same as if you were on land."

"It's all in the mind," Mat said.

As they reached their spacious cabin—Murakami had negotiated the best—Yaso lay down with Peggy beside her.

Mat exchanged glances with Suzuki and shrugged. Suzuki, casting a worried glance behind him, departed at the last "All ashore!"

"Mama! Get up!" Mat said. It was the first time Tora had heard Papa speak so sternly to Mama. "We will walk around the deck. The fresh air will make you feel better."

Yaso looked up furtively, like a guilty child. She got up and they all went outside. Peggy was sound asleep, drugged by the cold air. It was so cold and windy that after a couple of turns about the deck they were glad to retire to the warmth of the carpeted lounge. Mat made Yaso walk and walk so she wouldn't think about the motion of the ship as she left the shelter of Elliott Bay and headed up Puget Sound toward the Strait of Juan de Fuca. The last sight they had was the volcanic cone of Mount Rainier. I hope it is an omen for good, Mat thought.

The Inside Passage is formed and protected by hundreds of islands through most of its thousand-mile length from Juan de Fuca to Skagway. It is exposed to the ravages of the Pacific Ocean at the Strait, for fifty miles at Queen Charlotte Sound north of Vancouver Island, and again at Dixon Entrance. At the Strait long swells made the ship rise and fall with a slow, sickening motion that sent Yaso straightaway to her berth, from which she refused to stir during the four days of the voyage.

In their cabin Mat realized that the throb of the ship's engine had stopped. He heard the growl of the anchor chain. He remembered when the S.S. *Yukon* had stopped here so many years ago. Dangerous Seymour Narrows! Carrying Helen he took Tora and George on deck. He had been right. The *City of Seattle* had cast anchor at the entrance to Seymour Narrows to wait for twenty minutes of slack water during which passage could be safely made. It was a mile-and-a-half-long channel, about half a mile wide, through which the sea raced except at the turn of the tide.

What made it treacherous was Ripple Rock, a pinnacle in mid-channel. It was hidden, but close enough to the surface to rip a fatal gash in the hull of a ship pulled helplessly through by the irresistible current. It was a northern Scylla and Charybdis, a haunt of native superstition, where an evil god lurked to destroy canoes and devour victims. Many years later, through a major engineering feat, the pinnacle was blasted away so that ships could pass safely at all times.

Mat crossed Queen Charlotte Sound and Dixon's Entrance on the memory of his youthful dreams. As the ship entered Alaskan waters he was enveloped by the heady fragrance of spruce, hemlock, cedar, and fir. His entrancement was broken by Tora, sent by an anxious Yaso. The ship continued its tortuous course along the straits and fjords of the Tongass National Forest, a government preserve which comprises all Southeastern Alaska.

North of Wrangell the ship ran into a heavy fog bank that gave the captain and pilot some anxious hours. Abruptly—it seemed like magic to Mat who had come on deck—the fog was gone and the ship was hit by a strong gale and wind-lashed gray seas. As he turned his back on this new enemy he saw astern the fog overrun by this savage adversary, its gray ranks scattered in confusion and dispersed like the ghostly pennants of a defeated army. Hailstones large as marbles drove him into the salon.

When was it that the gods had vented their wrath on him? He recalled the scene at the family graveyard. Was this an omen of Alaskan oracles?

The storm continued to hound the ship for the last miles up Gastineau Channel, which separated Douglas Island from the mainland.

The pilot turned to the captain. "This is the worst storm I've experienced. I'm glad we have deep water beneath our bottom."

On the Douglas pier Ken Fuse, dressed in a red hooded mackinaw and wearing miner's heavy moleskin pants and a blue knitted wool cap which almost hid his features, huddled in the lee of the small dock warehouse. Beneath his boots the pier shuddered and swayed before the onslaught of wind and wave.

Occasionally he peered down channel, but visibility was only a few hundred yards. Suddenly the *City of Seattle*, armored in ice, loomed like a ghost ship out of snow driven horizontal by the gale. Her stays glistened in sunlight that was trying to break through a battleground of clouds.

To Yaso, who appeared on deck wan and frail-looking, this was a brutal welcome that fulfilled the warnings of Mrs. Tanaka in Seattle. Snuggling into her wool coat, she looked at the ice-locked land, the forlorn buildings savaged by the wind, the menacing mountains that towered around her like a prison.

"Hidoi kuni!" she exclaimed. "What a cruel country." She

shivered as much from fear as the cold.

She thought wistfully of the hot valley of the Yakimas and of her ancestral home in Yonezawa, where snow fell heavily but the winters were not slashed by the cruel teeth of a wind. But no ordeal, she thought, could be worse than the past four days. She dreaded the very thought of retracing that watery course. She could look only forward.

Mat grabbed Tora's arm. He had climbed on the lower cable in his efforts to locate his older brother. "Kiotsuke," Mat said. "Be careful."

"I see him," Tora cried. "There's Niisan. Over there."

Yaso saw him, too. A snow-whitened form waving an arm. She felt a sense of security but questioned his judgment. Was this a place to bring up children? But they had come this far. They were committed.

As the family disembarked, the wind snatched away their greetings. They fought its breathtaking fury as they struggled across the shaking wooden bridge built on piles that led ashore. Mat carried Helen, who was not quite three years old, Mama bore Peggy, while Tora and George, who was four, clung to Ken's hands. The ice-paved way was treacherous. An extra strong gust drove Yaso to the railing and Mat had to grab her.

They reached the shelter of two buildings, Shitanda's Restaurant on the right and the Alaskan Pharmacy on the left, that formed the entry to the dockway. Ken turned left and two doors from the corner led the way into a shop that had a barber's chair facing the ubiquitous barbershop mirror. They spread their hands around a potbellied stove resting on a zinc board. It had mica windows behind which fire danced. Ken opened the damper.

"Don't you lock the door?" Yaso asked.

"Nobody locks their doors," Ken said. "You won't need keys."

Tora never remembered having keys during his boyhood.

He threw off his jacket and went exploring. At the doorway he shouted, "Two bathtubs. We're rich."

"For the miners who want to take a bath," Ken said. "Mama, we have to do this to make extra money."

She nodded. What had to be, would be. She was ready to pin up her sleeves. Come what may.

The house had two bedrooms and a living room–kitchen with a double bed. She examined the four-lid wood-and-coal-burning stove and the porcelain-lined water reservoir. Ken had bought a brand-new washtub, she noticed, and a copper water boiler, together with a clothes wringer and a wicker basket.

"You have thought of everything," she smiled. Then she remembered. "How is your side? The scar?"

"It is all right. Nothing to worry."

Ken had cooked a large pot of rice, pulled a roast of beef from the oven, and placed a large apple pie on the table. "We'll have to eat this today," he said. "I hope you brought some Japanese food along."

Yaso nodded. "As much as we could. No fresh vegetables but takuwan, rakkyo, and umeboshi."

Ken smiled when she mentioned *umeboshi*.

So the Fuse family sat down to European food as their first meal on Alaskan soil. Normally, rice was the mainstay in the diet of the immigrant Japanese families. Those who endured hard physical labor found that only rice "stuck to their ribs." They demanded rice morning, noon, and night, for taste, economy, and staying power.

During lulls in the storm Yaso kept craning her neck as if sensing danger. "What is that noise?" she asked, bringing complete silence to the room. The 100 candlepower globe highlighted their faces in a group that Rembrandt might have wanted to capture on canvas.

Ken listened intently. "Oh, you mean that hum." He laughed. "That's the noise of the gold stamp mills. These heavy machines crush—make small—big rocks so they can get gold out of them. After a while you won't notice. Like the ticking of a clock. Now, Mama, don't you worry. Everything is going to be all right. And will you sit down and relax. Eat."

Yaso served Mat first and then Ken as he was the oldest of the children—and male. Then Tora, George, Helen, and Peggy in chronological order with the males first. Similarly Papa was always first to take a bath, as Mama was always the last. The children got into the tub together.

As they ate Ken told them about his work. He and the other young Japanese immigrants worked in the kitchens of the company boarding houses and waited on about two thousand miners who ate in shifts at long wooden sawbuck tables. Most of the Japanese workers were in their teens and early twenties. Like the majority of their countrymen, they had come to the United States to make a stake and return to Japan. Some had given up this dream or changed their goals.

A few, Ken said, remained permanently in a fenced-in section of the town graveyard. Their graves were marked by wooden stakes bearing their names in Japanese ideographs. Among them was a friend who had saved three thousand dollars and was waiting to catch the next ship to Seattle en route to Japan. An innocent bystander, he had been shot and killed in a quarrel between two miners.

"Kawaisō," Yaso said. "How pitiful."

"It is fate," Ken said, looking at his mother, who tended to be fatalistic.

Yaso nodded, her small, kindly eyes thoughtful.

"Come," Ken said, rising. "You must all be tired. Papa, why don't you take a hot bath? And you children, into the other tub."

Ken pulled down the shade of the large front window, shutting out the deserted street where only a tiring wind was prowling.

Mat was examining the barber chair as he draped a bath towel over his shoulder. He tried the lever that straightened the chair to shaving position and the hydraulic pedal that raised and lowered the chair. "It is in excellent condition," he said. "Thank you so much. You have saved our future."

Their eyes met in quick understanding.

"You will do well," Ken assured his father. "I will refer friends and miners here, and Mama can do their laundry and prepare baths for them. There are barbers at the mills, but they can't take care of everybody."

"You have been so helpful," his mother said, a catch in her soft voice.

Ken laughed abashed. "I will sleep on the couch tonight,

right here in the barbershop. The fire will keep me warm." As he listened to the cries and laughter of the children he said, "It's like home again."

"You must have been lonesome," Yaso said.

"And you have lost a lot of weight. Papa says you did not eat all that time on the boat. We must fatten you up."

"Kurushii katta," she said. "Painful. Good night." she touched his arm lightly. "Oyasumi nasai."

During the night she covered him with a blanket. Papa will keep me warm, she thought. Ken was relaxed in sleep but as usual he was grinding his teeth. Whether this strengthened his teeth and gums is subject to question, but he never had a cavity in his life. He opened bottle caps with his teeth to show how strong they were.

In the morning Ken left for his job at Treadwell. Yaso, who had risen in the dark, saw him to the front door. The storm had vanished southward, leaving behind a crystalline blue sky and a rugged landscape that looked like a fairyland adorned with snow and ice. Long rays of sunlight were harvesting diamonds from tree crystals.

"Utsukushii!" Yaso exclaimed. "How beautiful!"

Ken nodded, his breath a plume of white. He pulled his woolen cap over his ears and drew the collar of his mackinaw up around his neck.

"Feel better this morning?" he asked "Yesterday was a cruel day."

Yaso nodded, looked up at Mount Jumbo. "Just like Fujiyama," she said. "Like Japan."

"You will get to like this country," Ken said.

"In good weather you feel better," Yaso said.

"Yes. Now get inside before you catch cold." He turned and crunched away through the crusted snow.

Yaso closed the door and looked through the frost-etched window at her son's retreating figure. Her apprehension had vanished with the storm. She felt confident and secure. There was so much work to do.

The community of Douglas through which Ken trudged was a company town, the residential appendage of the Alaska

Treadwell Gold Mining Company. It had grown northward, the only direction in which it could expand, hemmed in as it was by the channel in front and the steep slopes of Mount Jumbo in back. Like most coastal towns in Alaska, it featured a planked Front Street built on piles and lined with stores, restaurants, poolhalls, and saloons. One Japanese family, the Shitandas, ran a restaurant. Because of the forcible evacuation of the Chinese in 1886, there was no Chinese laundry or restaurant.

One planked street ran from Douglas to Treadwell, lined with small stores, a sawmill with a giant sawdust pit into which the local children liked to jump, and the Alaska Foundry, which cast iron parts for the mine's machinery.

On the waterfront below this main street was the village of about fifty souls of the Auk tribe of the Tlingits, where the Indians spent the winter months. Tora and his friends never went through the area, nor did they have much contact with the children, who went to a separate Territorial school. It was like another world.

The heartbeat of the town was the roar of the Treadwell stamp mills day and night throughout the year. The townspeople had become inured to its noise. When the mill closed down for the Fourth of July holiday they became acutely aware of a vast silence, an absence from their world. When the stamps resumed their beat the world returned to normal.

The claims that made up the Treadwell mining complex bore such names as Ready Bullion, Old Mexican, Seven Hundred, and the Glory Hole. Tora never forgot the names, possibly because Ken mentioned them from time to time. Such as: "Glory Hole claimed another life."

Open pit mining at Treadwell had excavated an awesome, canyon-like hole. A grim jest went the rounds that a miner was killed or maimed everyday there, or in one of the two-thousand-foot-deep tunnels. The Glory Hole got its name, like so many other mine tunnels, because it sent so many men on the road to glory.

The mines got their start in 1881, when John Treadwell, a San Francisco financier, bought four claims. A year earlier Joe Juneau and Richard Harris made their strike across the channel, leading to Alaska's first stampede. By mass production Treadwell made the low grade gold quartz, some of it running as low as $1.25 a ton, a profitable operation until a cave-in flooded the mines in 1917.

Gold mines and stamp mills such as those at Treadwell, the Alaska Juneau, and the Alaska Gastineau at Thane four miles south of Juneau, provided grubstakes for prospectors heading north or for the unsuccessful who returned from the interior to restock their resources.

10

Alaskan Roots

K EN ENROLLED Tora in the Douglas elementary school, which was maintained for the children of miners, independent businessmen, professionals, and townspeople. Like most children, Tora was apprehensive as he faced his first day in a strange school. The teacher looked at his birth certificate. She turned to Ken. "You say he is seven years old. According to this, he is six."

"Oh," Ken laughed. "It is Japanese custom. When baby is born, baby is considered one year old on New Year's Day. When his real birthday comes, he is two."

"Well, this is the United States. Joe Toranosuke Fuse," she read from the birth certificate, "is six years old. How is his English?"

"Better than me," Ken said.

The teacher wisely decided not to correct Ken's grammar. "How did he get the name Joe?"

"American friend of family say he should have English name." This was a statement many other Japanese American parents could have made. But for some unknown reason, Joe, once given, was never used.

The teacher nodded. So it was that Tora was enrolled as the first American of Japanese descent in the Douglas educational system. He soon discovered, as most children do, that apprehension was worse than reality.

On his first day Tora learned to sing in unison with the class,

"Good morning to you, Miss Jameson" (an easy way to remember teacher's name), to recite "Twinkle, twinkle little star" as he pointed his chubby hand at the ceiling, and to "pledge allegiance to the flag of the United States of America and to the republic for which it stands, one nation, indivisible, with liberty and justice for all." (The words "under God" were added by an act of Congress in 1954.) Every morning, like the rest, Tora was a parrot.

A grownup European immigrant caused a minor sensation among the children when he attended class for a few days. Why would a man spend time with them? It was incomprehensible that a grownup could not read or write. He moved up through the grades and was granted an elementary school certificate at the end of the year. The pupils turned their attention to the adventures of Peter Rabbit, Goldilocks, and Little Red Riding Hood.

That winter when the picture of the entire school was taken in front of the school, someone jabbed Tora in the back so that he turned his head just when the photographer pressed the bulb. There is no photograph of him as a schoolchild, only the back of his uncombed head. Seen from the front, he had two dimples in plump cheeks. His countenance was ingenuous, quick to betray hurt or sadness, or illuminate anger or joy. Throughout his life he found it almost impossible to dissimulate.

The miners who patronized Mat's barbershop were amused by the name Fuse, as they used fuses in their work. Mat tried to explain that his name was pronounced with two syllables, Fuseh. But they continued to call him Fuse. He gave up. Scandinavians were a hard-headed lot.

Mat discovered that many of the miners, especially those from Eastern Europe, knew less English than he. After nearly twenty years in America he had a fair command of both English and Spanish. Now here, among these foreign Americans, he was amused that he had to resort to sign language and gestures in order to communicate.

As the first and oldest Japanese American boy in town, Tora was regarded as somewhat of a novelty. Most of the miners were bachelors who had dreams of marrying some girl from the old country, just like the Japanese. All the children of their fellow workers drew their attention and largess.

Miners coming into the warmth of Mat's shop would tousle Tora's hair and affectionately greet him with "Hello, Togo." Admiral Heihachiro Togo's role in defeating the Russian Baltic Fleet during the 1904–5 Russo-Japanese War was still fresh in their memories.

The Scandinavians, who made up more than twenty percent of the residents, were unable to pronounce such a tongue-twisting name as Toranosuke. They instantly gave him the name Thor, by which he was known thereafter. They were vastly amused by the name they had given the Japanese barber's son.

When Thor grew older he was pleased to learn the identity of the Nordic god of war. Here was a hero he could dream of being. The extrovert god in his Valhalla would have roared with laughter and slammed his hammer on his anvil. Thor, the human being, was by nature just the opposite: shy, sensitive, and introverted, with enough resources within to enjoy solitude and yet with the intelligence to get along with his peers and elders.

Thor was also a darling of the Japanese immigrants. They too dreamed of the time they would marry and have children. In the person of Thor they could project their future. Thor was not above taking advantage of this affection. If he felt hungry he would drop in at Shitanda's restaurant. He would be given a glass of milk and a cookie. On his way home he invariably stopped in front of a saloon that displayed Anheuser Busch's gory "Custer's Last Stand." He was fascinated by the tableau of horror that portrayed Custer standing alone among his dead and dying men, who were being scalped and looted while their bodies were still warm. The scene impressed his young mind with a fear of violence that became ingrained.

That winter two Japanese got into an argument in the barbershop when his father was absent. One pushed the hot stovepipe, soot, smoke and all, into the other's face. The latter grabbed a whetstone and gashed the first man's scalp. Although this ended the fight, the sight of blood made Thor throw up. He hid his face in a chair seat.

Thor's first spring in Alaska came gently. One sunny day

Terisaki the plumber, who still bore the scar of his fight, invited Thor for a boatride. He let Thor proudly carry one of the oars.

On their way across the bridge to the pier they met Tom Kubota, the town handyman. He had caged a huge rat in Shitanda's restaurant. He tied a long rope to the cage and lowered it into the seawater. Thor gazed in horrified fascination as the struggling creature drowned. Kubota noticed his frightened expression. "It's either them or us," he said.

Terisaki's rowboat was moored to the float. After he stowed the oars he untied the mooring rope and jumped into the boat. As he tried to draw it close to the float so Thor could board, it drifted with the strong tide. Like a human bridge, Terisaki collapsed into the water. With fearful eyes Thor watched him vanish into the green darkness. Then he reappeared like a shadow, took shape, dog-paddled upward, his face all screwed up as he held his breath. He swam to the boat and hauled himself in.

"For me, a Hiroshima fisherman. Hazukashii," he laughed. "Embarrassing." Thor didn't understand but felt relieved that the other could laugh at his mishap.

Although forbidden to him by his overly anxious mother, the float fascinated Thor. As part of a lifeline to Juneau and Thane, it was a local institution. The three towns were connected by a ferry, the *Lone Fisherman,* a tugboat converted to carry passengers and freight. It made its sedate rounds frequently throughout the day, summer and winter, good weather or storm.

The float was a plank platform resting on huge logs. It was kept captive from the strong tides by pilings that formed a cage. The gangplank was cleated on one side for pedestrians, with the other side left clear so freight, trunks, and other heavy items could be slid down or pulled up. Its incline, fearfully steep at low tides, diminished to almost level at the sixteen-foot and sometimes higher tides. Its pilings and logs were encrusted with barnacles and tiny blue-black mussels.

On sunny days Thor loved to lie prone on the planks, feeling the warmth through his cotton shirt and trousers, and to stare between the cracks at the shadowy forms of dogfish, tomcod, and other marine life. In winter the gangplank and float were plated with ice, the footing treacherous. Thor marveled at the agility of the deckhands who could jump from the icy deck of the ferry with mooring rope in hand to the ice-sheathed float. It was a hazardous feat during strong winds and storms. Under such conditions and especially at low tide, passengers had to pull themselves up the icy gangplank hand over hand, using the railing almost like a ladder.

An older boy Thor knew was not so fortunate as Terisaki. Enamored of the seine boats, he aped the fishermen by wearing hip boots and haunted the marina. One day he disappeared. Rumors of kidnapping gave way to the belief that he had fallen overboard and drowned. More often than not the tides returned the dead, but in this instance the sea kept its secret. The search was given up.

One day Yaso caught Thor returning alone from the float. "Bad boy," she scolded. That evening she told her husband, "Tell him that the float is forbidden to him."

"You will do as we say or I will punish you with okyū," Papa said.

In *okyū* therapy a piece of *moxa,* which to Thor looked like the wax that came out of his ears, was placed on the skin at key points and lighted with an incense stick. As it burned to the skin the heat stimulated the surface and drew blood to that area. The improved circulation, it was believed, would help to cure any local ailment. Although none of the children had been punished in this manner, the fear of being burned made them behave.

Mat believed in *okyū*. On the kitchen wall he had a large chart outlining a human figure on which key points were represented by black dots. In theory there were 657 vital spots, but Mat's chart was simplified to fewer dots, ones associated with rheumatism, neuralgia, and stomach disorders. Among Fuse's patients were Hayashi, Terisaki, and Kubota. Occasionally, Shitanda would come in with sore shoulder muscles and Mat would give him a massage.

Thor's parents also maintained traditional holidays. On the Emperor's birthday the Japanese gathered at the pavilion on Deer

Island to celebrate *Tenchō setsu*. A rear room of Thor's home overlooked the dark mass of the small island, which was reached by a walkway from the bridge that led to the pier.

Thor watched the lights of the pavilion and listened to the singing and clapping which were punctuated with cries of "Tenno heika, banzai! Tenno heika, banzai! Tenno heika, banzai!" The toasts to Emperor Yoshihito, who succeeded Emperor Matsuhito July 30, 1912, upon the death of the Meiji era ruler, roared out into the dimness of an Alaskan summer night.

On such festive occasions, his father would always be called upon to sing *nagauta*. He had a mellow, pleasant voice, but to Thor it seemed as if he were straining his vocal cords to get out certain sound effects. When Thor sang American songs they came out naturally. Once Mat turned to his wife and said, "He has a good voice. He could sing nagauta."

At times, Mat, who liked to sing even when not under the influence, would croon lullabies to Thor's sisters, who remembered them as they grew up. Thor never recalled that his father ever sang him to sleep. He was so charged with energy during the day that as soon as his head touched his pillow he fell sound asleep.

Among Mat's favorites was "The Firefly" or "Hotaru" lullaby nursemaids would sing as they carried infants in their arms through the warm night of a garden or on a riverbank in Japan:

Ho ho hotaru koi	Ho ho firefly come
Kochi no mizu wa amaizo	this water is sweet
achi no mizu wa nigaizo	that water is bitter
ho ho hotaru koi	ho ho firefly come

Mat, as was the Japanese custom, left the upbringing of the children to Mama. She liked to give the children small moral lessons. Like the one on honesty:

She held up two twigs, one straight to the sun, the other bent to the west. "You must grow straight like this." She held up the other twig. "Kore mitai ni magattara bachi ataru," she said. "If you bend like this one you will be punished."

Or on waste at the dinner table: If they left a few grains of rice on their plates she would scold them. "Me ga tsubureru," she said. "You will go blind." She made Thor write on both sides of his notebook paper.

Like most Japanese women whose duties were confined to the home, Mama did not speak much English. Nor did the Nisei speak much Japanese. Thor understood her Japanese and spoke fragments of the language, enough to maintain communication with her. In the morning she would give him a nickel. She did not have to say *buredo*. He enjoyed going up the hill to the baker. All the bakers in Douglas and Juneau were German.

As he waited for the door to open, he listened to the raucous challenge of the crows and the thin screams of angry seagulls fighting over scraps from the restaurant kitchen. The channel tides were the town's dumping ground. He returned with a loaf of French bread liberally sprinkled with blue poppy seeds. He never forgot the belly hungry odor of fresh baked bread, crusty in his hands and warm under his arm. How crunchy it was, how tasty yellow with butter. She would smile at him as she prepared warm milk for the cocoa. In some respects, as with animals unable to verbalize, there was an osmosis of empathy resulting in understanding.

Thor loved the Japanese fairy tales Mama told the children. The lessons these stories taught helped form his moral fiber, as much as the parables of Jesus. Human beings talked with birds, beasts, and denizens of the deep. Among the animals, birds, and insects, the mischievous badger and fox were the good guys, and demons, ogres, and dragons were the bad guys. Goodness and virtue were rewarded and villainy and evil punished.

The story of Momotaro was his favorite. "This childless couple lived in the forest," Mama began. "They were poor but longed for a child. One day they found a large peach floating down a stream. When they opened it they found a tiny baby inside whom they named Momotaro.

"He grew up strong and brave. When he was fifteen, he determined to attack the ogres living on an island who were raiding the mainland and despoiling it of its treasures. Before he set off, his foster mother gave him some rice cakes.

"On the way a dog, a pheasant, and a monkey joined him. He rewarded each one with a rice cake. Taking a boat to the island, they attacked and destroyed the ogres. Momotaro killed the chief ogre in a personal duel.

"They liberated all the prisoners, returned the treasures to their rightful owners, but had enough left over to take care of Momotaro's foster parents forever after."

Mama smiled at Thor's entranced expression. He was thinking: I want to help and reward Mama and Papa when I grow up. "Now off to bed, all of you."

On the family's first Memorial Day in Douglas, the family visited the Japanese graveyard where Ken's unfortunate friend was buried. Thor gazed curiously at the wooden stakes, some more weatherbeaten than others. Inscribed in black paint on the wood were the names in Japanese ideographs of those whose dreams had ended here.

"This was Mr. Murata," Ken said, pointing to a second stake. He turned to Thor. "Remember the man we visited on his fishing boat? He was dying and asked me to take care of his belongings. I sold his boat and sent the money to his family in Japan, but they never answered. Very strange and unusual for Japanese. I wrote again but received no reply."

On the way home they paused briefly at the Indian graveyard. "Instead of wood like the Japanese used here, or stone like the Americans, the Indians build tiny houses as monuments. I don't know why but maybe they give shelter to the dead before they leave for the next world."

As they reached the front of the barbershop, George dropped a fistful of coins through a crack in the sidewalk.

"Baka," Mat said. "Fool. Why did you do that?"

None of them, not even Mama, understood that George was begging for attention. It was the first outward sign of the psychological problems he was to face.

Thor was growing up self-reliant and consequently somewhat self-centered. He was oblivious rather than insensitive to the feelings of others, in particular to the nuances of emotion. He was too young to perceive the effect this trait had on his siblings, especially on his younger brother. George's distress was beyond his comprehension.

One day George asked him what people meant by "no thank you." Why thank someone for nothing? Because Thor wasn't certain, he airily dismissed the question. He did not realize that he had rebuffed and hurt his brother. He recognized this fact later because it stayed in his mind.

He had his own problem when the circus came to Douglas. A summerlike day had slipped into a rain-filled June. Miss Jameson dismissed the class for lunch with the caution, "Be sure to be back by one o'clock. Now don't forget." As a treat they were to attend a small itinerant circus show that had set up a tent on the town's ballfield.

Thor finished eating early and sat at the small table by the picture window of the deserted barbershop, idly leafing through the latest pink copy of the *Police Gazette*. He dozed off and awoke with a start. He looked at the clock on the wall and almost fell off the chair. He ran up the hill to the schoolhouse. There was not a soul around.

He ran toward the ballpark, panic in his heart, hoping to catch up with his class. There was no one outside the huge brown tent. He prowled around the entrance, afraid to go in and wishing someone would come out to invite him in. What would Miss Jameson say? For the first time in his life he was not only tardy, he was absent. Catastrophe. He couldn't go home and tell his envious siblings that he had missed the circus. Miserably he sat on a bench during an afternoon that stretched on forever.

As a result of this experience, attendance and punctuality became an obsession with Thor. On occasion it ceased to be a virtue, causing him fear and anxiety and contributing to a pervasive tension in his life. The long minutes spent waiting for an appointed hour added up to months as they poured through the sieve of time. He never fathomed this conscience within. Otherwise, like all boys, he was profligate with his hours.

In early summer Ken, as he had promised, found an unfurnished house on a high bank overlooking a stream. A wooden frame building like all the residences in town, it could have stood another coat of gray paint and white trim, but it had three bedrooms. Mama was excited by the kitchen stove, a deluxe Sears

Princess model, Ken explained, that burned coal and wood. It had four lids with a lift, a hot water reservoir, and an oven.

"Ii, ne," Mama said, shaking the grating and examining the oven.

"It came with the house," Ken said, happily enjoying his mother's pleasure. "The rent is only ten dollars a month."

It was their first real home in Alaska, separate from Papa's business and large enough to invite friends. One afternoon when his mother was away shopping with the children, Thor invited a friend into the kitchen. The latter saw some leftover rice. "Let's have some rice pudding," he suggested.

"What's that?"

They put rice in two bowls, poured sugar and milk over it and were eating when Mama returned. She was horrified at such sacrilege. "Putting milk and sugar on rice!" she exclaimed.

"This is rice pudding," Thor's friend said. "It tastes even better with cinnamon and raisins. It's just like eating oatmeal with milk."

"Barbaric," Mama muttered, or words to that effect. "Whoever heard of such a thing!"

The Fuses' second winter in Douglas was as cold but not as stormy as their first. One morning Thor awoke early beneath his heavy quilts. Dawn was gray at a window pane opaque with a Jack Frost canvas. His breath condensed in the frigid air. He heard the rush of water through the pipes, the thud of water under strong pressure as his mother shut the faucet.

In his flannel pajamas he rushed to the tiny secondary bathroom where, without turning on the small light, he brushed his teeth with the Colgate's toothpaste he preferred to Dr. Lyon's tooth powder, which came in a tiny wooden box and was used by his parents. He danced a foxtrot on the icy linoleum to keep his soles from freezing. He pressed one fingertip against the windowpane to melt a peephole to the white world outside. His mother brought a kettle of hot water and poured it into the tin washbasin.

"Why don't you wear your zori?" she scolded him in Japanese as he hopped about. She laughed and returned to the kitchen.

She had cooked Quaker's oatmeal mush, fried him an egg, and toasted bread on an asbestos toaster, which could be used over any kind of fire or heat. These asbestos disks with steel wire mesh on one side and a corrugated steel rim were a fixture in every Japanese kitchen, as they were used to keep rice pots warm for the final steaming. They had what was called an Alaskan handle, coiled steel instead of solid iron, so they would not get hot. For drink he had a choice of Baker's red breakfast cocoa, Ghirardelli's brown chocolate, or Postum.

When he had finished, Mama pointed to the Japanned coal hod so Thor took it outside and refilled it from the bin.

On occasion Ken brought home from the boardinghouse a slab of bacon, leftover meat, or crusty apple pie heavily spiced with cinnamon. These were treats they could not otherwise afford.

On Christmas morning when Thor wanted to try on his ice skates, Mama made him change from his good shoes to clodhoppers because the edge of the clamps would cut into the leather soles and heels. She tied the skate key to a loop of string which she hung around his neck. "Keep it there," she said, "so you won't lose it."

Thor ventured unsteadily out on the uneven surface of the sidewalk where snow had been packed to ice by passing feet. This was the first skating rink of boys as they grew up. Some shopkeepers and home owners were inconsiderate enough to throw ashes or sand on the icy surface. You could come barreling along and when you hit one of these spots your skates would stick, your head would keep on going, and said sand or ashes would scrape your face raw.

The sidewalk in front of the Fuse home was clear of such dangers, but Thor discovered that maintaining his balance was as much of a problem. After one particularly heavy bump he sat stunned. Papa happened to pass and laughed indulgently. Angrily, Thor looked after the retreating back and repressed an urge to throw a snowball at the black derby hat.

"He never helps me," he thought, unaware that this was in Mama's domain. He labored stubbornly and made such progress that he complied reluctantly when his mother called him to lunch.

From his peers he learned a variation of skating, not practical but one of the things boys do to be doing. He would take two large empty Carnation milk cans and crush them in the middle with his feet until they clung to his shoes. Then he would walk on them or slide down short inclines. It was a challenge to keep them stuck to his shoes.

There was magic when the first lacy ice of winter formed on the edges of a small stream and protruding boulders wore collars of ice. A procession of freezing nights proclaimed the mastery of ice over water until one fine morning, ice through which Thor could almost see bridged the stream behind his home.

It seemed a crime to even scratch that mirrored surface. But the challenge of skating along a stream that was more sporting than the flat surface of a pond drew him on. As his blades flashed over the meandering course he had to be on the alert for the heads of stones that stuck out here and there, or partially imbedded branches that lay like snakes to trip his unwary feet.

The joy of each day was complete when older boys built a fire of pitch-veined spruce and balsam on the bank. He loved to sit on a log and look into the flames that whispered, talked, and sometimes popped, and with the cold predatory at his back and the heat on his face, watch the myriad red and yellow flames paint canvases as varied as his imagination.

He embraced the fragrance of burning needles that tore at his heart, nor did he mind the acrid fumes that made him cry and cough. And at night there were dancing shadows thrown against the opposite bank of the stream as the fire shot sparks into the darkness where tree trunks wore long faces of light. Thor's imagination prospered and his storehouse of memories was enriched.

Late that winter, shortly before the Fuse family moved to Juneau, Thor beheld the most beautiful sight in his young life. The earth had rotated into a zone of black silence. The air was still as though all its molecules had stopped moving. Only the sniper fire of exploding branches rent the forest. The deep freeze of outer space had contracted its brake bands upon the spinning earth.

In front of Thor the surface of the channel stretched like black glass beneath starlight and the shine of the moon before its rise. Across the water, beneath the north star, Mount Juneau loomed against the bejeweled sky. Snow on its shoulders gave it an ethereal quality. The ghostly hulk of the mountain was mirrored perfectly on the surface of the water, appearing like a subterranean counterpart in the black depths of a nether world. Entranced, Thor walked softly to the end of the porch to have an unobstructed view, fearful that at any instant the beauty might vanish like magic.

Mama came with a blanket and they stood together beneath its warmth.

"Utsukushii! Hontō ni utsukushii!" she said. "Beautiful! So really beautiful!" It was another jewel, if not a diamond, on the necklace of her life's lovely moments.

Thor glanced up and saw tears in her eyes. Silent and motionless, they became one with the night.

I I

Channel Crossing

T HE NEXT DAY, the family rode the *Lone Fisherman* across the channel to Juneau. Ken had learned that Sadao Suda wanted to sell his barbershop to go prospecting again. Suda looked much the same as he had when Mat had met him in the Japanese bathhouse in Seattle: the same stooped shoulders, the gargle-like laugh, the bare scalp with the divot of hair above his nose.

"I will buy your business," Mat said. "I will have more opportunity here." He shook Suda's hand. In parting he said, "I wish you success, you old ishi atama."

The personal shaving mugs of Mat's regular customers posed a problem. The Austrian Hapsburg and German Carlsbad china cups, with floral designs and a heavy gold stipple on rim and handle, were kept in a pigeonhole rack. Surprisingly, many customers asked that he take the mugs with him. They would go to Juneau when they needed a shave and a haircut. Mat was humbly touched. "They are loyal," he said.

They could have told him that he had mastered the techniques of his trade: a flair for hair styling, a light touch with the razor, his insistence on a preliminary shampoo. They looked forward to the massage he gave their shoulders as well as their scalps.

"We should get rid of everything we don't need," Ken said, as families have said since the cave man.

"How about these old Japanese magazines?" Thor said,

grabbing up an armload. The paper was thin newsprint, not glossy.

"We use those for toilet paper," Mama said. She would make a hole near one corner, run a cord through it, and hang it up so they could use it. When Thor picked up an old Sears, Roebuck catalogue: "No, Papa use that to wipe his razor on." Papa would cut a catalogue in half, make a hole in one corner, and hang it by a loop of cord from the shelf in front of the barber chair. He would wipe bristle-filled lather on each sheet.

Mama insisted on taking all the old clothing. "I can use them for patching and making quilts." Everything had to go, she said: the coal, kindling, even the cube of ice in the icebox. Ken was going to put up an argument but changed his mind when Mama pinched her lips together. She patted the cold Princess stove with regret. That belonged with the house. She did not like the two-lid stove Suda had used to cook his bachelor meals. Ken assured her that if the Juneau Hardware did not have a Princess he would order it.

So the Fuse family settled down in Juneau for five years, the formative years of Thor's sojourn in Alaska.

Juneau, the capital of Alaska, was a frontier mining town of about 3,500 souls in 1914. It had been a major supply point for the gold rushers of '98, but now was not much more than a backwater of a once mighty human flood.

Juneau got its start as the site of Alaska's first major stampede. John Muir, the naturalist, had camped in the area in 1879 and noticed a quantity of gold quartz rock. No fortune hunter, he continued on, but he passed the word to a pair of prospectors, Joe Juneau and Richard Harris. George Pilz, an engineer from Sitka, offered the two a grubstake in exchange for two of every three claims they staked. He also offered 100 blankets to their Indian guides if they found gold.

The two men squandered the first grubstake on hooch, women, and song, but Cowee, an Auk Indian leader who was one of the guides, showed Pilz a sample of gold-bearing quartz. Pilz outfitted the prospectors again, and this time they ventured further up the creek Muir had visited, into a great basin where they found gold in unbelievable quantities—including nuggets the size of beans. They named their find Silver Bow after a mining district in Montana. Gold Creek came by its name naturally. As the fevers of the successive gold rushes subsided, the Japanese pioneers settled among their white neighbors in the residual towns of the Territory: Nome, Fairbanks, Anchorage, Seward, Cordova, Skagway, Sitka, Ketchikan, Petersburg, Wrangell, Douglas, and Juneau.

Their number ranged from a handful to a few dozen in each town, the total determined by seasonal work. They established restaurants and laundries (their favorite choices), grocery stores, bakeries, variety stores, rooming houses, and barbershops. The owners of these became the more prominent and successful members of their communities. Others, often those with less education or less English, worked for these establishments or settled for service jobs as cooks, waiters, kitchen help, porters, janitors, and general handymen.

Among them, too, were Japanese prostitutes who, like their sisters of the Rocky Mountain mining camps, became camp followers. The story is told that in Cordova the pimps and madames forbade Japanese customers, not because of prejudice, but because they were afraid their girls might fall in love and run away. Some of them married into respectability, after the fashion of those in San Francisco's Gold Coast.

The three other Japanese families in Juneau when the Fuses arrived owned a laundry (the Fukuyamas), a restaurant (the Tanakas), and a variety store (the Makinos). There were also about a dozen or so bachelors who had odd jobs about town.

Juneau grew on a toehold of land at the feet of Mount Juneau and Mount Roberts. Gold Creek ran through its western limits. The delta of the creek was a tideflat in front of the Tlingit village, an isolated enclave like the one in Douglas. The village, the U.S. government hospital, and Evergreen Cemetery were in the western part of the town.

Gold Creek ran between the two mountains, which towered almost straight up, dwarfing the town. From its source up in the mountains beyond the small mining camp of Perseverance, the creek had carved, with an assist from a snout of the glacial icecap, the great bowl of the canyon that some referred to also as Last Chance Basin. Its floor was flat for acres across and seeded with rocks and boulders. Through it Gold Creek, with many a twist and turn, brawled its way. This was the scene of many of Thor's adventures.

Aside from the waterfront, the four main streets of Juneau—Gold, Franklin, Seward, and Main—ran northward up a steep slope to a ridge of land, actually the big toe of Mount Roberts, which Thor knew as Chicken Ridge. On this highest part of town the rich built their homes. The other side of the ridge dropped sharply into a bowl containing Evergreen Pond, whose frozen surface in winter was the town's skating rink. During winter Thor practically lived on it.

The Fuses' rented house was on Front Street, opposite the entrance to Ferry Way, which led to the Alaska Steamship Company pier and the float where the *Lone Fisherman* moored its lines. This was the road to Outside. Front Street was built on pilings, surfaced with two-by-twelve planks laid at an angle. The sidewalks were built of two-by-six boards constructed at right angles to the buildings and a few inches above street level.

The lumber came from the sawmill at the southern, lower end of town, where the marina for the fishing fleet was also located. The sawmill's steam whistle announced the time for reporting to work, the lunch hour, and the end of the working day. The whine of its huge saws sang tenor to the gold stamp mill's bass. The large, gray buildings of the mill, built in steps up the mountainside, were the most prominent features of the town. On this side of town the steep rise of Mount Roberts posed a constant threat of landslides.

The Juneau Cold Storage Plant produced 200-pound blocks of ice for fishermen and froze halibut, salmon, cod, and other fish for local use and export. Thor was ever intrigued by the seagulls that soared on the thermals of warm air that rose above the roof of the cold storage plant. In winter cold they perched in a line along the top edge of the roof. He was moved to write a poem about the seagulls. His creative urge was awakened, too, by the sight of smoke rising from a hundred chimneys that he likened to pipes of peace.

Beyond the cold storage plant, on the mountain side of

Front Street, was a row of whorehouses, the despair of the female members of the dozen churches in town and of the wom-
en's auxiliaries of the dozen fraternal brotherhoods. It could not
be said that the softening influence of culture had not reached
this pioneer town. But since the majority of the miners in
Douglas and Juneau were bachelors, the town fathers were not
about to run the whores out of town. Not while they valued their
lives.

Soon after the Fuses had settled down in their new home,
the last Taku storm of the winter, named after the glacier south
of the town, roared up the channel herding snow and twenty-
foot waves before it. It blotted out the world as though the town
alone had become its target.

Mama looked through the frost-etched window at the deserted street. Tentatively she started to open the front door. A
gust of wind almost tore it from her hands. She put her hundred
pounds behind her shoulder and managed to get the door closed.
She felt afraid as gusts shook the house, protected though it was
by its neighbors and the steep hill behind it. In the kitchen Thor
was eating breakfast and getting ready to go to school.

Mama tried to dissuade him from venturing out, but he was
adamant. He was not going to miss a day of school. Nor was
he going to be tardy, he thought grimly, recalling his Douglas
experience. Mama compromised by bringing out a wool coat
with a narrow band of fur around the collar. Thor looked at
himself in the mirror, at the fur around his neck, and yanked off
the coat. To him it was a girl's coat and sissy. Boys didn't wear
girls' things.

"But it will keep you warm," Mama insisted.

In the gray, shrieking dawn he left the house dressed in a
sweater and muffler (a concession to Mama), and a jacket and
knickers. Swept off his feet when he tried to walk on the sidewalk, he trudged in the crusted snow along Front Street and up
Franklin to the school. When he reported to his teacher she was
shocked. She pinned the lapels of his jacket under his chin with
a safety pin and sent him home.

Dutifully having reported when almost every pupil had
stayed at home, he returned to Mama. She wrapped a blanket

around his shivering frame and served him steaming cocoa.

"Baka!" she said, but squeezed his shoulder affectionately.

Thor's first introduction to the Juneau community was through religion. He joined the Methodist Church Sunday School through the introduction of a Swedish friend, Lars Tolquist. Lars's younger brother, Gus, was Thor's closest friend.

Thor's parents did not go to church because there was no Buddhist temple or Shinto shrine in Alaska. Mama had an altar-like shelf where on certain anniversaries, festivals, and on New Year's Day she placed a round *mochi* (rice cake) on top of a larger one with a *mikan* or Japanese tangerine completing a pyramid. She put a small plate of *osekihan* (red bean rice) next to the tower, and burned incense. All these products were imported in advance from Seattle.

On the Sunday before Thor's first Sunday School class, Mama took him to the Emporium on Seward Street to buy him his first suit. He tried on the most expensive eight-dollar suits, but settled on a black clay worsted two-piece knee-pants suit for five dollars. The lining of the jacket was of good quality and the pants had double seat and knees. For the first time in his life he felt dressed up.

"That size is a bit large," the salesman said, reaching for the rack.

Mama looked at him from the corners of her small eyes. Any suspicion she might have harbored she hid behind a placid expression. If she bought a suit to exact size, she would have to buy Thor a suit every year or more often, which she felt might be in the salesman's mind.

Sunday School became a fixture in Thor's boyhood. If he were early, as he usually was, he would drop into Billy Taylor's, a chocolate shop famous in the Panhandle and even Outside. Cruise ships made it a port of call, and passengers spread the word. Thor would buy walnut creams or molasses kisses and go up to the library reading room in the City Hall to while away time.

In church the boys snickered among themselves when the minister, until he caught on, chose "Bringing in the Sheaves" for the congregation to sing. Gus would poke Thor in the ribs.

The boys in the class tried to drown out the rest by singing at the top of their voices, "Bringing in the Cheese," with a heavy downbeat on the cheese. The hymn became a neglected orphan in the hymnal.

A new minister to the church caused a schism in the congregation. In order to build membership among the younger people, he introduced boxing gloves and a pool table into the basement social room. This shocked the fundamentalists who, after a controversial discussion, withdrew and joined the Bethel Pentecostal Church and Mission.

It was the leader of the dissidents who frightened the living daylights out of Thor one Sunday after church. He invited Thor into the study and tried to convert him. He got on his knees, his hands together, and prayed with eyes uplifted to the ceiling, calling on God to forgive and accept this poor sinner into His Kingdom. Thor stood dumbfounded, confused and frightened by the intensity of the man's emotion. Finally, he escaped outdoors. It was the most soul-shattering experience of his young life. The mystery of salvation was beyond his comprehension.

In later years, especially on the Fourth of July when out-of-town celebrants thronged the streets, Thor would see him on the bandstand, preaching and exhorting the poor sinners to be saved. Thor wondered what possessed the man.

As in the Douglas school, Thor was the only Oriental, a term that was to fall into disfavor in another era. He never saw a Negro or Indian native among his white, mostly Anglo-Saxon Protestant classmates. Their names were Peterson, Padermeister, Krugness, Holmquist, Oja, Meyer, Messerschmidt. They were children of sourdoughs, of government employees, of immigrants, of insurance agents, merchants and shopkeepers, of doctors, lawyers and dentists, of representatives of steamship lines, of miners, fishermen and sawmill workers. In a territory once owned and ruled by Russia, there were very few of this descent. Catholics, for the most part, attended the parochial school near St. Ann's Hospital, which also was maintained by the Catholic Church.

The Tlingit children from the Auk village on Juneau's

tideflats attended a Territorial government school. Originally, Sheldon Jackson, the United States' first General Agent of Education for the Territory, had planned an integrated school system but was forced to change because of opposition from the whites.

It never occurred to Thor to question or even think about the ethnic or religious composition of his classmates. They were all white, but he was one of them and was never given cause to think otherwise. Many were children of immigrants who had just "stepped off the boat," and in a sense he was too.

Although Thor learned moral and ethical conduct at home and in Sunday School, the Juneau school and the public library were his main founts of learning.

Each fall the teachers for the school year would arrive from Outside in time for the opening of classes after Labor Day. Their names would be on the list of cabin-class passengers that was carried in the newspaper. There were only three hotels in town—the Alaskan, the Hotel Zynda, and the largest, the Gastineau, where most of the teachers stayed until late in June. Thor looked forward with expectation to see what kind of teacher he would have.

The opening of each semester had a sense of freshness and expectancy. The blackboards were almost pristine, the desks dusted and oiled, the inkwells clean. Thor walked down the aisles looking at the carved initials (his respect for authority prevented him from doing this) and sensed the ghosts of former years. He was intrigued by the differences in newcomers, such as the girl from the South who pronounced her state name *Tinnissee,* or the one from Norway who had trouble pronouncing *v. Valley* came out *walley.*

Thor was resented by one boy. The son of an English father and an Eskimo mother, he was sensitive about his parentage. Although he was treated without prejudice, he envied Thor's status. A further aggravation to him was that Thor was a teacher's pet, a favor he had won because of his deportment and his impressive memory, which earned him grades of mostly E or excellent—97 to 100 percent.

Thor remembered by rote. Instead of loitering on his way

home from school, he would go straight home, throw himself on his bed, and with one or two readings know the location of a state, its capital, its principal products and industries. Then he would go out to play. If called upon the next day he would read the facts off the screen of his memory and watch teacher following the list of products in the geography book.

Only rarely did his gift fail him. He was mortified when he could not locate Lake Chad in northern Africa or define fortnight. Teacher was relieved and humanly gratified to learn that she could stump her star pupil.

Otherwise, she was amazed at his memory. One day, as an experiment, she instructed a part of the class to memorize a twenty-line poem stanza by stanza, and the rest of the pupils to memorize it as a whole, to see which method was faster. Thor read the poem once, reviewed it in his mind, with a couple of quick peeks at the text, and raised his hand. Teacher looked at the watch on her lapel, held it to her ear to see if it was running, and then shook her head. Unbelievable.

One characteristic that evolved from Thor's school years was a pose to make others think he knew everything. To some extent he was successful, even to the point where he would grunt—it could mean yes or no—when he wasn't certain and the others would think he knew.

In spelling bees Thor was almost infallible. At the start all the pupils would be standing. A miss, even a false start, and the pupil sat down. It was guaranteed that the son of the school janitor—who got his nickname Doughhead because of his white hair, or because his surname was White, or possibly from the lack of quality of his gray cells—would be the first to sit down. It was almost as certain that Thor would be standing at the end.

At this time he read a novel about a boy named Limpy who let a girl win and was considered a hero. Thor thought if you were given something, that wasn't winning. He felt that he had to win to maintain his reputation. Chivalry was for someone else.

Thor's facile memory became a weakness when school curricula began to emphasize reasoning rather than rote. Instead of photographic impressions, logic took a lot of dark-room work, which he had never trained himself to do.

Of all the teachers, Thor remembered Miss Nelson best. She entered his life in the latter years of his grammar-school education. In those days the school system was eight-four-four: eight grammar, four high, and four college, unlike the six-three-three-four of more recent times. To the smaller boys, Miss Nelson loomed large and tall. She had fine features, gray eyes that looked into a boy's mind, trim ankles below the dust-sweeping dresses of the day, and she bore herself like a queen. As vice principal she was a symbol of authority. She gave Thor a sense of security, for even the rowdiest boy stepped lightly in her presence.

"When she looks at you you want to sink through the floor," Doughhead said. He had laughed as he spoke but respect was in his tone.

Doughhead himself was an authority on a different level. He was neither a brain nor a bully, but was strong, tough, and fearless and was tacitly acknowledged as the physical superior of his peers. Prestige was on an individual basis. There were no gangs as such, though the boys who lived in the west end of town beyond the Governor's Mansion referred to themselves as the River Rats because they lived along Gold Creek, and called those living in and around the piers the Wharf Rats. But it was all in good-humored jest.

A new boy in town, to gain instant prestige, challenged Doughhead without provocation to a fight. The next morning he appeared in school with a black eye, Doughhead's trademark. The boys snickered. Not many had seen the encounter, but Doughhead only laughed when he was questioned, saying "He wanted to fight." The new boy had gained instant recognition.

On Fridays in English class Miss Nelson would read a chapter from *Ivanhoe* or some other work of fiction. Even Doughhead looked forward to this treat, and Miss Nelson quelled any unruly behavior by threatening to withdraw this favor. She had a well-modulated voice and clear diction, and could bring a scene to emotional life.

On one occasion she had the class act out a scene from

Midsummer Night's Dream. Thor was assigned the role of Bottom. The incongruity of a man with the head of a donkey speaking Shakespeare's lines struck Thor as so ridiculous that he was convulsed with laughter and hysteria ruled his voice. He had the class in stitches.

12

Frontier Home

T HOR DISCOVERED in the streets of the town and in the wilderness of the mountains and creeks almost inexhaustible opportunities to develop his initiative and resourcefulness. Although he was neither avaricious nor needy, if some of his numerous activities brought him income he considered it sugar on his buttered bread. Mama could not afford cake except on birthdays. She was saving what she could for the family's future.

Much of the money he earned went to buy sweets. He did not correlate sugar with his frequent toothaches and reluctant visits to the dentist. Mama scolded but to no end.

On most Saturday mornings Thor turned scavenger. It took Mama several weeks to realize that it was impractical to lay out freshly laundered clothing for him on Saturdays. At least her son had sense enough to wear his clodhoppers on his forays. He would tuck a gunnysack under his arm and disappear beneath the piers.

The sandy beach of this underworld was slimy and the acrid air smelled of sewage. He learned to avoid the sudden flushing of toilets but could not evade the constant drops of water that fell from the street planks. Overhead he heard the *clip, clop, clip, clop* of hooves and the rumble of steel-tired wagon wheels. The log pilings, eroded by tide and marine life into elongated hourglass shapes, were encrusted with knife-edged barnacles and tiny mussel shells. In the dim light emanating from the edge of the pier, he searched for soda-water bottles and an occasional reed-encased demijohn bottle that was worth a quarter.

He emerged on the street with a sack full of bottles, smelling of hemp, stale beer, seaweed, and slimy clay. Dampness had climbed the ironed legs of his denim pants, water had darkened his blue cambric shirt, and his shoes were soaked and caked with brine.

One Saturday Mama met him emerging from the netherworld. "Komaru ne!" she said, her voice betraying all the meanings of the word: embarrassment, perplexity, annoyance. "What will the neighbors think! Not of you!" she emphasized. "Of me! Me!"

She threw up her hands in defeat as he bore his clinking burden to Dolly Gray's bottling works, where he dumped the bottles into a large wooden tank of water. He scraped off the labels and emptied the sand out of the bottles. He watched in fascination as Dolly placed the bottles over the whirling brushes of a machine that thoroughly cleansed the insides.

The bottles were filled with fruit syrup and carbonated water, capped, and labeled. Dolly rewarded Thor with two cents a bottle and a soda. His favorite flavor was strawberry. Instead of removing the cap he would drive a nail through it and so prolong his enjoyment.

At the bowling alley across the street—he was always on call—he attained a speed setting up pins on ten black dots that earned him a nickel a game. The charge was twenty-five cents a line, with the winner paying ten cents and the loser fifteen. Thor usually received a tip from the bowlers, who skidded the money down the maple alleys. He dreaded the big Swedes who used brute force rather than finesse just to see the pins fly.

One night at the pool hall up the street, Thor and Gus were watching Ken when the butt of Ken's cue hit Gus in the eye. Ken apologized, though Gus was wrong, standing too close, and gave him a silver dollar.

"What an easy way to make a buck," Thor said.

"You know, that hurt. I saw stars."

Thor examined the eye. "Yeah, it's going to get black."

"Your brother's a sport. C'mon, let's go have a soda."

The two boys, one of Swedish forebears, the other of Japanese, were the closest of friends and almost inseparable. Gus was about the same height, with flaxen hair, blue eyes, and a round face. Gus had a habit of ducking his head when he made a mischievous remark, as if he were trying to hide his expression. He had a flexible and loose scalp so he was able to wiggle his ears. This ability was Thor's despair because no matter how much he tried, he could not duplicate what he considered a remarkable feat.

Gus had round shoulders, partly the consequence of a fall he had taken up on the mountainside. He had fallen from the lip of a frozen waterfall, and escaped serious injury only because he landed on a steep, icy slope, sliding rather than falling flat. Thor had been shaken by his friend's close call, but was relieved to find him in good spirits when he visited him in the hospital.

Thor also had misadventures. One Saturday at the pier he was helping George the Greek lower provisions to a boat by means of a rope. The weight of a sack of potatoes pulled his hand forward before he could even think of letting go. His first and middle fingers were caught between the edge of the pier and the running rope that burned off the flesh.

The doctor applied salve to his wounds; he never forgot the smell of the yellow ointment, the stained gauze and adhesive tape which became soiled and had to be changed. He watched with awe as nature healed the raw flesh and covered it with skin. He bore the scars for years.

In July George commissioned Thor to pick some blueberries at ten cents a pound. He expected Thor to fill a five-pound, Swift lard pail, but he returned with a water pail more than half full. George wanted to pay him with an equivalent value of fruit, but Thor wanted cash. He had risen before the sun, raided his favorite patches on the Silver Bow Basin road where the berries grew as big as nickels. Now he thought of the time and labor spent and his resentment grew.

Angrily he stalked the stand, strongly tempted to push over some of the displays in revenge. Fear restrained him. His home was just across the street.

"I won't buy anything from you for my mother," he threatened. When George offered him half of what he had earned, Thor slapped the coins out of the extended hand. As he started to run away George grabbed him. He struggled furiously as the strong arms carried him toward the cash register. Three silver dollars were placed in his hand and his fingers were closed over the money. He stood wiping the tears from his eyes. He returned one dollar. "You owe me only two dollars," he said.

George threw up his hands and raised his eyes to the twilight sky. "All this commotion for what. I was only teasing."

"You were not," Thor retorted hotly. "You're a mean man."

Mama wondered why he went blocks out of his way to buy green groceries when all he had to do was walk across the street. He refused to tell her what was wrong. This was between him and that bugger. It was weeks before George could mollify him. After that Mama would wonder why Thor brought home more fruit and vegetables than her money would normally buy.

Weddings were of more than romantic interest to the boys. At the reception, usually held in the dining room of a hotel, the boys would gather in the street outside and wait for the ushers or friends of the groom to come out. Invariably they would toss silver dollars and two-and-a-half-dollar gold pieces out into the street, and the boys would scramble for their share.

At one of the wedding receptions, Thor snatched a gold piece from under the hand of Ettore Lucano, a newcomer who tended to bully the younger boys. Ettore had a complexion that always looked flushed, with a white scar across his left jawbone.

"Gimme," Ettore said. "That's mine."

Thor backed away. "Is not. I got it first." He added, "Slowpoke."

That was a mistake. Ettore reddened to the roots of his badger-colored hair. He stalked Thor and suddenly grabbed for him. Thor took to his heels, closely pursued by the older boy. Thor sought refuge in his home, slamming the door on Ettore's panting breath.

As Thor stood gasping for breath in the kitchen, his sister

Helen reported to him, "Ettore says the money is his."

"Tell him it's mine and I'm going to keep it."

Helen returned. "He says he is going to come in after you."

"I dare him to."

"He's much larger than you," Helen observed.

"I don't care."

Helen carried the message. "He says he will split with you."

Thor was tempted but said, "I beat him to it. He's a slow-poke."

"He's going to get real mad."

"See if I care,"

"You want me to say slowpoke?"

"Sure."

Ettore entered the kitchen, casting uneasy glances over his shoulder.

"Now, you going to give me that money?"

"No!"

As they glared at each other, Thor glimpsed his father coming down the hall from the barbershop. On impulse Thor hit Ettore in the mouth as hard as he could. As Ettore staggered back, Papa entered the room.

"What is going on here?" he asked.

"Nothing," Thor said.

Ettore slipped away through the kitchen door. Helen reported that he was real mad. He was walking back and forth like a lion in a cage. He was red in the face and talking to himself. Sometimes he would hit his hand with his fist. Oh, he was real mad!

As the saying goes, Thor thought discretion was the better part of valor.

The next day he was playing casino with Gus on the front porch. From time to time he would stand up and glance up and down the street. He was apprehensive and couldn't keep his mind on the cards. Gus sensed what was bothering Thor but kept silent. Thor had done what none of them dared to do, but now he had to take the consequences. Ettore appeared but Thor remained on his knees, dealing the cards without a break. Ettore nudged him in the back with his knee.

"What you mean, hitting me?"

"You had no business coming into the house."

"I ought to sock you one."

Thor played a card, but remained silent. He was on edge, aware of the menace that kept muttering threats over his head.

"One of these days," Ettore said, and left.

Gus took a deep breath. "I'll be a son of a gun," he said. It was a favorite expression of his. "Man, you really must have socked him."

Thor disclaimed any hint of prowess. He would rather run than fight. He was never forced to do either. Although Juneau was a frontier town, its residents were relatively quiet and peaceful. His encounter with Ettore was a rare exception.

Thor never saw knives used as weapons. If two boys were to fight it was fair and square, with bare fists. Knives were used to whittle, make whistles out of an elderberry twig, cut bait, but mostly for mumbletypeg. In one version the small blade was kept extended straight out, with the large blade at right angles. In another version the game was played with only the small blade extended straight out. The loser had to pull a peg out of the ground with his teeth.

With regional variations and modifications the childhood games of Main Street, U.S.A., were borne to the territorial appendage of Alaska. Thor disdained the games his sisters played: jackstraws, jump rope, hopscotch, and beanbags. The only interest Thor had was in trying to juggle three or four beanbags at a time.

Thor's childhood games ran the gamut of kick the can, pom pom pullaway, and Annie, Annie over. In kick the can, Thor griped that the smaller boys always seemed to be "it." More to his liking was pom pom pullaway. The one who was "it" stood in the center of the street while the rest lined up on the edge of the sidewalk.

"Pom, pom, pullaway, if you don't come I'll pull you away."

The boys tried to run across the street without being tagged. Those tagged joined the one who was "it" until all the boys were caught. The space for crossing was limited by outside boundaries. The game ended when the last boy was tagged. The first one tagged became "it" for the next game. This was a game he never saw played when he went Outside.

In "Annie, Annie over, dachshund free" (or that was the way it sounded to Thor), in which girls also joined, those on one side of a house would throw the ball over the roof while those on the other side would try to catch the ball before it hit the ground.

In a mining town of fewer than four thousand residents, many of them bachelors, there were not enough children to have organized sports. The boys occasionally played pick-up base-ball on the sand flats along Willoughby Avenue until the in-coming tide was washing around their shoes. One Saturday when the rising tide was lapping at Thor's heels, the ball was hit over his head and plopped into the sea. He stood a moment in indecision, took off his shoes and stockings, waded knee-deep to the ball, and retrieved it while the batter circled the bases for a home run. There was no ground-rule double.

Except for a game of catch, he hung up his glove for many years. He disliked making a fool of himself and the traumatic experience of being the last one picked to a side.

Perhaps the most important influence in his life at this time was Toby Thompson, the son of the town foundryman who cast parts for the machinery in the stamp mills and mines. Every vil-lage and town has a genius who grows up with a hammer in one hand and a monkeywrench in the other. He could fix his moth-er's wringer or sewing machine, adjust his father's boat engine, learn to drive and repair the first automobile, and make his own crystal radio set from raw material.

One day Thor labored industriously on a model car he felt would beat all the others in town. It ran well on the planked streets, but when he tried it out on a gravel road, the rear axle assembly collapsed under him. His vexation was so great he was tempted to leave his creation on the spot.

Toby came upon him wiping tears that left smears on his cheeks. He squatted on his haunches and examined the two-by-fours Thor had spiked together to hold the axles.

"You was thinkin' wishful," Toby said. "You need long bolts and nuts to hold those two-by-fours together. You got a bit and augur? You bore holes all the way through; thick bolts will hold those boards together. The blacksmith should have some long enough."

Toby looked at Thor. "I could do it for you but then it wouldn't be yours."

"I'll feel like a fool dragging that thing through the streets."

"Let them laugh. If they don't like it they can lump it." It was Toby's favorite expression. "Never quit. See it through."

"Like shooting a shotgun. Or carrying that stove up to our treehouse."

"Sure. That's what I mean."

Thor nodded. He watched the older boy walk away. He's someone special, he thought. He's not mean like Cecil Rhodes, the son of Old Man Rhodes who had named his son after the British Empire builder. The town egotist would jeer, "That's for me to know and for you to find out."

Toby would say, "When your time comes will be soon enough."

Toby had taken Thor, Gus, and George Oja up to Silver Bow Basin and spent an entire afternoon teaching them how to shoot his shotgun. He had labored over several weekends helping them build a treehouse. Like most playthings it fell into neglect as the boys moved on to other things, but it had been a game more important than most.

Thor watched winter approach on the mountain tops. The days were usually raw and threatening. He went to bed with rain pattering on the window pane. In the morning, as clouds climbed the sky, the bald heads of the three mountains were crowned with snow. Each day the snowline crept further down into the timber belt. He rescued his ice skates from the corner of a closet and industriously sharpened and oiled them each night by lamplight.

Then one evening large, fat snowflakes floated down and peered through the windows. Winter had come. Restless days were spent testing the ice on Evergreen Pond. After one heavy rainstorm, an Arctic front moved in and the pond was a huge sheet of glass.

On this Saturday morning Thor emptied the last of the

condensed milk from a can—mystified Mama was certain she had had enough for Papa's morning coffee—and with can and a branch shaped like a hockey stick hied himself to the pond. His skates cut the first strokes on the deserted and virgin surface of the ice. He never forgot the intoxication of that first stride, the cold bite of the air on his cheeks, of unused muscles quivering in their sheaths of thigh, calf, and ankle. He loved to play shinny and because of his skill on skates was a match for the older boys.

Reality brought him back to earth. One enchanted moonlit night as he was guiding a can up the ice, a high school student picked up his can and threw it far into the woods. The act was so unexpected that Thor stood dumbfounded. The anger came later, but what could he do about it? He reasoned that the skittering noise of the can had annoyed the student's girlfriend.

Thor literally grew up on skates in winter. After school and on weekends, Evergreen Pond, moonlit or starlit, was the home of his soul.

A big thrill was to be allowed to ride on a bobsled with the older boys. Toby Thompson saw to that. He had taken a two-by-twelve plank and attached small wooden sleds with steel runners at front and back, with a steering wheel assembly to guide the front sled.

At the top of frozen Gold Street the boys, alternating sides, would give the bobsled a running start, swing on in unison, and race downward, gaining momentum every second. Hugging the boy in front of him Thor lifted his legs as high as he could for fear they might be snapped off by the hurtling ground underneath.

On either side the sidewalks with their wooden railings posed the constant threat of death or mutilation should the human juggernaut hurtle off course. The ride was especially thrilling at night, as there were only the dim street-corner lights, the shadows of the houses, and the white gleam of the snow to guide Toby. The younger boys had the honor of pulling the heavy bobsled up the hill.

When northern lights shuttled across the loom of the sky Thor was aware of some force beyond his ken. One night as he skated on Auk Lake in the starlight, the northern lights hung like celestial curtains above the stage of Mendenhall Glacier, parting and then drawing together as if at some ghostly standing ovation. He felt that he was seeing the colors of the spheres. He was transported beyond himself as though in religious ecstasy. His trance held him captive, although mechanically he went home in Toby's truck with his noisy peers and lay sleepless in his bed.

Another treat was the class sleigh ride in winter, with hay softening the wooden floor of the sled and blankets to keep warm. The night chosen for the outing came clear and cold. Starshine etched its spell among the trees that lined Glacier Highway, the crusty blanket of snow, the sleeping giants of mountains. After the tittering and snickering subsided the class sang Christmas carols, and what was more appropriate than "Jingle Bells"? There was nothing, he thought, to equal the smoothness of steel runners on ice, like a magic carpet flying through the air. He listened to the muffled plop of the horse's hooves, the rustle of the runners, the wind whispering in his ears. The sleigh ride went into a treasury of little hours gathered to exalt his heart.

An abiding influence in Thor's growth and development was his inheritance, the wilderness, in which Juneau was set like an anachronism. At one with nature and its living creatures among his beloved mountains and waters, he lived from day to day unfettered by the concerns that warped and deformed his elders.

Mat envied Thor and tried through meditation to reach his son's state of grace. Thor watched curiously as Papa sat Turkish fashion on the floor, his back straight as Mama's broomstick, his hands resting on his lap, his eyes closed. Twenty minutes every morning before breakfast. Sometimes he would hold his hands in prayer position and vibrate them as if he were calling on invisible powers. Practical Mama wished Papa would use his meditation to stop his drinking.

Mat tried to bring nature into the home in the form of *bonkei*, a miniature tray landscape. George the Greek brought him a flat cherry crate. Mat had Thor gather white sand, pebbles, and the short moss that grew on Gold Creek's boulders, and the longer moss found on forest floors. Using wooden match sticks and a piece of windowpane glass for a lake, he created a creditable *bonkei*. Displayed in the barbershop window, it drew favorable comment. In his fashion Mat brought one of the arts of Japan to this outpost of civilization.

Thor's first efforts at expressing himself were to copy what he saw, such as the labels on the ends of orange crates that depicted the blossoms, leaves, and fruit. He drew by rote, just as he memorized his lessons. The symbolism of Papa's landscape, unsophisticated as it was, escaped him.

As he grew, his inclination was more toward the visual than the aural. To him the earth was a palette of color that appealed more to his senses than the sound of music. Of all his joys the greatest was to find remnants of the rainbow reborn in field and wood, on mountain and in the sea.

He admired the courage of the crocuses, as strong in their instincts as the salmon running upriver, reaching for the pale sun through imprisoning snow. He feasted his eyes on the rash yellow flowerlets of pussywillows nurtured in nooks of Silver Bow Basin, a vast bowl concentrating solar heat. He loved to run his fingers over the silvery down of the catkins, a sensual pleasure. He would bring shoots of the first pussywillows to school and for art class he would draw brownish-green shoots and—such sacrilege—paste catkins on the drawing to imitate nature.

On the road to Thane he sought the shy gold of the first yellow violets near rivulets, knowing almost to the day when they would greet him, winking their tiny purple lashes. Pink carillons of blueberry flowers swung on crimson branches along Glacier Highway, while the salmonberry flowers were pink stars on bright brown shoots.

In the Mendenhall meadows of the delta dairy lands, buttercups, clover, and marigolds wove designs richer than Persian rugs. Wild roses were a treasure infrequently found, their fragrance more subtle than all the perfumes of Grasse. Acres of pink lupine shot spikes into the summer sky and lavender iris grew in the marshes. Alaskan cotton, Michaelmas daisies, and goldenrod decorated earth's autumn canvas.

The Alaskan spring came in various guises: cold driving rains, cloudless skies, or dangerous white cloaks of snow. All winter long Thor walked the treacherous streets with guarded tension in his calves, but when spring came the feeling was different. As the last ice melted on the planked streets beneath the young sun, the soles of his feet, through leather, through wood, held communion with earth. Never mind the calendar, this was his vernal equinox.

One morning he left his sleeping family and went out on the deserted Sunday street. He looked at the refuse of winter and had a thought. He walked up Front Street, turned left on First Street, and passed Seward. He looked up Main Street toward City Hall. Yes, he was right.

The town firemen had brought out their truck, unreeled their hose and started down Main Street, washing it from sidewalk to sidewalk. The stream of water cleansed the wooden planks of gravel, sand, salt and coal ashes—all the grime of winter, until the wet wood surfaces sparkled in the sunlight. He retreated before the spray that made small rainbows in the air.

He kept pace with the firemen, sometimes ahead, sometimes behind, as they moved from hydrant to hydrant down Front Street. When he mocked them they directed the water at his flying feet and he would race away simulating terror. Once he dodged the wrong way and was bowled over. A fireman in his rubber boots ran over, swung him high in the air and said, "That didn't hurt, young man, did it?"

He wiped the tears from his eyes and laughed. "I was scared." At City Dock the firemen completed their chore, rolled up their hose and returned to the firehouse. He watched them leave with regret.

Thor held the firemen in deep respect. Every Fourth of July program listed a firemen's hose contest. Two teams of firemen dressed in slicker hats with chin straps, oilskin coats, and rubber hip boots lined up ahead of two hydrants. Leading from each hydrant lay three lengths of hose, like a white snake ready to be coupled together.

At a given signal, two men coupled the hose and nozzle

together while another attached the hose to the hydrant and turned on the water. As the men finished coupling the hose they ran to help anchor their leader, who directed his stream of water at the leader of the other team.

At five to ten yards the force of the water could bowl a man over or stagger a team of four as each side struggled to score a direct hit on the other. The team that drove the other behind a designated line won the contest.

On an unseasonably warm day Thor walked up the gravel road that ran beside Gold Creek into Silver Bow Basin. High overhead where the eagles soar, on the shoulders of Mount Juneau, acres of snow trembled on their uneasy beds. Underneath, water from melting ice leaped from the lip of each ravine and poured a thousand feet into the canyon, living columns as graceful as any in Ionia. Through the spring, sitting in his classroom, Thor had heard the roar of avalanches and longed to dash outside to watch the spectacle.

The roar of a minor avalanche from a neighboring ravine made Thor jump. The reverberations should have alerted him. He looked across the creek and up the rocky slope created by previous avalanches. He stared straight up at the snow mass that was bulging over the mountain's shoulder.

He disobeyed the premonition that told him to flee. He was spellbound, as though the white mass was a predatory animal ready to pounce on him. Even as he watched the overhang of snow a thousand feet above his head started to move. It was like slow motion. So engrossed was he, like a cameraman shooting oblivious to a danger threatening him, that he only started to run when it was almost too late.

The roar as tons of white hit the slope across Gold Creek several hundred feet away shattered the air. Snow and ice, clawing up gravel and boulders, raced downward toward the creek. He glanced back once and forever remembered the fearful grandeur of the oncoming tide, a wave crested with clouds of snow that glowed like glory in the sunlight.

Another fleeting glimpse from the corner of his eye and he felt he was out of danger. The snow dust devils escorting the main mass of snow could hardly harm him.

Just then the concussion hit him as if he had fallen from the roof of his home. A live force tumbled and rolled him over until he fetched up against a snowbank. Bruised and uncomprehending, he watched as the flying snow dissipated, leaving an awesome mass blocking the highway.

He lay in a state of shock. It did not occur to him that his body could have been entombed without anyone knowing until the trucks and snowplows came to clear the road. He got up and started walking toward town. Soon he was running with a fixed look in his eyes, down Gold Street and then Front Street to his home.

At the kitchen table he sat unseeing, unrecognizing, as though in a trance. Mama hovered over him with small questions and his siblings stared at him as though he were a stranger. The trembling left his limbs and a deep lassitude possessed him. He lay down for a nap. By evening he was enjoying his dinner. Not to alarm his mother, he kept his adventure a secret. Between mouthfuls he considered the invisible force that had almost killed him. So, an explosion is accompanied by concussion.

This homing instinct possessed him on at least two other brushes with nature—and possible death. With Gus and George he was fishing a pool in Gold Creek up in the basin. This was no quiescent water but more like a whirlpool formed as the spring-swollen stream poured into a large pool, made a complete circle, and dashed out on the other side.

A piece of the decaying stump to which he was clinging with one hand while he cast with the other gave way, and he was plunged into the white water. Unable to swim, he held his breath and thrashed the numbing cold, trying to keep afloat. Gus and George were too petrified to even move.

Thor circled the whirlpool once and on his second round the force of the circling water cast him ashore near the outlet. He clawed his way out of the tugging waters and lay several moments gasping to regain his breath.

The chill penetrated his body and drove him to his feet. Without a word to his friends he started walking toward town. Soon he was running past the melting mass of the avalanche that had almost sent him into oblivion. In his eyes was the same fixed, unnatural stare. His wet pants rubbed the skin between his thighs. Warmth had returned to his body by the time he reached home and changed into dry clothing. He did not analyze his actions. He had run to keep warm; he had sought the refuge of his home. To Mama he explained that he had falled into Gold Creek.

A third accident occurred one spring dusk on the steepest part of Gold Street near St. Ann's Hospital. Instead of cycling down the steep wooden sidewalk, he chose the unpaved street. When he tried to brake his momentum he realized his rear tire could not get traction on the gravel and large stones.

Frightened and desperate, his arms like steel rods and his hands clamped like vises around the handlebars, he bounced crazily from stone to stone, steering as straight as he could toward where the wood planking started on Gold Street. He was short of safety when the front wheel hit a large stone. He was catapulted from the bicycle, slammed against the ground with stunning force, and almost knocked senseless. He lay prone for moments regaining his wits.

In the corner playground some girls were swinging and singing in the Alaskan dusk. They couldn't care less if I'd been killed, he thought, bitterly though unjustly. They could not see him where he lay. Painfully he picked himself up and limped home because his handlebars had been twisted askew. No fixed stare in his eyes this time. He hurt too much in every bone of his body.

Mama happened to be standing on the porch. In the dusk she did not see that gravel had scraped one cheek raw. She was looking for the other children to call them in for dinner. She could not know that he had bitten the inside of his lower lip. A lump formed there that his tongue toyed with over many years.

13
Backwaters of War

A T AGE SIX, Thor had been recruited by the Douglas tobacco shop man, David Stern, next door to sell one-week-
old Sunday newspapers that the ships brought in from
Seattle. He transferred this activity to Juneau by accepting a
paper route offered by the *Alaska Press*. On his first morning he
dressed in the dawn light. Not wanting to disturb his brother,
he did not turn on the light. He failed to notice he had on one
black and one brown shoe until he reached the newspaper office. Despite his mortification he finished his route. For a few
weeks the operator of the flatbed press called him Thor Two
Shoes.

Among Thor's jobs as he grew older was to melt the lines
of lead into ingots that the linotype operator could slip into his
pot. He built a fire in a potbellied stove that had a bowl-like top.
As the lead melted he skimmed off impurities. He used an iron
ladle to pour the molten lead into cast-iron molds that formed
ingots. When these were cool he piled them in neat stacks near
the linotyper.

One Sunday he neglected his weekly chore. When he went
in to pick up a bundle of papers for delivery he was given an angry and memorable dressing down by the editor. For the first
time he was made aware of deadlines, the interdependence of
the editorial and the mechanical departments.

Whether these early exposures to the newspaper business
influenced his future in journalism is subject to question. Dur-

ing his teen years he had no thought of his future, no attraction to printer's ink.

When the United States declared war on Germany on April 6, 1917, a form of military training was instituted at the school. Using wooden guns made in the manual training class, the boys learned the manual of arms, close-order drill, and marching formations, complete with color guard. At one inspection, A. B. Phillips, the principal, who also taught manual training, looked down at Thor's shoes and asked when he had shined them.

"Last week," Thor said. He got one demerit. Gus, who was standing next to him, suppressed a snicker, and when asked the question gave the same answer.

Phillips looked into Thor's eyes, glanced at the color guard, and said, "I'd like to see you make up the demerit."

Thor got the impression that if he did so, he would have the honor of carrying the flag. For some reason the principal had taken a liking to him.

After school that afternoon Thor looked through the window into the gym and watched an upperclassman put a few sweating pupils through a series of close-order drills. The martinet was Cecil Rhodes, whom he feared and disliked. In front of Gus and George he had called their attention to Thor's "slitty" eyes for no reason. There was no racial connotation, for he would have used a similar remark about anyone he disliked. Thor was aware that the older boy would take particular pleasure in putting him through the ropes. He would not submit his pride to such humiliation.

The only casualty Thor knew of from Juneau was a high school graduate who returned shell shocked. The townspeople talked in hushed tones and in school the teachers told their pupils not to talk about the war to the young man.

One day in class Miss Seleen distributed magazines. Thor's landed face down, so she turned it over. Pointing an accusing finger at Thor was James Montgomery Flagg's Uncle Sam. He sat back startled. His teacher saw the consternation on his face. "You are doing your bit," she said.

In class Thor knitted little squares that were to be used for hot water bottle covers. Religiously each week he brought a quarter to buy a Liberty Bond stamp that he stuck into a holder. When this was full he turned it in for a bond. Enterprising as ever, he sold a map of the world at war that was bordered by photographs of the Allied leaders. He had been delayed in securing the maps. He had filled in a coupon and put it in the mail drop. The postal clerk had called him to the window.

"Young man," he had said, "when you want to mail one of these coupons you have to put it in an addressed envelope. And don't forget the stamp."

When he eventually received the maps he had a brisk sale. A great many of the residents were immigrants from Europe. The family and friends they had left were now killing, dying, and starving in war-ravaged lands. When Thor offered a map to Rupert Gruben, the German dairyman said, "Those butchers!"

At Thor's surprised and crestfallen look, he gave Thor a quarter.

"I mean the butchers on both sides, young man. War is stupid and don't you ever forget that."

Thor returned thoughtfully home. Gruben intrigued him. He was always saying unexpected things that made the townspeople look at him sideways. Some said he was a nut, a few that he was an anarchist, and others said he talked plain common sense. As Thor thought it over, war meant more than a chance to make money.

The next day he met Gruben, who asked, "How are you making out?"

"I tore them up and burned them." Thor said.

Gruben held his fat sides, threw back his crewcut head and laughed. "You catch on fast."

Thor rather liked Gruben. Although his wife boiled his overalls until they were a pale blue, he smelled of old milk, cow dung, and the stables.

One day he had lectured Papa, who had a habit of tipping his derby to everyone he met.

"You tip your hat to the ladies," Gruben said. "That is good manners. But you don't tip your hat to other men. In America we are all equal. Or we try to be."

The war hysteria was so insane that the town council had the German dairymen sign a paper that they would not poison the milk they distributed. This had Gruben talking to himself. He signed because, as he said, "What can sane men do in a cuckoo's nest?" The German owners of the two bakeries also came under surveillance. Thor thought it odd that these irreproachable citizens should come under suspicion. Or that German fries should become French fries, or that German pot roast assumed the name of Yankee pot roast, or that hamburgers turned up as Liberty burgers. Or that he should catch Liberty measles.

As he recuperated his sheet was littered with scales of his skin as if Mama had scaled a fish over his bed. One of his closest friends, John Rundall, who was also stricken at the same time, claimed that their subsequent nearsightedness was a result of this illness.

Thor was not quarantined but he remembered that in Douglas when a household was stricken the health authorities would tack bright red or orange signs bearing in large black type SMALLPOX or SCARLET FEVER or the name of some other serious, communicable disease on the front of the house. Those inside were quarantined for days.

April proved to be an eventful month. The schoolhouse built in 1892 was to be demolished and a new one constructed. Plans were announced for the formation of a Boy Scout troop, the first in the territory, of which Thor became a member.

On April 13 Edward Krause, a convicted murderer who was suspected, among other crimes, of killing a Japanese man named Yamamoto in Wrangell, escaped from the federal jail. Three days later he was shot and killed by Arvin Franzen at Doty's Cove on Admiralty Island. Franzen, who claimed he had shot in defense of his family, laid claim to the $1,000 reward that had been offered.

On April 17, Thor appeared in a school performance of a musical, *The Pixies' Triumph,* as one of the brownies. He was not too disappointed that Mama (although she made his costume) and Papa did not attend his stage debut. The spheres of his life at school and at home hardly ever intersected. Mama knew little English and Papa did not speak fluently enough to feel at home among the other parents.

On the heels of the musical show came the cave-in at the Treadwell mines. It was not totally unexpected. For some time the swimming pool walls of the Natatorium had been cracking and being repaired. The foundations of the oil tanks and fire-hall were settling unevenly. As a result, a safety signal system was instituted.

Even with this precaution it was a miracle that of the 350 men underground on April 21, only one was reported missing. The major cave-in occurred between Mine 700 and Bunkhouse 4. The Natatorium, the oil tanks, and the firehouse dropped instantly. More than a thousand miners were put out of work. Guards were posted around the disaster area, not to prevent looting but to keep out the unwary should further cave-ins occur.

Ken was out of a job, together with all the other Japanese workers, and the miners and stamp mill hands. Close to two thousand jobs were lost overnight among a combined population of about five thousand in the two channel towns.

Fortunately for the Fuse family, Ken found a job as a waiter at Johnson's City Cafe, while Papa's business, though it suffered, earned enough to see the family through the crisis. Thor continued his schooling without interruption. He was almost unaware of the problems the townspeople met and overcame. Like pioneers they tightened their belts and made do with what they had.

14

The Wreck of the Princess Sophia

T HE WRECK of the *Princess Sophia* in October 1918 cast a
gloom over the residents of Juneau. Inured though they
were to the savage ways of the Alaskan wilderness, they
were deeply wounded by this cruel and total destruction.

A few days before the *Princess Sophia* was scheduled to pick
up passengers at Skagway, Sadao Suda sat astride his trail pack
watching with envy the bon voyage gaiety around him. A puff
of steam issued from the whistle on the stack of the S.S. *Alaska,*
followed by the universal blast warning passengers that the ship
would cast off in fifteen minutes. He looked wistfully at the last-
minute arrivals scurrying up the gangplank.

Unconsciously his hand rested on his money belt hidden
beneath his blue flannel shirt. He had offered a premium to those
lucky enough to have secured a berth, but money meant nothing to those eager to go Outside. He had pleaded with the purser that he did not need a cabin, not even a berth—it was only
to Juneau—but for some fateful reason the purser refused.

A knee gently nudged his back. He looked up and jumped
to his feet. "'Lo, Frank," he grinned. "Long time no see."

Suda half-bowed, a habit he had kept through years of living in the United States. He still felt a bit embarrassed by the
bearhug that Frank Dulac gave him, but in the warmth of affection he felt, he thought, "never mind." In their eyes was the
recollection of a bug-infested summer they had spent prospecting for gold along the Koyukuk River and a cold, black

winter trapping for furs in the Brooks Range. There they had spent the winter with Frank Yasuda, his Eskimo wife, and their people. It was a measure of the empathy they had that even in the most trying times they never caught cabin fever. As the years passed their trails had crossed during stampedes to Nome, Tanana, Chandalar, Iditarod, and Ruby, finally converging on this Skagway pier.

Dulac looked down at Suda's pack. "Trying to board the *Alaska,* eh?"

"No luck. Not even to Juneau."

"You got passage on the *Princess Sophia?*" Suda nodded. "Want to exchange tickets?"

"No, no."

"You know damn well you mean hai, hai." Dulac nudged Suda's pack with his toe. They laughed. "C'mon, let's go see the purser."

As the *Alaska* warped away from the pier, Suda waved back. Mist blurred Frank's form. His last words had been, "See you in Juneau."

In the few minutes before the "All ashore" cry, emphasized by the ringing of a triangular gong, Frank had told Suda of his plans to homestead on Glacier Highway outside the capital town. He had met a girl booked on the *Princess Sophia* who seemed interested in joining his venture.

"I'm plumb fed up on chasing rumors," Frank had said. "It's time I settled down. I think I've found the right woman."

Suda had no doubt that Frank would captivate the woman. He had proved that in a hundred dancehalls throughout the Klondike and Alaska.

The hundred miles down Lynn Canal and up Gastineau Channel passed without incident, but when the *Alaska* docked at Juneau, Suda was detained by a deputy from the U.S. Marshal's office. At the City Cafe, Ken received a call from the deputy.

"Hi, Ken, this is Jerry. There's a Chink down here at the dock, says he's a Jap. Claims to know you. Want to come down and identify him?"

Ken laughed when he saw Suda. He was known among the

Japanese as Shin-san because he looked Chinese. "He's Japanese all right, Jerry."

"Can't tell the difference since they started cutting off their pigtails," Jerry said.

"We all look alike, eh, Jerry."

"You're different. Johnson's different. You work hard. You mind your own business. The Chinks are a menace. I remember my uncle telling me about the time the miners loaded all of them on a ship and got rid of the lot. They were taking the jobs away from the Indians and whites. Guess that was about 1886. The governor ordered them back to the mines, but the miners said they would line the shore with shotguns to keep them out."

"From what I heard the Indians couldn't stand the noise and the confinement," Ken said. "It was like a prison. They were used to the sea and the woods. Same way with the prospectors. They would work until they had a grubstake and then take off. Undependable. That's why Treadwell imported Chinese workers."

"They was too many of them. They stuck like leeches. The miners tried dynamiting their houses but even that didn't work. Finally they put them on ship and packed them off to Wrangell."

"I hear it took eight days and they almost starved."

"Served them right."

"I don't get you. You got a good heart, right instincts, but when it comes to the Chinese . . ." Ken shrugged.

Ken felt comfortable with his younger friend, who always spoke his mind. He was impressionable, with the lean, cleancut features of his Nordic forebears, with eyes the blue of glacial caverns and hair the color of straws in Mendenhall meadows. No shadow of race fell across their relationship.

Once Jerry, who was an only son, said, "You're like an older brother."

They would drink up at Donovan's bar or shoot pool at his tables. They schemed to take the unwary, for they were as expert as any pool shark and frequently earned their dinners with their cues.

One evening a drunken miner, newly arrived from Outside, called Ken a Jap with intent to insult. Ken would have let it pass, for like most of the immigrant Japanese he knowingly cultivated a low profile to avoid unnecessary trouble.

"Deru kugi wa utareru," as Mat would say. "The nail that sticks out gets pounded."

Jerry though, sensing the insult, invited the miner to step outside.

Ken elbowed him aside. "This is my fight."

The miner was restrained by his companions. Or by the sight of Ken holding a cue in a bayonet stance.

Jerry looked at him curiously. "Would you have used that?"

"I never ask for trouble, but when it comes—I could have used this like a bayonet against his Adam's apple, or brought up the butt and broken his jaw," Ken said. "Let's go have a bowl of noodles."

They seated themselves in one of a row of green-curtained booths that opened off a narrow hall running behind the back bar wall of the restaurant proper.

Ken said, "I still have to report by mail every year to the Japanese Consulate in Seattle. This is in place of compulsory military training."

"But you're in the United States. You're an American."

"Not yet, Jerry. There's a law on the books says I can't become a naturalized citizen because I'm a Jap. Now, you take my kid brother, he was born in America so he's a United States citizen. Or, you take your father, he was born in Norway or Sweden, I forget which."

"Sweden. Peterson, ending in *son*. Remember, if the ending is *sen* it's Norwegian, *son* is Swedish. Not always, but most of the time."

"Well, anyway, your father became a naturalized citizen. He could because he's white."

Jerry nodded. He toyed with a piece of pork in his bowl. Ken had taught him how to use chopsticks.

"What did that guy mean, that I'm a Jap lover?"

"Anybody who sympathizes or is friendly with us Japs."

"But what the hell. Man to man what's the difference?"

"What about the Chinese?"

"They threatened to take away our jobs."

Ken laughed. "That's exactly what they're saying about Japanese on the Pacific Coast. Economic competition. "That's the whole thing in a nutshell. Things are going to get worse. Remember that I told you."

Jerry looked at Ken. A frown wrinkled his brow.

"Confused?"

Jerry's blue eyes were dark. "Meaning I shouldn't use Jap?"

"Between us friends, I wouldn't fuss. But don't use Chink."

Jerry put his hand across the table. "I didn't know." Their handclasp tightened.

"I know," Ken said.

The dark green curtain parted in the adjoining booth. A Tlingit couple, possibly in their thirties, stood up.

Ken, who was facing them, looked up. "Hi, Brant. How's things?"

"Can't complain. Couldn't help overhearing you." Brant looked at his wife. Elsie giggled. All the mobile features of her handsome face wreathed in a smile. "Sorry about that," she said.

"Come to think about it, Jerry," Ken said, "did you know that none of the Natives have citizenship?"

"You're kidding. I just took it for granted. Why, they're the original Americans. I may be naive, but I know that much." Jerry shifted over and patted the bench seat beside him. Across the table Ken moved over. "Join us."

Brant, a tall man with a genial countenance, hesitated, then laughed as he sat down. "I'm not used to being treated like a white man."

"Aw, come off it, Brant. You're raising my dander. You're the best guide in these parts and you know you're one of us."

A shadow darkened Brant's face. "As I listened to you two talking I couldn't help making comparisons with our lot."

Elsie's hand rested on her husband's. "Now, Brant, don't you get riled up."

"Those signs in the saloon and restaurant windows: NO NATIVES. But the one that gets my goat is Greene's NO DOGS OR NATIVES. Some day I'm going to shoot out his window." He looked at Jerry's deputy marshall's badge. "Of course, my gun went off by accident."

"I could talk to Greene," Jerry said, his face red.

"Don't bother. That ignorant bastard isn't worth noticing."

There was silence as Brant cooled off.

"Johnson's decent. I've come in to eat and sat at the counter talking to Ken. He's all right." Brant smiled. "He had a bright idea when he had these booths put in. Gives young people privacy." Elsie blushed at his look.

"My people find them convenient. Of course, he would let them sit at the tables out there but they feel more at home and comfy sitting in the booths. Saves embarrassment all around. One thing I've got to say, Johnson makes the best chow mein and chop suey around."

He stood up. "Got to make tracks." He slapped Jerry on the back. "When we going deer hunting?"

"Make it two Sundays from now."

As the couple left, Jerry and Ken exchanged glances. "Why do things have to be this way?"

"Because we're stupid!"

The first report that the *Princess Sophia* had run aground on Vanderbilt Reef in Lynn Canal aroused little alarm. The Canadian Pacific steamer had sailed from Skagway on October 22, a Wednesday, toward evening. Her passenger manifest was a cross section of Alaskans: Yukon River pilots and deckhands heading South before the big freeze. Miners and prospectors who wanted Outside to escape the long dark winter and bitter cold. Families of servicemen who had departed from Fort Haines earlier aboard troop transports. Business men, transient workers, and prostitutes who were headed toward more lucrative fields. An ill-fated shipload of 268 passengers and 75 crewmen aboard a 3,000-ton steamship.

A few hours south of Skagway an arctic snowstorm overtook the ship. The driven snow was as blinding as fog, blotting out all landmarks. Visibility was almost zero. Her speed reduced, the ship crept through the night, guided only by the echoes of the whistle rebounding from unseen mountains to port and starboard. Distance from either shore was estimated by the speed of sound, counting off echoes in seconds.

But disaster lurked below. With a jar that shook the ship, she ran on and up Vanderbilt Reef until two thirds of her was cradled on solid rock. She remained on even keel, though on a slant from bow to stern.

Alaskan curio shops abound with photographs of ships in similar positions. Low tide finds them perched high and dry on rocky cradles. While the radio operator tapped out the marine distress signal, Captain F. L. Locke saw no reason for alarm. No wind nor wild water threatened the ship's security. Only the heavily falling snow was turning her into a ghost ship.

Captain Locke made his fateful decision. The sky and sea were calm, the rocky shore was not many yards away. The parent steamship company had dispatched a sister ship, the *Princess Alice,* and a salvage tug, which were racing to the scene. Locke asked the *Cedar,* a Coast Guard ship that had sped to the rescue, to stand by. Thursday and most of Friday passed uneventfully. The passengers tended to treat the stranding as an adventure to be related to admiring friends and relatives. Wait till Suda hears about this, Frank Dulac thought.

But late Friday afternoon a storm front from the Arctic regions roared down Lynn Canal, herding rollers made enormous by the narrow confines of the waterway. Thirty-foot waves forced smaller rescue craft to take to the shelter of nearby inlets and islands.

The *Cedar,* with anchor dragging, approached to within a few hundred yards of the stricken ship, but when the force of the gale threatened to pile it on the reef, the captain had to withdraw into deeper water. Darkness became a discord of caterwauling wind, booming surf, crashing walls of water.

The last wireless message received from the radio operator aboard the *Princess Sophia* was that she had been driven over the reef into deep water. The *Cedar* raced back to the scene, but its searchlight disclosed only a barren reef over which white-fanged waters prowled like a pack of angry wolves.

Toward daylight, as though the storm had achieved its objective, the wind slackened. When the *Cedar* returned on Saturday morning, only the foremast of the sunken ship was visible above the sullen, gray, restless waters. If there's a judgment seat upstairs, the skipper thought, I'd hate to be Locke standing before it.

Silent and subdued, the crew members went about the job of salvaging human bodies. They were joined by seiners and other small craft. For days the bodies, most of them fully clothed and wearing lifebelts, were cast ashore for miles along the forlorn coast. Some watches were found stopped at 7:30, indicating that the ship had taken its death plunge shortly before the *Cedar* steamed up to the scene the night before. Recovered bodies were taken to Skagway and to Juneau, where they were laid out in mute rows, covered by canvas, in the warehouses on the piers.

The story of the three-day tragedy had been carried on bulletins at the *Daily Alaska Empire* building, and details were printed in its columns. A somber mood haunted the town. A few among the dead were townspeople who had gone to Skagway on business or who had intended the round trip as a diversionary cruise.

After a sleepless night, Suda was having a late breakfast at the City Cafe Saturday morning. Ferns and flowers of frost had grown halfway up the windows. Snow was crusty on the ledges outside, a token of the storm whose evil deed was not yet known in town.

A newsboy burst through the front door. "*Princess Sophia* sinks!" he shouted, waving a newspaper in the air. "No survivors! Extra!"

Suda's first anxiety was fear for his friend. Frank Dulac could not be dead. No, it was impossible! Suda could see him walking through that door, a whimsical smile on his round, lively face. But there it was, in black print on a roll call of death: Frank Dulac.

The awful realization struck him that he, Sadao Suda, would have been listed there, except for a chance meeting on a Skagway pier. *Kangaete minasaiyo*, he thought. Just think about it.

There but for a prank of fate would be I.

Subtly woven into his thoughts was a feeling of guilt. He had no reason to feel as he did. The initiative in exchanging berths had been taken by his friend. In their decades of friendship there had been crises when either would have given his life for the other.

That evening as Suda was having dinner, Jerry and two fishermen dropped in for a bite. Weariness seamed their unshaven faces.

"Four more bodies," Jerry told Ken. "God! One was only a little girl. It was awful."

He clasped his lean hands around the coffee mug to warm his fingers.

"The boats are going twenty miles up and down that damn canal. Down Stephens Passage," Jerry said. "If the tides took any bodies out Icy Strait, good-bye. How we're going to identify them, especially the kids without identification, is beyond me. Damn that Locke, anyway."

"Maybe his decision was influenced by the head office. Salvage costs, you know."

"It's going to cost the company a damn sight more. When I think about it. God." He slammed the counter with his fist. To Suda, who had edged up, "What do you want?"

"I can identify one of them."

"Which one?"

"Frank Dulac."

Jerry pulled a crumpled sheet of paper from his mackinaw pocket. "Nope, he's not on the list yet."

"I volunteer to help," Suda said. "He my best friend."

As Jerry hesitated one of the fishermen said, "He can spell me. I have my family to look after."

Jerry nodded. "We're leaving at four in the morning. Meet us at the City Dock. I'm going to get me some shut-eye."

It was about noon of the second day, the sun a disk in the clouds, when they found Frank Dulac. They gaffed the body close to the seiner. As they pulled him aboard he was cradled in Suda's arms. Suda rocked back and forth. Tears flowed down his cheeks. "My friend, my friend," he murmured. "Kawaiso,

kawaiso. So pitiful, so pitiful." Suda helped bear Dulac's body to the warehouse deck, where he was placed among the rows of bodies covered with blankets, tarpaulins, and canvas. Suda was inconsolable.

The hours were moving slowly in the cozy warmth of the City Cafe, an isolated glow in the darkened streets of lower Juneau. In the raw cold outside an uneasy wind moaned and prowled about the windows. Embers settled on the grate in the cooking range. Amano made noises with his big wooden pestle as he mixed lye with fat skimmed from cooking meat to make soap. The alkaline smell of wood ash blended with that of sourdough rising on the upper shelves of the work counter. On this island of warmth, Suda was remorseful.

Thor knew he should be home in bed. Johnson had donned his heavy wool overcoat, arctics, and his sealskin cap with the band that could be pulled down to cover his ears, but he lingered to listen. Ken as usual was standing behind the counter. Thor had never seen his brother sit down on the job except to eat. Sometimes he even stood while he ate off the counter top. He was polishing a fork until it was dry as an old bone.

Jerry Peterson pulled off his mackinaw. "Whew, it's hot in here."

"What do you expect." Ken cast him a quick, humorous glance, and returned his attention to Suda.

Two whores from a house up the street entered the cafe and sat down at a table. Ken went to serve them.

Alicia, the plump one with the baby face and blond hair, was saying, "You'd think sex was out of style."

"Maybe it's all them people dying in the wreck." Annie was not much more than a tiny, living skeleton. Her brown eyes looked the color and size of chestnuts between hollow cheeks and thin brown hair.

Back at the counter Suda was saying, "In a way we exchanged life and death."

"I know it hit you in the guts," Jerry said. "But you don't have to feel so God damn guilty about it." He had been deeply touched by the compassion Suda had shown his dead friend. He could never forget the way Suda had embraced Dulac. "He asked you to exchange tickets, didn't he? It was one of those things."

Suda was not consoled. "He could be alive."

"Would you rather be dead?" Jerry studied Suda's face. "Huh, maybe you would. But think of all those others. Their time had come. It was in the cards."

"You sound like a fatalist." Ken had returned to lean against the counter.

"I'd fight like hell to keep alive," Jerry said. "Anytime. But . . . ." He shrugged his shoulders. "You got some booze? Suda needs it. I could use a drink, too."

"We don't have a liquor license."

"Aw, come off it."

Ken glanced at Johnson, looked at the deputy's badge on Jerry's shirt. "Remember, you asked. I didn't. I got witnesses."

Ken's hands disappeared below the counter and his shoulders moved. Three shot glasses appeared filled with an amber liquid. He offered one to Johnson, who shook his head. He did not approve of drinking on the job, but this was an exceptional time.

"Here's mud in your eye," Ken said. He and Jerry threw back their heads.

Suda took a sip and toyed with his glass. He stood up. "I go for walk."

As he walked by the two women Alicia said, "Come over and see me sometime, honey."

Suda whirled on her, then lowered his fist. The door slammed behind him.

"What's eatin' him?"

Jerry turned on his stool, his elbows on the counter. "You wouldn't understand. His best friend was on the *Princess Sophia*."

Alicia stood up, knocking over her chair. She strode over to Jerry. "What makes you think I got no feelings you, you . . ." Her voice, warm and mellow, was edged with tears. Her body trembled.

"You sure look pretty when you're mad."

Alicia slapped Jerry so hard he almost fell off his stool.

"Why, you . . ." He saw tears in her eyes and said, "I'm

sorry. I really am. Kind of on edge. Fishing up dead bodies."

Alicia made a visible effort to control herself. Her voice softened as she said, "I know. I was down at the wharf today. I saw you. It makes me cry, all those people. I didn't know about his friend."

She turned to Ken. "A round of Irish coffee. I'm buying. C'mon now. I saw you fellows."

Suda walked the snowy sidewalks, his head down, his hands thrust into the pockets of his mackinaw. Overhead the electric wires strung from wooden pole to pole shed their strands of snow as they were nudged by the light wind.

Posters in the darkened marquee of the Coliseum Theater featured Mary Pickford in *The Little Princess* and Charlie Chaplin's *The Pawn Shop*. D. W. Griffith's *Civilization*, starring Thomas Ince, was billed as a coming attraction.

In the lobby of the Alaskan Hotel a poker game had drawn a ring of onlookers. Further up the street, at the foot of Franklin, the lights of the Gastineau Hotel lobby fell across the street. Here and there lights of cafes and saloons emphasized the loneliness of the street.

Suda seldom had cause to evaluate his life or the lives of others. Dulac's death had brought him up short. Frank had been on the threshold of a dream, but was destined never to pass through the door.

Suda turned his steps toward the aloneness of his cubbyhole of a room on the second floor of the City Cafe.

15

Into the Unknown

T HOR UNHOOKED THE LAST of a dozen brook trout into
a pail of water. His fingertips still tingled with the quick,
impatient tugs of his captives. On this April dawn in the
year 1919, when he was twelve years old, the trout had bit at
preserved salmon eggs as if there would be no sunrise. Now they
nosed around their galvanized prison, seeking the indepen-
dence they had lost. He sensed their bewilderment: he was a
kindred soul in a wilderness where he also felt most at home.

For one vanishing moment he was tempted to empty his
pail back into the pool. He reconsidered. He saw ten- and fif-
teen-cent price tags on their tails, the sum they would fetch him
in the world on the other side of Chicken Ridge, where to live
he had to be practical.

In the gray shadows of the night around him the pulse of
awakening day throbbed in harmony. Crystal-clear Gold Creek,
swollen by April thaw in the mountain icefields beyond the
mining camp of Perseverance, brawled at Thor's feet. He looked
up the watercourse where granite boulders, some as large as
woodsheds, were taking shape in the dawn light. A gray squir-
rel hustled over a bridge of stones across the impatient water.
A piece of sky in the shape of a bluejay glided past a robin that
regarded Thor with eyes unafraid. Thor lifted his head and listened to the voices of his wilderness: among the tall spruce and
fir that clad the knees of Mount Roberts a grouse drummed
wings larger than its body, a ptarmigan cried, and a wood-

pecker telegraphed a random message. He knelt in salaam and drank ice-cold water from his image in the pool.

He suppressed a twinge of pity as he picked up his captives and fishing gear: a sapling to which was tied a line, with one buckshot sinker, leader, and bare hook. He would have to make tracks if he didn't want his trout to suffocate. It was a grueling mile to his market.

In front of the City Cafe he set his pail down and rubbed the fatigue from his hands and arms. He looked at the tank that ran the width of the plate-glass window facing Front Street. Gushing from an upright pipe, mountain water was a continuous current that kept the fish alive and healthy. He saw two speckled trout about a foot long, but the supply was depleted. He had banked on this to sell his catch.

He had not asked the proprietor if he wanted to buy any trout. He walked through the front door and presented him with a *fait accompli*. He could never be certain if Johnson would buy. Occasionally he could be in a foul mood, especially if he had been crossed by a salesman, a customer, or one of his help. Like many chefs he was of impatient temperament.

Thor placed his reliance, too, on the fact that Johnson was impressed by initiative, resourcefulness, and hard work. He glanced at his brother. Ken straightened his black bow tie, adjusted his immaculate waiter's apron, and nodded. Johnson was in a receptive mood.

Johnson stepped around the work counter. He was a large-framed Japanese in his forties. Though he was fleshy, his pounds were so well distributed he did not look fat, nor had they warped his straight back. His large eyes beneath heavy eyebrows were shrewd and appraising. Those close to him knew he was not to be trifled with. His jowls could not hide the fine lines of his strong jaw. He wore his normally pleasant expression as he greeted Thor.

Johnson had bought Johnson's Saloon, converted it and renamed it the City Cafe. Thereafter, S. Tanaka was known as Johnson, much to the puzzlement of strangers. The townspeople and even the Japanese referred to him as Johnson. It was a mark of distinction in which he took pride. Everyone knew

"Johnson," though there were several Johnsons in town. To the dry-humored Scandinavians there was a bit of irony in the nickname.

Thor felt good with himself. He had put in an early morning's work. This gave him the confidence and positive air of a salesman as he approached Johnson with his waterpail. One of the larger trout, a ten-incher, slapped the surface of the water with its tail.

Thor set the pail on the floor. The Messerschmidts' son who delivered rye bread and rolls for his father's bakery was wont to say that the kitchen floor was so clean you could eat off it. After closing each night, Frank Amano, the dishwasher, pot cleaner and man of all dirty work, would take a long-handled bristle brush, scrub the floor with soapy water and mop it up until the wood shone.

He and Ken gathered around the pail with Johnson, who remarked on the size and beauty of the trout.

"Five cents," he said to Thor. He laughed at Thor's long face. His gold-capped teeth gleamed. He turned to Ken. "Give him two bits."

Ken emptied the pail into the tank. The trout nosed up and down, measuring the limits of their confinement. From the cash register Ken took three silver dollars and placed them in Thor's hand.

This was riches beyond Thor's expectation. "Oh, thank you, Mr. Johnson!" He thumped his fishing pole on the floor. "Thank you!"

Johnson threw back his head and laughed. He was pleased when his generosity was appreciated. It was known about that he had staked prospectors down on their luck. Most of them had repaid his trust. He turned a tough eye on town bums. They can work, was his thinking. Hard work and long hours had made him proprietor of a thriving restaurant.

Thor was intrigued by the sight of gold-capped molars in Johnson's mouth. There were times he tried to make Johnson laugh so he could see the gold gleam. Once he had asked his dentist if he could have a gold crown on his tooth like Johnson, but the dentist had laughed.

"You had better brush your teeth well and stop eating candy. If you don't," the dentist prophesied, "you won't have any teeth by the time you're thirty. You have teeth like chalk."

Johnson said to Ken. "Give him pie and milk. Bonus." He was indeed in a good mood.

Although sorely tempted by the offer, Thor said to Johnson, "Thank you, Mr. Johnson. But you pay me, I pay you."

Johnson laughed his approval and Thor was rewarded with the gleam of gold.

Thor jumped on his favorite stool at the end of the long counter.

Tom Kubota had dropped in for a cup of coffee. He carried a mug of hot water to Thor, who carefully measured a teaspoon of Baker's Cocoa and another of sugar into the mug. Kubota, his red, weather-wrinkled features bent in a smile, watched in amusement.

"Why do you measure?" he asked. He poured the equivalent of four teaspoons of sugar into his coffee and whitened it with condensed milk poured through one of two holes punched in the top of a Carnation can.

"Because it says so on the can."

It was said that Kubota had not taken a bath for years because the last time he did he had caught cold and almost died. Some credence might be given this story because he was brown as a walnut. When Ken visited him once when he was sick, he could barely make out his body. The sheets were as brown as he was. The laundryman had refused the linen because he said they would dye the rest of the clothing. Ever since his brush with death, he wore army surplus shirt and pants and, no matter what the weather, an army overcoat. This idiosyncrasy caused Thor's sisters to tease him, calling him punkin head.

When he had a spare nickel, and even when he didn't, he would drop in at the City Cafe and nurse a cup of coffee for an hour or two by refilling his cup from time to time. Johnson tolerated him because he was a homespun philosopher who could hold his own in any badinage and helped to pass the slow hours between meals. He was always available for errands and in emergencies.

During the morning, light and shadow had been playing through the windows of the restaurant as clouds dawdled across the face of the sun. Johnson was wiping the top of the kitchen range with a larded gunnysack when the sound of a ship's whistle made him straighten up. He stood listening intently. The sound came again, echoing off the rocky cliffs of the two mountains that towered above town.

"That's the *City of Seattle!*" Thor shouted. Everyone in the restaurant and on the streets of the town recognized the whistle.

"Oi!" Johnson's shout galvanized the restaurant workers. "Wash another pot of rice," he ordered Amano.

Kubota, who always seemed to be around during emergencies, donned a white waiter's bib-fronted apron that intensified the greasiness of his khaki flannel shirt. Ken thrust the Japanese newspaper he had been reading beneath the counter. He brought chopsticks out from the back bar. He piled them into empty water glasses that he spaced down the length of the counter. Kubota placed others on each of the tables. Rice bowls and tea cups were placed before each stool and the chairs at the tables.

Johnson stoked the kitchen range. He filled a second nine-quart kettle and placed the kettle directly on the flames to heat up water for tea. Thor watched, puzzled. Was an army coming? From earthenware crocks Johnson dredged up pickled Chinese cabbage and cucumbers that to Thor smelled to the Pearly Gates. Johnson sliced the vegetables into bite-sized pieces.

"Here!" Ken thrust white paper napkins in front of Thor. "Fold these."

Thor surveyed the purposeful confusion. "Who's coming?" he asked, but everyone was too busy to answer.

Ken had just finished a cigarette when the front door opened. Thor was unprepared for what looked to him like an invasion of strange Japanese and Chinese men. They looked like Ken, Amano, Kubota, and Johnson, but so many of them. A plump Chinese about forty years of age led the motley crew, who dispersed themselves on the stools and at the tables.

From the babel emerged requests for rice, rice, and more

rice, strong green tea, and pickled cabbage. Never mind the entrees. During the four days of the voyage from Seattle the men, who had existed on scrambled eggs, corned beef hash, frankfurters and beans, and similar mainstays, had been starved for their favorite food.

Apprehensive, Thor was of a mind to flee this alien onslaught. A young man of about thirty whom he was to know as Abe (Ah-beh) stopped him with a crinkly-eyed smile. He reminded Thor of his father. He had friendly eyes, a thick mustache, and bushy eyebrows. As Thor responded to his warmth he became aware that Abe greeted his words with innocent candor. He would say, "You don't say!" Or "How interesting!" Or "Naruhodo!" Thor found this a bit disconcerting as his information wasn't that earth-shaking.

Thor looked into Abe's eyes seeking an answer, but found no guile or foolishness in their clear depths. His new-found friend seemed genuinely interested. He wanted to know what a boy like Thor was doing in such an isolated place. How had he come here? Did he like to live here? To Abe these were legitimate questions. Although he was a veteran of the Russo-Japanese war and had endured the hardships of a frontline soldier, he could not see himself living in this kind of environment.

"It's the only place I know," Thor said. He could not answer the other questions, so he told Abe of his parents, his younger brother and two sisters. "And this is my older brother, Ken."

"Mezurashii," Abe said. "Unusual." He shook hands with Ken. "Nihon wa?"

"Yamagata-ken," Ken said.

"Tohoku ka." Abe shook his head. "Not many Japanese from there. Honto ni mezurashii," he said. "Really unusual."

Ken laughed. "Father had wandering feet. He liked faraway places. And had the courage to do what others talk of doing."

"I would like to meet him sometime," Abe said.

He accepted the bowl of green tea over rice, with the red eyes of two *umeboshi* in it, that Ken handed him. He ate standing up. Ken also gave a bowl of rice to the man standing beside Abe.

Thor felt uneasy, as if someone were staring at the back of his neck. He slanted a glance at Abe's companion. Though silent, he had listened attentively. Their eyes met. Thor felt a thrill of the unknown. Of mysterious, enigmatic depths. The man's eyes were cool, objective, like a judge's weighing evidence. Mature, rough men had shifted uneasily before that gaze. Thor turned his head away.

Abe suddenly realized he had been remiss. "This Hotta," he said. "My friend. My best friend. We be in war together. He my captain."

Hotta nodded stiffly as if an army collar was binding his neck. His crewcut crowned a commanding, handsome, square face that wore a resolute expression as of one born to lead. The scar of a saber cut was white-lipped on his jaw. His complexion was clear as Thor's.

Hotta seemed out of place among these men. Although it was warm in the room he wore his lumberman's duck coat buttoned neatly to the top. His thick, broad shoulders gave an impression of latent power.

Hotta held out his hand. Thor was surprised at the softness of his hand but sensed the strength of muscles sheathed like a cat's claws. The hand tightened. Thor was surprised but pressed back. He wanted to add the strength of his other hand to the unequal contest. Their eyes locked, and Thor was infuriated by Hotta's cool, detached gaze. He clenched his free hand. The sudden light of laughter that shone in Hotta's eyes made him take a mental step back.

"Yūki da." Hotta laughed, loosening his grip. "Courageous."

Sternness vanished from his face like a fleeting cloud. His strong features were warm and admiring. He patted Thor on the shoulder, but took the precaution of holding his open hand in front of Thor's clenched fist.

Thor had felt cornered and was ready to lash out. The consequences be damned. His anger ran hot in the blood that suffused his cheeks. He turned his back. He refused to be mollified by Hotta's advances.

Abe had caught the byplay. His displeasure showed on his face. "Someday you will go too far," he told Hotta.

Meanwhile, Billy Tang, the round-faced cannery labor contractor, had walked with short, quick steps to the kitchen. He pushed his gold spectacles up on his receding thin hair as the lenses clouded in the humid warmth of the kitchen. He shook hands with Johnson. They had known each other for years and a strong friendship had developed between them, even though they met only briefly during the salmon-canning season. Whenever Tang was in town he made it a point to visit Johnson. Beside the stolid Johnson, Tang was like a bantam rooster, forever on the move, strutting, restless.

"Was expecting you," Johnson said, "Geese been flying north couple of weeks. I made plenty rice. Lots of pickled cabbage and cucumbers."

"Know I could depend on you. Boys been starving for rice." He moved around as though the floor was hot. "Same old place. Like home."

"How many cases you contract for?"

"Forty thousand at fifty cents. You know, forty-eight one-pound cans per case. Twenty thousand dollars even if we have bad season and pack less."

"Guaranteed, eh. Good. How much if over?"

"Thirty cents a case." Tang made a face. "Cheap company. But I got 'nother cannery, get fifty cents for every case over fifty thousand. Good deal."

Tang snapped his fingers. "Hey, Johnson, you want become boy contractor? Japanese taking over in Seattle. Can't get China boys anymore. You know, immigration."

"You got job for Tora? This summer." He led Tang over to the end of the counter where Thor was talking to Abe.

"How old he?"

"Fourteen," Johnson said, squeezing Thor's shoulder as he opened his mouth to protest.

Tang pretended he hadn't seen.

"Big and strong for his age."

"Okay." Each knew he was not fooling the other. To Tang it was a favor for a friend.

Johnson appreciated the gesture but had no intention of lowering his asking price.

"Eighty a month." Board and room was understood.

Tang choked on the tea he was sipping. "Too much." Tang shook his head. Favor or no favor.

"You need men. He is right here. No pay for passage."

"War makes prices sky high. You know how much I pay for sack rice?"

"You get more contract pay for your boys." Johnson waved out toward the counter where the young men were guzzling their food with a great smacking of lips.

"You tough," Tang complained. Their glances met in understanding. "You send boy by boat 'bout 'Fourt'' of July. What his name?"

"Tora. Real name Toranosuke, but too hard. Friends call him Thor. Last name Fuse. F-u-s-e. Like miners use. Only pronounced Fu-seh. You remember, Tora Fuse. Tell your bookkeeper."

Tang shook hands and got his men to their feet. Green tea over rice had brought an aura of contentment and well-being to their faces. Tang paid Ken at the front cash register. The amount could have been more, but Johnson had a generous heart with friends.

Johnson recognized Abe and Hotta. "Mata kita no ka." he said. "Again you come!" He laughed, his gold teeth gleaming. "Again you would not come, you said."

"Alaska boy is Alaska boy," Hotta said, using the description applied with condescension, in some instances with contempt, by the more established Japanese to the seasonal cannery workers. Hotta, confident in himself, could jest about his condition. The independent son of a baron, he took pride in his status and the military reputation earned at the storming of Port Arthur.

Johnson followed them to the door. "Oi, Tora be coming to your cannery. Take good care of him."

"So young." Hotta rubbed the scar on his jaw.

Abe put his hand on Thor's shoulder. "You be okay. We wait."

"Tanomu yo," Johnson said, asking their favor.

Johnson turned to Ken, who had been working for him since the 1917 cave-in closed the Treadwell mines.

"Be his first job. Make money. Two months, he come back with one hundred sixty dollars."

Ken nodded above his black bow tie. To him the tie was the badge of a waiter. Despite the hurry and confusion of serving so many men, his shirt sleeves and apron were spotless.

"You never ask Tora." His tone was respectful on two counts: Johnson was his employer and he was also his elder.

"Ah, so." Johnson turned to Thor, who had been engrossed by the rough manners and loud talk of the cannery boys. He had caught the last part of the bargaining between Johnson and Tang.

"You want to make one hundred and sixty dollars? Right? All that money working this summer between schools."

Johnson was an old-timer who was like a counselor to the pliant Fuse family, a bit overbearing at times, but tolerated. He was an initiator; he proposed and disposed in one breath. The fast-growing Alaska grass never grew under his No. 12 bluchers. He got things done.

Thor was apprehensive as he thought of the boisterous men he had seen, but the memory of the kindly Abe's friendliness and the thought of all those silver dollars reassured him. Why, he'd be rich. He nodded.

The Chinese he had observed were a rarity in his world.

Living in a little two-story house he had built on Third Street down Main Street from the City Hall, "China Joe" maintained a store, with a bakery in the rear. He used the top floor for living quarters. Beside the house he had a vegetable garden; its produce he would sell to green grocers. Sometimes mischievous boys would throw cans and bottles over the fence. On Chinese New Year's he remembered who they were and did not give them goodies that he gave to others.

Sometimes Thor, accompanied by friends, would drop in

to buy rock candy and sweet-sour plums. Thor watched fascinated as the elderly Chinese held up a delicate brass balancing scale to weigh their purchases. He would put a tiny brass weight on one pan and the candy on the other until the crossbeam was horizontal. He would smile indulgently and thank them gravely for their nickels.

Joe had wide eyes beneath eyebrows that crowded down on his eyelids. His cheekbones were prominent on either side of his broad nose. His wide, mobile mouth was quirky at the corners, quick to express his moods. Normally he wore his pigtail wound tightly around his head. Occasionally, he could be seen smoking a Chinese pipe that was about a foot-and-a-half long.

"China Joe" was one of the few Chinese, if any, left in Alaska after the anti-Chinese agitation of the 1880s. Arriving in Victoria, B.C., in 1864, he was among the three to five hundred Chinese who joined the 1874 gold rush to the Cassiar district in British Columbia, north of Wrangell. It was here that Joe, during a winter famine, shared his entire stock of flour with the starving miners. He earned their everlasting gratitude.

After a couple of years, 1878–79, in Wrangell, where he beached the *Hope*, an old sternwheeler, and ran it as a hotel, and a brief stint in Sitka, he arrived in Juneau in early 1881, following the miners to this first Alaskan gold rush.

On July 18 he bought from Mike Duquette for sixty dollars a corner lot at Third and Main streets where he built his house. The deed from M. Duquette was assigned to: "As Hie, known as Joe the Baker." When he registered in 1893 under the new Chinese Registration Act he gave his name as Ting Tu Wee. He was also known as Chung Tuwee and Chung Thui. When he joined the '87 Pioneers Association in 1907 his name was listed as Hi Chung.

Joe died alone in his home on the night of May 17, 1917, and was buried in Evergreen Cemetery. Whatever his name, "China Joe" was remembered by Thor as the greatest of the Chinese sourdoughs, a pioneer Alaska could call one of its sons.

Joe was the only Chinese in Juneau. In the 1880s, in an extension of the anti-Chinese demonstrations on the Pacific Slope, vigilantes tried to drive the Chinese workers from the Treadwell mines. Dynamite was used on their dwellings. The Chinese asked for guns to protect themselves but their employer, fearful that they, so greatly outnumbered, would be massacred, had refused. Finally, they were loaded at gunpoint on a schooner and set adrift down Gastineau Channel. They almost starved before reaching Wrangell. The governor intervened, but the miners threatened to line the shore with shotguns to prevent the Chinese from landing.

An exception was made for "China Joe." The miners remembered well the famine-stalked winter up at Cassiar.

As Ken told the story to Thor he had muttered, "Big deal." Thor wondered what he meant but his brother never elaborated.

The first time Thor had seen Chinese was back in 1913 when the family was living in Douglas. Through a concealing curtain he had seen them shuffle by, the hands of their crossed arms hidden in big sleeves. They looked like his brother and his friends, but some wore round, flat-topped black hats, suits that looked like black satin pajamas, and open sandals. What engrossed him most were the pigtails some of the men wore.

"Just like my sisters," he thought. "Look, Mama," he shouted, but not so loud that he would be heard outside. "The funny dressed men."

Mama told him they were Chinese cannery boys on their way to work in canneries that dotted the Inside Passage from Ketchikan to Skagway. They had to make cans and boxes in preparation for the salmon run in July and August.

At the City Cafe Thor had seen a representative sampling of Alaska boys. They were a mixed lot of unskilled laborers, or *rōdōsha*. Most of them were from farming regions of southern Japan. A majority had become set in the mold of itinerants. From the canneries of Alaska they would disperse to the logging camps and sawmills of Enumclaw, Selleck, Snoqualmie, and other sites of the lumber industry. Or they would follow the uncertain seasons of the harvest, from the potato crops of the Yakima

Valley and Idaho, the fruit of eastern Oregon, the vineyards of California all the way to the cantaloupe of the Imperial Valley on the Mexican border.

By contrast, an industrious few saved their pennies for nest eggs that would take them back to Japan. Others set themselves up in business, usually catering to the needs of their landsmen. They set roots and flowered into communities. A handful, like those in Juneau, had pioneered far afield.

From their positions of stability the entrepreneurs regarded the migratory workers, and in particular the Alaska boys, with tolerance and condescension if not contempt. Contempt might be too harsh a term, for in face-to-face situations they had a delicate Japanese reticence about hurting another's pride. On their part, the itinerant workers, from callousness or because their sensitivity had been demeaned by drudgery and hopelessness, had learned to live with the opprobrious term.

The Alaska boys also were referred to as *atama ga nai* drifters. Literally, *atama ga nai* means "without a head." The expression cannot be translated in a word, or without a qualifying phrase. In its broadest connotation *atama ga nai* might be translated as senseless, in the meaning of not using one's head or mind. Each definition requires refinements of meaning.

An example was the worker who labored from April into September and October at some remote salmon cannery and gambled away his wages, returning to Seattle penniless. This was the epitome of futility. They lived for today, yielded to temptation, and did not consider the future. They did not use their heads.

The Alaska boys who at first sight had intimidated Thor worked conscientiously, like most Japanese. They endured small portions of miserable food—just enough to keep body and "samurai" spirit together—primitive sleeping quarters, and poor wages, not to mention deadening working days running from twelve to twenty hours at the height of the salmon run. They performed *hone no oreru*, "bone-breaking" work. The small laughter they had they expended on each other and the human condition they endured.

Thor had no prescience of the summer. His innocence and

naivete were certain to be targets. The supreme test came from an unexpected quarter. It was an omen that foreshadowed his entire life.

On a warm summer night as the northern lights shuttled among the stars Thor got packed. Mama's small face wore the anxious expression of a mother seeing her son leaving home for the first time. She took a bit of *umeboshi* on the end of her chopsticks and made him eat it as protection against misfortune. He screwed up his face at the sour taste.

"It it safe?" Mama fluttered around Thor.

"Shinpai shinai de," Ken said, getting impatient. 'Don't worry."

Papa, who had been standing all day cutting hair, was relaxing in a rocking chair with sake and cigarettes. At sight of the blanket roll he retired to memories of his days of freedom when wanderlust was a fever in his blood. Back then in Japan, so many years ago, he had mounted his hope like a white charger for the land where recruiters said "money grew on trees." Barriers of language, prejudice, and discrimination had turned him down the path of least resistance.

He looked into his sake cup—of late these had become endless—where he had found surcease from the disappointments and frustrations of shattered dreams. His health had been failing lately, and his thoughts had turned to the mountains of Yamagata beyond the ocean.

He supposed he should be helping his son pack, but Ken was here to assume responsibility. Papa had abdicated to his eldest son. Now his second son was embarking on his first adventure at a much younger age than he or Ken had. He would surely take the high road. He knew the language and in this free land of Alaska he did not face prejudice and discrimination. He had a healthy body and a good, enterprising mind. The odds were in his favor.

Thor's brother and two little sisters looked on curiously. Big brother was going away for a while, whatever two months was. At parting they did not kiss or embrace. It was not the Japanese custom.

Shortly before midnight Ken escorted Thor through the

sleeping dusk of Front Street to City Dock. In the dark hulk of the City Cafe, only Amano's window showed a light. The summer nights, about four or five hours long, were never pitch black even without benefit of starshine.

Thor's transportation was a ferry launch that made the rounds of isolated truck farms, mink and fox ranches, and canneries, delivering food, supplies, and mail in the Douglas Island and Admiralty Island districts. The deckhand cast off the lines for the fifty-mile run to Funter Bay. The boat became a tiny black island distinguished only by the riding light on its mast, the red port and green starboard gleams, and the ghostly glow at the captain's wheel in the cabin.

Thor turned for a last look at the scattered street lamps of the town sleeping in the cradle of Mount Juneau, whose close immensity was a part of the night sky. As he watched, the first fireflies of carbide lamps on the miners' caps danced out of the tunnel mouth of the gold mine on the steep side of Mount Roberts and performed their choreography down the switchback trail. In closeup he could visualize the aura of light around the head of each miner as he leaped from rock to rock.

Thor listened to the chuckle of the waves at the bow and felt the light breeze that sang softly in his ears and caressed them as the boat cleared the dark, protective promontory of the breakwater. Off the starboard side they passed the scattered lights of Douglas and the deserted darkness of Treadwell, now a ghost town. High above, the cone of snowcapped Mount Jumbo floated ethereally in the starlight.

Thor lay on his back on deck and watched shooting stars scratch the shoulder blades of midnight and could almost hear them hiss as they faded away like fireworks. The cadence of waves slapping the hull was a lullaby. As he dozed off the ebbing tide was draining the waters from 34,000 miles of Alaskan coastline.

The boat rounded the southern tip of Douglas Island and turned its bow northward up Stephens Passage with the huge, bear-shaped bulk of Admiralty Island to port. When Thor awoke the mountain range on the mainland was afire as the hidden sun struck spokes of light from its peaks. Thor was reminded of the flag of the Imperial Navy of Japan. The waters of the cool morning trembled like mercury, turned roseate, and as the sun mounted the heavens the sea turned blue, then green where massed ranks of evergreens marched down to their reflections in the mirror of the sea.

The boat rounded the northern tip of Admiralty Island and reached Funter Bay as the cooks were stoking their stoves. The pale blue smoke of cooking fires rose straight from the chimneys of the Chinese mess hall and the white maintenance crew, and from the campfires of the Tlingit villagers down the beach.

Accustomed to the amenities of even such a small town as Juneau, Thor was dismayed at first glance by the isolation and seeming lack of life around the buildings that made up the cannery compound. He was tempted to remain aboard and return home, but vetoed the weakness. As he had grown up, much on his own in a frontier town, he had faced up to all challenges. This was the biggest of them all.

16

The Initiation

BILLY TANG, who was in Funter to prepare for the coming of the guarantee boys, was at dockside along with Shin Nagatani, the Japanese foreman, Seiji Abe, and Jun Hotta. The tide was full and the top of the pilot house was even with the pier deck.

Thor was heartened by the sight of Abe.

"Hello, Tora-chan," Abe said. He extended a hand to help Thor ashore. His smile, crinkly around the eyes, and the warmth of his greeting reassured Thor.

Thor looked askance at Hotta, who stood near a hand truck with his arms folded aross his chest like some artist's conception of a noble Indian. His enigmatic eyes troubled Thor. Time had interred his resentment toward Hotta, but he looked uneasily into a future overcast by Hotta's shadow. He took refuge in Abe's protective friendliness. At least Abe seemed to understand that he was only a kid among grown-up strangers.

Supplies and provisions were unloaded on the dock in separate piles: Canned goods, staples and supplies for the company store patronized by the Tlingits and the cannery workers to supplement their daily rations. Ham, slabs of bacon, crates of eggs, sides of beef, and sacks of potatoes for the white kitchen. Vegetables and greens, eggs, and a pittance of pork for the Chinese and Japanese. Thor missed the significance of this inequitable distribution until he sat down to future meals.

Throughout his stay he was tormented between his determination to spend as little money as he could and his desire to buy bread, canned fruit, and cookies to fill his stomach. When he went into the store to buy some essential like toothpaste, his eyes would feast on the round ginger cookies frosted in white and pink, almost the size of his spread-out hand. They made him hunger for the rich yellow cream puffs sold at the Peerless Bakery. In town he could always satiate himself; here he was always a little hungry. But he was determined to return home with 160 dollars. Not a cent less.

The salmon cannery located at Funter Bay, near the great halibut fishing banks of Icy Strait and Cross Sound, was one of the earliest in Alaska. Most of the canneries in the Southeastern Panhandle were located in isolated inlets and coves of the Inside Passage, such as Yes Bay, Hidden Inlet, and Waterfall, accessible only by water. The primary criterion for cannery sites was a source of fresh water to wash and process the salmon. Funter was closed down about a decade later because the supply of water became insufficient.

In this summer of 1919, the cannery consisted of a small bunkhouse for the Japanese workers, a larger one for the Chinese that included the common dining room, and a building with a company store, accommodations, dining room, and kitchen for the white maintenance crew, all appendages to the main cannery building. A small house on the hill was used by the superintendent and his wife. Even in such a small social unit there was a hierarchical order. A path led through the woods beside the beach to the temporary encampment of the Natives who were season workers, the men fishing and the women laboring in the cannery.

Hotta loaded his hand truck with the fresh provisions. He kicked a crate of Chinese cabbage. Abe took the hint and was about to lift the box on his shoulder when Thor grabbed one end and together they headed toward the kitchen. Abe had slung Thor's blanket roll across his shoulder.

Hotta looked on with disapproval. "Let him carry his own blankets."

"Mind your own business," Abe snapped in Japanese.

"Aho," Hotta retorted. "Fool."

Abe flung the crate beside the kitchen door and said to Thor, "Come."

Abe showed Thor to an empty room in the Japanese bunkhouse that had two double-tiered bunks that would hold four men. Still angry with Hotta, Abe flung the blanket roll on a lower bunk that held a two-inch-thick, excelsior-stuffed mattress resting on boards. No springs.

"Look like silkworm racks," Abe said, using a term favored by Japanese immigrants when referring to bunks in a ship's steerage class.

Thor looked with dismay around the unpainted wooden walls pockmarked with nail holes. The whites said that when the workers mounted pictures, "the Chinks paste, the Japs nail." A few old, torn, brownstained pin-ups, some of Japanese girls, added to the room's bleakness. The air smelled of burnt coal oil.

"We kill all bedbugs," Abe said, as he caught the expression on Thor's face. He added, "Guarantee boys arrive couple days."

It was Sunday and most of the season boys were asleep. They were awakened by the sound of the triangular gong. Some of the Japanese workers straggled over the walkway to the dining room. The tables were square, built to seat four. Abe explained that the Chinese have a superstition that it was bad luck to seat more at one table. Thor sat with Abe, Hotta, and Gen Wakabayashi, who had skipped the spring semester at the University of Washington to earn tuition and living expenses.

Thor looked at the table and wondered where the food was. To save space a shallow baking pan filled with cooked rice hung above the table suspended from a ceiling beam. A communal pan of omelet, a small piece of salted salmon, and pickled *bok choy*, or Chinese cabbage, completed the menu.

"I need a fork," Thor said.

A roomful of chopsticks hung suspended in midair. A Japanese unable to use *hashi*! A Chinese unable to use *k'uai-tzu*! A Korean unable to use *chokkai*!

"Fork! Fork!" There was a commotion in the kitchen, an Asian *l* sound playing havoc with the English *r* in the word. Thor walked into the kitchen.

"Hoya! Hoya! Little boy need fork! Where fork? Any fork?"

Thor returned red-faced to the table. Abe smiled sympathetically. Hotta held up his chopsticks. Abe groaned. His friend was about to embark on one of his discourses. Abe had never known anyone as talkative as Hotta. He referred to him as a *benjo no bengoshi*, a toilet lawyer. Servicemen of another age called them latrine lawyers.

"In ancient times," Hotta said, "hashi made of bamboo in one piece shaped like a *U*, like a cooking tong. Historically"— he repeated the word as though it were a recent acquisition— "historically, it was first mentioned in book of *I ching*, before Christ. Oi, Yee Sing," he called to an elderly Chinese at the next table, "how old *I ching*?"

Yee Sing shook his head as he gulped a mouthful of rice and tea. "Old. Old."

Hotta nodded. "Hashi mean tip, end, or edge," he said to Thor. "First it was made of bamboo because it is pliable and can be bent like *U*. When chopstick became two sticks . . ."

"When?" Abe asked. He had learned enough English to follow Hotta. Wakabayashi was listening intently to improve his English.

"First time I read about hashi made in two pieces in *Ko-jiki*, a Japanese history. Written, oh, about 700 A.D. When chopsticks became two sticks they use willow, pine, chestnut, and cedar. Cedar smell good. You smell cedar today," he said to Thor. "They use cedar to make wari-bashi, the kind you pull apart in restaurant. Later hashi made of gold and silver and ivory for Emperor and high-class nobles. Now custom in Japan to give you new hashi on birthday.

"Only countries influenced by Chinese culture in all Asia use hashi. Korea, Japan, Taiwan. But not Philippines. You know why? Their culture come from east, from Polynesia and Austronesia." Hotta's smile was a slight softening of his taut features.

"In beginning all people eat with fingers. In most parts of world they invent spoons. Japanese no. Only recent times. Chinese invent chopsticks. Great people, eh, Yee Sing?"

"Start one of three great civilizations."

"Eh! How you know?"

"I like read. Like you."

Hotta started off on a new tack. Abe stood up, but Hotta pulled him down. "You stay. You listen. Maybe you learn good English."

Abe made a mock face of dismay at Thor.

Hotta nodded his squarish head. "Three civilizations start on banks of great rivers. Chinese on Yangtze and Yellow Rivers, Hindu on Indus, Eurasian on Tigris and Euphrates. Scholars still trying to find out why, all about same time, six thousand years ago. Man much older but no record except bones and artifacts."

"Artifacts?" Thor asked.

"Pieces of chawan. Like this." Hotta held up his rice bowl. "Arrowheads."

"But how do we know?"

"In beginning by speech and memory. I tell you, you tell your children, they tell their children, like that. Mukashi—" The Japanese word for ancient times came most naturally to Hotta's lips. He started again. "In ancient China they write one line at time, from top to bottom like your father, on inside of split bamboo stick. They tie sticks together and read from one bamboo stick to next, from right to left. They roll sticks up and carry them around. But this too much work. So they invent paper out of rice leaves and write on long scrolls. No pages like in your school books."

"I remember," Thor said. "In Europe, too, and Middle East. I saw them in the movies."

"Very interesting how they write hashi in Japanese. Under character for bamboo they write character for person. So hashi becomes person who uses bamboo. That is ideograph for hashi."

Hotta had been eating as he talked. Thor looked on with distaste as he saw the chopsticks dipping into the omelet. He was accustomed to being served individual portions by Mama.

Hotta, who was as perceptive if not as sensitive as Abe, sensed Thor's discomfort. "Your Mama serve you individual portions? She must be gentlewoman. That is how I was brought up. When I first came to these American camps I did not like to eat this way. I did not think it was clean habit. But it is custom. You cannot be high tone. You do same as everybody or you starve."

Thor was surprised. This was the first interest that Hotta had shown in Thor's well-being. He had paid Thor a subtle compliment. Thor glanced sidelong at Hotta's poker face, and then across the table at Abe, who winked.

Thor speared a good-sized piece of salmon and stuck it into his mouth. As he chewed a startled expression froze on his face. "Whew! Is that salty!"

Abe laughed. "You take small piece and eat it with rice and tea."

"Boss man has cook make it real salty so you won't eat so much," Hotta said. "That way they save money."

Abe picked up the last piece of onion from the pan and rose. "Come," he said. "Bring bowl and, er, fork."

In the kitchen the Chinese cook was scraping chunks of burnt rice from a wok-shaped cooker about three feet across. The wok was set in a brick frame over a fireplace. The cook was about to pour hot water over the burnt rice. "Wait," Hotta said. He picked up several sections of the rice and placed them on a plate. "Good with salt, eat like piece of pie," he said.

The cook emptied a pot of hot water into the wok. Abe scooped the burnt rice and water into Thor's bowl and helped himself. Hotta was at his elbow.

"Better eat," Abe said. "This way you no starve. Soon we have salmon. All day. Everyday. Make you sick."

Thor forced the mixture down his throat. When he had an upset stomach Mama would make a rice gruel, but it never tasted bitter or looked like charcoal. He had read somewhere that charcoal purifies the blood, but in this form—he had his doubts.

Abe handed him a salt shaker. "This make taste better."

To the cook: "Shin-san, make some sandwiches. We cut firewood for you. Four." He looked at Thor, "You want come?" Thor nodded. "Five."

The work detail, voluntary for lack of anything else to do, returned to the bunkhouse to pick up tools. Several men were already engaged in *hana fuda*, a Japanese card game. Although called flower cards, the pictures actually depict the four seasons.

Games of chance, particularly dice and poker, were a part of an Alaska boy's life. They filled the empty hours of May and June after the daily stint of making cans and boxes. A few of the men might go hunting or fishing for trout on weekends, but on the whole it was one dead day following another into limbo.

Each playing surface was a salmon case top nailed to an upended box. Stools were empty nail kegs cushioned with gunnysacking. Gen Wakabayashi, who had yet to win and was as hungry as he looked, had challenged Tanaka, whose name is legion in Japan, to a game of *shōgi*, a Japanese version of chess in which captured pieces can be replaced. The pieces were identically shaped like miniature yellow gravestones, the pawns smaller than the rest, each identified by an ideograph.

As the oldest Japanese in camp, Tanaka was called Oji-san or Uncle. In a fit of sentimentality his parents had named him Momotaro, whose legendary feats he was hardly likely to emulate, so he used the plain Taro. He had a round, merry face like that of the god of fortune in Japanese myth.

"Shall I remove my bishop and knight?" he needled blandly in Japanese.

"No!" Gen leaned across the board, his thin face sharp with irritation. "I want no favors. I'm going to beat you if it takes all season!"

Tanaka reared back with a loud laugh and almost fell off the backless stool. "Come. Your move."

At a neighboring table *Go*, a game of strategy for two players, was in progress. Skinny Frank Suzuki, whose name is more legion than Tanaka, was licking his broad lips opposite Shintaro Manabe. The fatty skin on Manabe's brow, above pig eyes almost buried in fat, was pleated in desperation. His pockets of white stones, shaped like tiddledywinks, were being surrounded and pinched off by Suzuki's attacking blacks.

He looked up at Hotta, whose military mind had made him *Go* champion of the camp. Hotta shook his head in commiseration.

On a nearby navy blue surplus blanket the assistant fore-man, Goro Obata, was running a crap game. The head of the wash-can gang was a smaller edition of Benkei, the giant Jap-anese folk hero, but without his shrewdness. A couple of losers who had borrowed to the limit of their credit—their season's pay plus anything they could beg or borrow—looked discon-solately on. One of them put down two bits.

Obata, a sheaf of dollar bills in his huge hand, looked at the quarter.

"What's that?" He flicked it away like a tiddledywink.

Shamefaced, the owner retrieved his quarter. He seemed to shrivel before Obata's scorn. A man like Akira Takahashi learned to live with his degradation. He was the popular con-ception of an Alaska boy. He never learned. When he returned to Seattle he would hang around Jackson Street trying to mooch a few dollars against next season's wages. Any labor contractor soft enough to be touched would be out this amount if the debtor never showed up the following season. A few such trusting contractors carried these unpaid debts on their books; over the course of years they amounted to several thousands of dollars.

The *atama ga nai* boys were subject to another form of ex-ploitation. An unscrupulous foreman or bookkeeper would keep a record of their credits and debits in a little black book. The hapless Alaska boy, usually illiterate, was never given a receipt or IOU note. He had no proof of his financial status. When he wanted money he could be brushed off with the remark that he had no money on account or in overtime pay. There was noth-ing the poor soul could say or do. A foreman of this ilk had a revolver locked up in his field desk.

Takahashi crept away with his humiliation, like a dog from an arrogant master. Hotta looked after him with pity. When he turned around he saw Obata regarding him with an attitude that said, "What are you going to do about it?" Hotta, his face im-passive, stared him down. The air was taut with silence. Thor could almost taste the tension, the fear that backed up in his throat.

Obata shifted uneasily on his feet. Abruptly he turned toward the blanket. "Place your bets," he said. Several times he looked over his shoulder as if he felt Hotta's stare. But Hotta was gone.

Hotta led the work detail to a clearing on a point of land that jutted into the bay. The smell of yellow cedar from the large chips of wood that littered the ground permeated the morning air. The men threw down their axes, wedges, and crosscut saws and relaxed over cigarettes before tackling fallen tree trunks. The detail consisted of Abe, Hotta, Yee Sing, and Peter Pagsan, the lone Filipino in camp. Among the supplies they had brought with them, Thor had seen a coffee pot, cups, and bottles of water from which the men took swigs.

"Want me to build a fire to make some hot coffee?" Thor asked Abe.

Abe nodded. "Good."

With his Boy Scout knife Thor sliced paper-thin shavings from a stick of yellow cedar, built a pyramid, and lit it with a match from his waterproof box. The almost invisible flame crept up the shavings, which curled in the heat. He added larger shavings until he had a blaze. He surrounded the fire with stones placed so that the water-filled coffee pot would rest on them. "There," he said, as the water started to boil. "I'm a Boy Scout," he announced.

Admiration touched the smile on Abe's face. He had watched Thor with a quizzical expression. Thor felt that Abe's regard for him always had this perplexed, questioning quality, as if he were not quite sure what to make of such a youngster.

For his part, Abe saw in Thor the embodiment of a dream that had died. A dream that had drawn him to the United States: of money, marriage, a son such as Thor, a family. A dream that had vanished in the heat waves of the Imperial Valley, in the mists of Oregon and Washington sawmills and logging camps, in the stink of Alaskan salmon canneries such as this.

He threw coffee into the pot and picked up an axe to attack a drum-sized cylinder of tree trunk. "Pour some cold water in the pot so the coffee settle," he told Thor.

The brilliant sun now shone with comforting warmth

through Thor's flannel shirt. In the clearing thudding axes bit large *V*s out of tree trunks while the crosscut saw buzzed like a giant bee. Near the cookhouse screaming seagulls swooped down on discarded food.

Abe wiped the sweat from his face with the blue bandanna he wore around his neck. He removed his shirt and unwound a couple of yards of flannel *haramaki* from around his waist. This cloth band, worn by many Japanese workers to support their abdominal muscles, was supposed to strengthen and protect their stomachs, the source of all power. Abe took off his undershirt and revealed a hairy chest, not a very common sight among Japanese. Hotta claimed Abe had Ainu blood in his veins, the Ainu being a hairy, Caucasoid race, the first inhabitants of Japan, and one of the oldest existing races of mankind.

As Abe studied a knot that defied his axe, his thoughts went back to the origins of his dream, to the end of the Russo-Japanese war. A private, he was on the same homeward-bound transport as his commanding officer, Colonel Jun Hotta, whom he met on deck as the *Yokohama Maru* entered Tokyo Bay.

"What will you do?" Hotta asked.

"I will go back to Hiroshima to pay my respects to my parents."

"Good, an obedient son. And then?"

"My oldest brother will inherit our father's land. I am the third son. I must make my own way."

"Have you considered going to America?"

"No." Abe shook his head. "I was too busy saving my life."

Hotta smiled. "I have considered this step seriously. Besides Japanese, I speak English, read German, and picked up some Russian."

"You have a good mind, Colonel."

"Thank you. And you—this is English expression I have just learned. I like it. You have shrewd, native intelligence. We might say yoku atama tsukau. You have this. That is why you came back alive."

"You trained me well. And you were a good leader."

"We sacrificed too many men." Hotta said, with a harshness that surprised Abe. "Too, too many men."

As the *Yokohama Maru* docked they were interrupted by shouts from the crowd that thronged the pier to greet the returning veterans. Hotta tore a sheet from the small black notebook he always carried with him. "This is my address," he said. "You must keep in touch with me. That's an order. I am also a third son. I am also what the Americans call a black sheep. I am too independent. I, too, must make my own way."

Abe had parted from Hotta with a deep sense of loss. He was eighteen then and though he had grown up overnight in the storming of Port Arthur, right at Hotta's shoulder, he missed the security and confidence the other inspired.

Thor's cry of "Coffee's ready!" broke through Abe's thoughts. He smiled at the boy's earnestness. The two exchanged glances and Thor, to hide his shyness, fed the fire with more chips. Abe, looking over the rim of the salmon can that served as a coffee cup, realized suddenly that here was a twelve-year-old boy (he had not been fooled by Johnson's white lie) who had suddenly been thrust into a man's world. It could be an ordeal.

He could not understand Hotta's attitude toward Thor. While not antagonistic, neither was it friendly. Then with a flash of insight he recalled a day in 1904. During basic training, while Japan and Russia were at war, Hotta had been so hard on Abe that the other recruits had pitied him. Sometimes he would think: he treats me like this because I am a farmer. He would grit his teeth and make mincemeat of a dummy with his bayonet.

On a day after basic when Hotta had been especially hard on him, Abe had lost his temper. He was beyond caring whether he got decapitated on the spot. He had marched up to Hotta, saluted smartly and said, "May I say a few words, Sir?"

"Yes?"

"When we go into combat I am going to shoot you down like a dog, like an inu."

To Abe's complete amazement Hotta had thrown back his head and roared with laughter. He had slapped Abe on the back and said, "That's the right spirit."

Dumbfounded, open-mouthed, Abe had stood petrified in his tracks as he watched Hotta stride away. A few recruits who had overheard the exchange had expected to see Abe's head rolling in the mud.

The man's mad, Abe thought. Absolutely mad.

Not much later, on the battlefield, he discovered that there was method in Hotta's madness. If it had not been for his captain's (later colonel's) rigorous training, the lessons he was taught, he could have been killed a dozen times. Was his experience, though on a smaller scale, in store for Thor? How would the boy take it?

The clamor of the cooks' triangle gong pulsed across the water. Hotta distributed sandwiches to all, bottles of beer to the men, and soda to Thor. How the cook had obtained meat Thor didn't know and cared less. He was so famished the roast beef sandwich tasted even better than Johnson's. A sacrilegious thought. And the canned pineapple. Um!

Peter Pagsan broke the silence. "Why they call you Lucky?" he asked Yee Sing.

"He lucky be alive," Hotta said.

Pagsan looked at Hotta gravely. "I ask Yee Sing."

"That okay," Sing said. "Him tell."

Nothing loath, Hotta said, "On boat coming here Yee Sing and I talk much." He looked at Pagsan disarmingly. "You excuse me? Good."

"He live through worst of anti-Chinese troubles. When small boy he escape Rock Spring massacre in Wyoming because family friend hide him. He escape lynching in California twice. But in 1908 he lucky. Most lucky.

"He almost die in wreck of ship. In 1908 *Star of Bengal* wrecked off place called Coronation Island near Wrangell. I read about investigation in newspaper and Yee Sing tell me more. One hundred thirty-two men on ship. Cannery workers and crew. Only twenty-two safe. Of seventy-four Chinese only Lucky and one more survive. Twenty-two Japanese, seven safe. Four Filipinos, three okay," he looked toward Pagsan.

"Three hundred and forty-three, everybody, died when the

Princess Sophia went down last year," Thor said with an intent to impress. He pointed northward in the direction of Lynn Canal not many miles away.

Hotta nodded. "But circumstances different. *Princess Sophia* wreck terrible tragedy. On *Star of Bengal*—Oi, Yee Sing, you tell."

"I work in salmon cannery. Wrangell. We pack forty thousand cases. Good pack. We load 'em on *Star of Bengal*. We load on empty oil drums, hundreds. Then two tugboats tow ship through channel toward ocean. Weather fine but then wind begin. It night now. Ship jumping around. Men get seasick."

"Story in paper," Hotta said, "say storm get so bad tugboats cut lines and leave for safety. Captains say at hearing, fifteen minutes, maybe half hour more, his ship be out on ocean and safe. He call tugboat pilots cowards. Anyway, he put down anchor, then one more, but giant waves smash ship, drive it toward rocks."

"After breakfast, captain ask for volunteers to take line to beach," Yee Sing resumed. "Four men volunteer. I look at big waves and think they going die. They get in boat and row away. One big wave catch boat. It go like arrow. Smash on rocks. I know they dead. Then we see one man crawl out of water, then one more, one more. Four safe. We cheer and laugh. Maybe hope. They tie end of line to tree. A few get ashore this way. One of your countrymen on rope. *Star* lean toward shore and line get loose. Then *Star* lean other way and line get tight as string on bow. He go like arrow into sky and fall down on ship. He killed."

The listening men were silent as the picture flashed on the screen of their minds.

"Story in paper say no time to use line. Less than hour *Star of Bengal* break up," Hotta said. "Salmon, oil drums and ship's wreckage all drive toward beach. Only mast of ship above water. More than hundred men fight to remain alive."

"Terrible," Yee Sing said, closing his eyes as if to blot out the memory. "I see two cases smash man's head like eggshell. I swim deep as can. I lucky. Reach beach. I see countryman, very weak. I go to help him. Big wave come. It carry lots of cases of salmon. They fall on man bury him in sand." Yee Sing turned his head away and looked at the ground. "Terrible. Never forget."

"Only twenty-two men of one hundred thirty-two live. Most killed by wreckage. Most killed by salmon they canned. Hiniku da," Hotta said to Abe. "In English?" He frowned. "Iron . . . Ironical. That is word."

He turned to Thor. "You see difference. When *Princess Sophia* go down nobody had chance. Like rats in trap. When *Star of Bengal* wrecked, men fight to live."

"We bury everybody in sand and put salmon cases on top so sea no take away bodies," Yee Sing said. "I go smoke my pipe."

The gaunt figure shuffled away with bent back, as though the weight of a century was on his shoulders.

Thor, though a bit piqued that his contribution had been downgraded, was impressed by the graphic pictures Hotta and Yee Sing had brought to life. It was like the movies he had seen at the Coliseum. Never having experienced death or dying at first hand, he could not fully comprehend the emotional depths of the drama that had been related. But his knowledge and experience had broadened. He was being initiated into the wider horizon of adults.

As Yee Sing disappeared into the woods, Hotta said, "He look so old. Maybe fifty-five, sixty. Not so many Chinese in canneries anymore. More Japanese coming. Then Filipinos come," he said to Pagsan. "And maybe Mexicans like Jose Gomez," referring to one of the wash can boys. "History of America like that. Newest immigrants start at bottom."

"Naruhodo," Abe said, using his favorite expression. "Really." Naruhodo can mean *indeed, really,* or *I see,* just as Thor might have said "No kidding" or "You don't say."

When Abe would use the word with wide-eyed wonder after one of Hotta's pronouncements, Hotta could never be certain whether Abe was agreeing, being sarcastic, or acting plain dumb. The expression, as Abe used it, irritated Hotta no end.

It set Hotta off now. He looked sharply at Abe. "Don't be sarcastic. I'm serious. Trouble with you, Abe, you don't think."

Abe hid a smile as he split a piece of log. He enjoyed getting under Hotta's skin. "Me just uneducated farmer."

"He is hopeless," Hotta said. He grabbed a crosscut saw. "Come," he said to Pagsan. They made the sawdust fly as Hotta vented his irritation on a tree trunk. As they paused for breath a faint smile livened Hotta's face. "Son of a gun. That what they say?" he asked the sun-dancing leaves. Like most foreigners he found slang the hardest to comprehend.

"That Abe, he son of a gun." The saw buzzed at a more leisurely pace. "He make me so mad. Me, a philosopher." He glanced at Abe, who was trying to free his axe from a knot. He chuckled. He thought back affectionately to the days when he had made a soldier out of this Hiroshima farmer.

"Where you from?" he asked Pagsan.

"Luzon. Near Baguio. Me farmer, like Abe." He exchanged a glance of kinship with Abe.

"You mean you grow up among famous rice terraces?" Hotta's voice was tinged with awe, as if Pagsan were a special person from a rare land.

"Lots of fun when boy climbing mountains." He patted his thigh. "Strong. Hard work, too. No money."

"Rice terraces. Baguio," Hotta said. "Famous."

Pagsan shrugged bony shoulders. "Grow rice. Get food."

"One of wonders of world and you don't know. Took centuries to build. Two thousand years ago."

Pagsan nodded. "Grandfather tell me story. His grandfather tell him. Go back many grandfathers."

"But why you come to America?" Hotta asked.

"Same why you come. Make money. Cousin in Manila come America. Say I come."

"So you work in cannery!"

Pagsan looked around at the group. "All of us. All same."

Hotta nodded. "Europeans come looking for streets paved with gold. Chinese expect mountains of gold. Gum sum. Japanese told money grow on trees. And Filipinos?"

"Much same," Pagsan said.

During a break a middle-aged man accompanied by an Indian woman appeared on the trail that led from the company store to the clearing. He was carrying a single barrel shotgun, while the woman bore a bundle wrapped Japanese-style in a *furoshiki*, a square of cloth with the opposite corners tied to form a sling. At first glance even Hotta had taken the newcomers for an Indian couple.

The sight of the *furoshiki* puzzled him. He examined the man's dark brown face more closely. He could be a native, he could be—Hotta drew on his anthropological knowledge—Japanese, maybe a Kyushu islander. "Sore da," he thought. "That's it."

"Konnichi wa," he bowed slightly. "Good day."

"Konnichi wa." The stranger did not bow.

Was he a native after all? Or had he lost the habit? "I have seen you before," Hotta said, "but this is first time—Hotta desu."

"Ibusuki desu. This is my wife."

Hotta bowed to her. She nodded her head, her round, weatherbeaten face impassive.

The dialect and accent the man used, the way he spoke, convinced Hotta the man was from Japan's southernmost large island. "Kyushu kara desu ka?"

The man straightened in surprise. "Hai, Kagoshima."

Hotta smiled, pleased. "I have made a study of ben. Tokyo ben, Osaka ben, Hiroshima ben. In a small country like Japan there are so many dialects."

"So desu."

"You do not work in the cannery. What do you do?"

"I am the cannery watchman."

"You mean—You stay here the year around?"

Ibusuki nodded.

"It must be a lonely life."

"Narete kimasu," Ibusuki said. "You get used to it. I prefer solitude, the simple life of my wife's people. My life now."

"Eh! If you have the temperament."

"When I left Kagoshima I lived in Tokyo, but even for one year I could not stand it. Like a cage it was."

"I understand," Hotta said.

"You are of nobility?" Ibusuki asked.

Hotta laughed. "I, too, escaped from a cage." He waved toward the cannery compound. "This is for today." He held out his hands.

Ibusuki handed him his gun.

Hotta hefted it. "Nice balance." He noticed the well-oiled stock and barrel, broke open the gun and looked down the barrel. He nodded. "Beautiful. You would make a good soldier."

Ibusuki took back his gun. He locked gazes with Hotta. "I kill to eat."

Their eyes remained unwavering. "You would give me trouble," Hotta said. "But sometimes a man must fight."

"I choose not to be a butcher of men."

"Eh. You interest me."

Ibusuki hefted his gun. "I must go get my supper."

"What?"

"Duck. Maybe grouse, maybe ptarmigan."

"I hear there are giant bears on this island."

"One thousand pounds, maybe. A few big as fifteen hundred pounds. Mostly inland, but come down to streams when salmon run."

"You hear that, Tora. You be careful when you hunt blueberries."

"Two lakes, Hasselberg and Florence. Catch trout two feet long, but lakes hard to reach. Sitka deer, too. Otter, marten, beaver, many." Ibusuki looked at the descending sun. "Must go if want grouse for dinner." He pushed a shell into the chamber and nodded good-bye.

"If you get more than you need we will buy some from you," Hotta said.

"Will remember," Ibusuki said.

As the couple disappeared into the undergrowth, Ibusuki leading the way, Hotta said, "Mezurashii na." He nodded. "Unusual. I have heard of Japanese marrying Indian women and living as Indians but this first time I meet one."

"Woman look Japanese," Abe said.

"Well, they say all Indians come from Asia, when Alaska and Siberia joined together. Animals crossed first, then men follow hunting them for food."

"Birds!"

"Baka, they flew."

"Naruhodo."

Hotta raised his arm as if to give Abe the back of his hand. Abe ducked and returned to his axe. Hotta measured the sun as if estimating how much daylight was left.

"Oi, Tora. Get hand truck from warehouse. And rope hanging from nail. We bring this wood back to cook."

At the warehouse Thor was about to start back to the clearing when he remembered Hotta had had a board with a crosspiece which fitted into the receiving lip of the truck and doubled its capacity. He laid the board on the truck and returned to the clearing. It was a struggle as he fought the truck over roots and rocks. He sweated profusely.

"You brought board, too," Hotta said. "Good. You use your head."

Thor felt six feet tall.

Thor was to remember this day all his life: all the yellow hours of sunlight, the green of leaf and sea, the blue of sky, and the warmth of men at primitive tasks. In the predawn hours he had embarked on an adventure not often given to one so young. Like the comforting warmth of the sun through his shirt, he felt a sense of peace and well-being, of achievement, of acceptance by the adult world. It seemed as if he had distilled life into one day. He fell asleep that night thinking: I never felt so good.

17

Breaking In

THE COOK'S TRIANGLE awoke Thor from a dream of home. For a bewildered moment he was disoriented. The sight of his roommate, Gen Wakabayashi, stirring in the other lower bunk, informed him that he had awakened in a new world. As he started to rise he bumped his head, the first of several knocks until pain conditioned his behavior. He washed his face and brushed his teeth in cold water from a faucet, one of three sticking out above a trough outside the bathhouse. At the next faucet Wakabayashi watched in amusement as Thor hopped around trying to lessen the numbing effect of the cold water.

"Like ice," Wakabayashi laughed.

Breakfast, if it could be called that, was a disappointment. Thor had expected bread at least.

"Is that all?" he asked. He looked in dismay at the pan of rice suspended from the ceiling. On the table was a piece of salted salmon, pickled greens, *misoshiru*, and a pot of tea.

"Sometimes not even soup. That was our breakfast, April, May, June."

"Is that all!" Thor repeated.

Abe and Hotta had joined them at the table.

"Is all," Abe said. He had bought Thor a can of beef.

Thor sat dejectedly on his stool. "I'm going to starve." He watched the others fill their bowls with rice and decided he had better follow suit.

"By and by you get salmon. Every meal. Come out ears."

Thor watched fascinated, like a starving creature, as Abe opened the can and shared the beef equally. Heat would have melted the fat and the gelatin in which it was preserved, but hungry stomachs are not finicky. Such canned beef, especially with the gelatin, became a prime favorite with Thor. A starving stomach remembers. It started this day off right. They also retired to the kitchen for a share of burnt rice. Substitute salmon for beef and this was an Alaska boy's breakfast until the cannery workers were unionized in the Thirties.

Five small native seine boats arrived early the next morning. Billy Tang had selected his season boys, who arrived in April and worked into September, with an eye to meet any unexpected early run of salmon. In this instance there were enough workers skilled at each machine to run at least one of the three canning lines. Guarantee boys, promised two months' wages, worked the months of July and August, the peak of the salmon run.

Thor was given knee-high rubber boots, a yellow bibbed oilskin apron, and white canvas gloves blue-ribbed at the wrists. In contrast to his moccasin shoes the boots felt heavy and clumsy as he clumped toward the cannery. Puffs of steam rose here and there from the cannery building as if it were awaking from hibernation. Thor walked to a vantage point at the front of the pier. He was wordering what his job would be. Would he be up to it?

The seiners were moored to a small float at the bottom of an escalator that would bring the salmon up to the fish deck. Two endless iron chains, to which wooden cleats about four inches high were attached at intervals, ran like a continuous belt designed to bring up the salmon, empty them on the deck, and then return under the escalator down to the float.

As the chains started to rattle upward the Tlingits on one boat, using a tool that looked like a broom handle with a single sharp stine attached, expertly speared the salmon at the gills and slid them into the escalator pit. Each cleat carried a salmon to the top, where the company bookkeeper, using a watch-like counter, tabulated each fish as it fell off the escalator.

Although this method of tabulating a catch was fair when the salmon were of a more or less uniform size, it was not equitable to the fishermen when they brought in the larger king and coho salmon. In some canneries these were put in large wooden boxes and weighed on a scale to compensate the seiners by weight rather than number. Whether the price paid the fishermen was fair is another matter.

Abe, who as a sorter was the highest paid workman at 150 dollars a month, had scattered rock salt freely over the fish deck so he could keep his footing on what would soon become a slimy, slippery surface.

"This king, or spring salmon," he told Thor, as he hooked a large salmon near the gills. "See dots on back and tail. Biggest salmon." He hefted it with his fishhook. "About thirty-five pounds. Sometimes grow hundred pounds. Not many."

He hooked the king into a box made of two-by-twelve lumber. It was balanced in the middle on an axle with two iron wheels, with a smaller pivot wheel at one end. Abe's movement was as smooth as a samurai stroking his sword. Abe slid a second quinnat, another name for the king, into the box.

"Indian name Tyee. Mean Chief. Also called spring."

The early salmon were mostly sockeye, he explained, the most prized because their red meat commanded the highest price. "Up here they call them Alaska Red. On Columbia River blueback. In busy time we get mostly pink or humpback. See hump on this one." He slid it into a separate corner from the sockeye. In the busy season he would slide them into bins separated by boards.

"Then come chum. Also call them dog salmon because they have teeth like dog. Coho or silver salmon come mixed all time. All mixed. That is why they need sorter like me."

"Oi, Wakabayashi," he called out, "Show Tora-chan around. You learn better English from him."

"Hai, hai, Abe-san."

In the bowels of the building, a two-foot-wide belt that would power all the machines in the cannery through a system of interlocking, smaller belts hummed to life. Each machine had a lever that would connect or disconnect it from its source of power.

Although the salmon continued to thump off the escalator, Abe now hooked sockeyes on to a raised, waist-high platform where a man—Thor recognized the jolly, round-faced "Uncle" Tanaka—was lining them up. He slid them along to Hotta, who was manning the Iron Chink. Tanaka controlled the flow of fish by means of a hinged, wooden lever that he lifted up and down.

Hotta wore yellow oilskin pants and jacket and a broad-brimmed black fisherman's hat to protect him from flying bits of salmon, though pieces could still be seen on his face. A few fish, stiff from *rigor mortis*, would not lie flat. Tanaka's cherubic face wore a frown as he wrestled with these.

Hotta fed the salmon tail first into a red-painted machine with a large revolving wheel that gripped the fish, beheaded and disemboweled it, and cut off its fins and tail. Thor looked on wide-eyed at the efficiency with which the machine did its work.

"That is called Iron Chink," Gen said. "Chinese workers did that before, so they call it Iron Chink."

Thor was too naive to catch the racial implications of the name.

A conveyor belt carried the salmon to the slimers, who washed and cleaned out what blood and intestines remained in the inside of the spine. The slimers worked on boards one foot wide, fixed above troughs into which the salmon fell from the belt. Two-by-four board gates controlled the number of salmon that fell into each trough.

Cold, fresh water from fixed-hose faucets poured on the board on which the slimers worked. Although the canvas gloves the workers wore conserved some heat, the exposure to cold running water over a long working day, day after day, favored the development of rheumatism and arthritis.

The cleaned salmon were thrown on another conveyor belt running above the incoming belt and carried to another bin in front of the slicing machine. Here a fat worker whom Thor recognized as Shintaro Manabe, dressed like Hotta, placed the salmon in wooden buckets fixed on an endless chain. A set of whirling, knife-edged disks sliced the salmon into can-length sizes.

Thor shuddered at the sight of the spinning disk knives. Suppose your hand got caught on a bucket and you were drawn up through the knives. He closed his eyes at the horrifying image. Abe told him once that such an accident had happened. A worker drugged by fourteen hours at the machine had gotten careless and his arm was caught by a bucket. His scream—

Thor had cut Abe short and turned away. He did not want to hear the rest of the story. He felt that Abe had meant to frighten him into being careful. He was more than successful. In fact, Thor felt uneasy in the presence of the machine, even when it was idle. It caused him a few nightmares.

As Thor and Gen walked on, the sliced salmon began thumping on the slanted deck of the filling machine. Takahashi, the man who had tried to enter the dice game for a quarter, jumped up on a narrow platform and began lining up the cut pieces on a small conveyor belt that drew the salmon along a narrow trough into the machine.

Frank Suzuki, who had been giving Manabe a hard time over the game of *Go,* took his post on a platform near a long lever that controlled the filling machine. To Thor, who was to work below him all summer, he stood up there like the pilot of a ship on a bridge. His job was to see that the salmon went into the machine closely packed, so that each time a piston pushed the fish into a can it would be full.

The machine automatically filled the empty cans, sixty a minute, as they came down a chute-like metal loader from the second floor. Upstairs workers kept the chute loaded with cans. The emptied wooden boxes, one stacked inside two others for economy of space, were taken to the warehouse where they would be filled with forty-eight one-pound cans of labeled salmon toward the end of the season.

"This where you work," Gen said. "Cans roll out of machine. You pick up two at a time and hit them down and push them on that belt. Indian women patch them up so they weigh one pound." As Suzuki pulled the lever, Gen said, "Time you go to work."

Thor drew on his dry, spotless canvas gloves, took a deep breath, and stepped to his post with the chugging machine at his right ear. On his left three Tlingit women sat on either side of the table through which the conveyor belt ran. They cut pieces of salmon for cans that looked imperfectly filled or registered too light on the small, red balance scale.

Thor was a bit apprehensive as the first filled cans came rolling down a short chute at the rate of one a second. He had a few pile-ups, which he took care of by pushing the cans onto the belt. The women laughed, thumped these and sent them on their way. Thor stole furtive glances at them. They were the first Natives with whom he had such close contact.

The women at the patching table normally wore stolid expressions, but at work they jested and laughed among themselves and were kindly indulgent toward Thor because of his youth and inexperience. Their attitude made him feel more relaxed. Their eyes were large, down slanted above wide cheekbones and thick upper lips suggestive of Mongol stock, like the Japanese and Chinese. They were short, plump with middle age, and wore their thick hair in braids. One of the women wore her hair cut at the shoulder, a sign of mourning, so Thor learned later. They were round-faced, with much darker skin than the Japanese.

After several minutes Thor adjusted to the rhythm of the machine and was soon looking around, enjoying the sights and sounds of a cannery in operation. From the filling table the belt carried the cans under a salt dispensing machine that automatically dropped several grains of rock salt on top of the salmon. The cans proceeded through a long steam box to the can-topping machine. It was Gen's job to keep the holder filled with lids, which he took from a stack of boxes beside him. His most important duty was to keep the machine from jamming and to change dies when different kinds of salmon were canned.

Thor was surprised to see Gen take a book from behind the bib of his apron and start reading. "I read about three pages and

I know it is time to refill the machine," Gen explained, "I study English this way."

Thor wondered how one got a job like that. Anybody could pick up two cans at a time and thump them on the table. Maybe you needed a college education to man the topping machine. At his age he did not have much choice about assignments. Besides, the politics of buttering up to a foreman to get a choice position was beyond his ken.

After being topped the cans were vacuum-sealed and went through another steambath. As they emerged they rolled down an inclined chute where the wash can boys, with a wooden board, would scoop up six cans at a time and place them in a tray made of strap iron. Two scoops to a row made twelve cans, times twelve rows made one hundred forty-four cans to a tray. As each case of salmon contained forty-eight tins, one tray filled three cases. When each tray was filled another empty one was placed on top, filled, and the process repeated until there was a stack six high.

Reaching down and out to fill the lower trays and stretching up and out for the higher trays was guaranteed to keep the stomach muscles flat. An exercise performed not for fifteen minutes but for ten, twelve, fourteen hours a day, day after day, for about sixty days, with members of the wash can crew taking turns.

Each stack was pushed along a narrow-gauge railroad track to the cooking retort, which looked like a locomotive boiler. When three stacks were ready they were pushed into the cooker, the door locked by means of a giant iron wheel, and steam at high pressure released into the retort for the cooking period at about 240 degrees.

When the door was opened the stacks were pulled out by the use of an iron hook about ten feet long with a loop of iron at the end for a handle. Using folded gunnysacks to protect their hands from the hot trays, the workers pushed the stacks to a knee-high wooden tank filled with a solution of lye water. With iron hooks, two men at a time unloaded each tray, which was conveyed through the water by moving chains. The men employed long-handled brushes to vigorously scrub the tops of each tray full of cans. As the trays emerged from the adjoining rinse tank they were stacked again, this time on wooden platforms. A hand lift truck was pushed under the platform and the stacks pulled away into the warehouse where they were left to cool off.

Before the trays were unloaded and the cans stacked in the warehouse for labeling, a man with a small hammer—it had a metal handle with a marble-sized head—went down each row of cans tapping the can tops. Any that gave off an unusual sound was removed as defectively sealed and retopped or discarded. Even one fish scale could cause leakage.

Back at the filling machine, Thor viewed his job with misgivings. Was he to pick up cans and thump them all summer long? At least ten hours a day, day after day, for sixty days. No Sundays. The work was boring. It was tedious. He was appalled. Why, he was a robot, an appendage of the filling machine that *chunked, chunked, chunked* in his right ear. But he had a mind, had feeling, he was blood and flesh. He shifted the weight of his body from one leg to the other to relieve his fatigue.

The cook's gong summoned the workers to a one-hour lunch. Thor's first fresh salmon of the season was a gourmet's treat, especially to an appetite sharpened by the fresh sea air. The rest of the lunch hour he spent sitting on the edge of the pier watching the last of the seine boats being hosed clean.

"We'll be finished at this end by three o'clock," Abe said.

He had dropped by to see how Thor was making out. He had finished with the sockeye and pink salmon. There would be a respite until the line was ready to take on the chum, king, and coho. With his forefinger Abe tapped tobacco from a Durham bag onto cigarette paper which he rolled into a cylinder with one hand. He moistened the edge of the paper with his tongue and sealed the contents by twisting one end together. He took his first drag with such obvious enjoyment that Thor looked on in envy.

As the filling machine chunked out the last can of salmon, Thor stepped back with relief. He went to the wooden trough where he washed out his gloves under a faucet. He was joined by the women, chatting in Tlingit.

He thought the day's work was done, but the men were using hoses which emitted steam under extreme pressure to whisk the last bits of salmon from the machines, leaving them in spotless condition for the next day's use. Each machine in the long building was engulfed in steam. Finally, the entire floor was hosed down. The water and refuse escaped down trapdoors or through the cracks between the wooden planks of the pier.

A sense of well-being lightened the weight of his fatigue. He had done a man's work and, he felt, acquitted himself well. A note to Ken, who would read it to the family, would make them aware of what he had achieved. As he clumped his way to the bunkhouse the sun setting behind the headland drew the light from the placid waters of the bay. Peace was all pervasive across the face of the darkling water.

He almost bumped into Gen, who appeared in the doorway wearing a *yukata* or light summer kimono. Over his shoulder were slung a bath towel and a *tenugui*.

"Come take a bath," he said.

So it was that Thor was introduced to the *furo*. The Japanese bath was more than a fringe benefit; it was an integral if unwritten part of every worker's contract, whether it was at a cannery, a railroad section, a logging camp, wherever the footsteps of Japanese itinerant workers led. The *furo* could be a barrel or shaped like a bathtub made of two-inch planks, with a pit underneath where logs were burned to heat the water. It was a cultural appendage brought by the immigrants from Japan, where godliness takes second place to cleanliness.

Uncle Tanaka was sitting in a foot of water. Thor stepped in and jumped out with a howl.

"It's boiling," he said. "How can you stand it?"

The old man laughed.

Gen tested the water. "He got in when water warm. Then his body get used to water as it hotted."

"As it got hot," Thor corrected. "Or, as it grew hotter."

"Grew hotter." Gen's thin, smooth face knotted around the word as if he were impressing it into the folds of his brain. "I must remember that."

He opened the cold water faucet and swished the cold water

around with a tin basin. "Now," he instructed Thor, "we never go into bath American way. They wash in their own dirt. Japanese way, we wash first with soap and scrub with this tenugui, rinse, and then go in and soak. And soak. Hotter the better. You no feel tired after. You feel good. Everybody can use same water. Especially if little water, like in some places. Like here."

18

The Omen

T HE NEXT MORNING only two seine boats arrived with salmon, but they were larger than those of the previous day and the silver-sheened fish overflowed the holds and covered the decks.

"Maybe take till about two o'clock," Abe estimated.

Feeling optimistic and content with his emotions of the day before, Thor approached his duties unaware that on this day he was to experience one of the most traumatic events of his life.

The morning passed without incident. After lunch the workers were at ease, lounging about in front of the bunk-house waiting for the work whistle. With few exceptions, they were in their late teens or early twenties, from *inaka* or coun-tryside villages of Wakayama, Hiroshima, Yamaguchi, Kago-shima, and other prefectures of southern Japan. Having ex-hausted chitchat they were ripe for some excitement.

Hotta threw a bombshell into the pregnant air. He asked Thor: "If there was a war between Japan and the United States, on which side would you fight?"

The workers formed a tableau of hushed expectancy. Un-cle Tanaka's round face became a doll's mask. Suzuki's ready smile wavered on the edge of uncertainty. Thor became aware of Gen's intelligent face thrust forward to catch the signifi-cance of this event. Hotta stood stiffly erect as if he were re-viewing troops.

Abe, from his wartime experience, realized at once that his

friend was putting Thor to the extreme test. He reddened, his anger surging with the blood in his veins. The question was cruel and unfair. Tora was a boy and naive at that. Abe tightened his lips to dam the protest that rose in his throat. He was curious to see how the boy would react.

Hotta, from the corner of his eye, had caught Abe's involuntary movement and understood how he felt. Even as he spoke he had wanted to retract his question. Although he had spoken half in jest, he felt that he had acted like a bully. But he had acted on impulse. Abe, with his exquisite sensitivity, was right as usual.

To Thor the scene had a sense of unreality, the quality of a dream.

Behind the men the sun-dancing face of the bay mirrored the shadowless forests of high noon. From the mess hall chimney pale smoke rose straight as a birch and spread out like branches. Wavelets whispered around the barnacle-encrusted piles and chuckled as they lapped the pristine shore that in a few days would stink of offal from gutted salmon. A flight of birds wheeled like a giant leaf showing its underside to the sight, and a leaping salmon flashed its silver side like a sword at the sun and splashed the silence. No scene could have been more peaceful, so unlikely a setting for talk of violence.

To Thor the challenge literally came out of the blue, a clear Alaskan sky through which a few clouds straggled. To him the words hung in the air like a string of ill-fated opals, iridescent and ominous, ominous though he did not comprehend why. He stepped back as though he saw an omen. He felt alone and as helpless as any animal caught by the steel teeth of a trap, a boy among men. Anger and distress warred within him. He saw the men's faces as through a yellow fog: laughing and jeering. He wanted to close his eyes and ears to this nightmare throng.

Most of the men facing him had been too young to fight, but the glory of the Sino-Japanese and Russo-Japanese victories that had made Japan a world power was proud in their hearts. In their ignorant arrogance they fancied taking on the United States at some future date with destiny.

Thor's only comfort was Abe, who stood near him facing

the others. Thor glanced at Abe, but he was facing Hotta in a crouch, his face red with anger.

Thor realized that this was a crisis only he himself must face.

He looked straight into Hotta's enigmatic eyes and said, "For the United States."

He failed to catch the fleeting smile that crossed Hotta's face. He was confused by the loud laughter that greeted his answer. He sensed that much of it was good-natured and that he should stand his ground, yet he did not want to feel estranged or left out. He wanted to be liked and accepted by these men. He wanted to belong.

"If they will have me," he said. His doubt was prophetic. At the outbreak of World War II Nisei service was placed on hold.

At the mixed laughter that followed, he realized that he had lost their respect.

Hotta's contemptuous words cut him like a sword. "You serve one lord or none."

Evading Abe's supportive hand, tearful, Thor fled with his shame and humiliation. It seemed to him that he was pursued by raucous laughter, and not only of the men: The crows cawed in derision, the seagulls screamed as if in angry pursuit, and a woodpecker hammered a tree. Miserable. Bitter. He hated himself. He fled blindly into the forest. The wilderness was always his refuge. He ignored the high-bush blueberries that plucked at his eyes. The undergrowth that tore at his clothes. The perfume of wild roses and the sight of their fragile beauty stopped his headlong plunge. A truce settled the turmoil in his heart. Under the trees he vacillated between "They can go to hell!" and "I've got a job to do!"

He returned because he knew they were depending upon him. Roughly he elbowed aside the worker who had substituted for him. As he savagely thumped the cans he thought, "I hate Hotta. I hate the whole gang of them." He even hated Abe because he had disgraced himself before him. That was the cruelest cut of all. Most of all he hated himself. "I won't talk to them, ever," he thought.

Abe was furious, his face flushed, as he turned on Hotta.

"That was an unfair question. He is too young to understand."

"I was only joking." Hotta tried to pass the incident off lightly.

"Gizen-sha!" Abe snapped. "Hypocrite! Why don't you say what you really meant! You're a bully and a coward!" Abe was beside himself.

"Baka," Hotta said. "Fool."

"Nani!" Abe lunged at him. "What did you say!" His high-pitched voice was shrill with anger.

Hotta fended him off. He was aware that Abe did not own a knife, pistol, or rifle because he knew from experience that he was not responsible when in one of his uncontrollable rages. As Hotta held him off he thought Abe didn't need any weapons. Like a man possessed, he seemed to have the strength of ten.

Hotta finally got Abe around the neck and put his arm in a hammerlock behind his back. Abe almost broke Hotta's shin-bone with a backward kick of his heel.

Hotta, who prided himself on never losing his composure, roared in Abe's ear, "Attention! That's an order!"

At the military command Abe straightened to attention. When he realized how he had reacted he was more than beside himself. He looked around for some weapon to attack Hotta.

Hotta hobbled to a nearby nail keg, sat down, and kneaded his left shin. "It was such a peaceful afternoon." He smiled wryly. "If I'd had a hundred men like you we could have walked into Port Arthur."

The other workers, who had been mesmerized by the struggle, burst into laughter.

Shin Nagatani emerged from his office and blew his nickel-plated whistle. "All right. Back to work."

Hotta threw his arm across his friend's shoulders, restraining him as he tried to shrug off this yoke.

"He is young but don't baby him," Hotta said. "He has the right instincts. I liked the way he spoke up to me. He weakened because he wanted to please us. He must beware of this trait. I have watched him and studied him since he came here. It is his biggest weakness. Unless he overcomes it he will never be strong."

He withdrew his arm from Abe's unresponsive shoulders. "The boy must be loyal to his country. In the Japanese tradition, loyal to his family, his village, his company when he grows up, to his country. But first he must be loyal to himself. This is good if instinct is good. If instinct bad, it is something to think about. Wakatta?" he emphasized. "Understand?"

"Wakatta, wakatta. If we fight America, Nisei like Thor be in most difficult position."

Hotta nodded. "If instinct is right, they will fight us. Fight their father and mother."

"Not that. Baka."

"Japanese history is full of torn loyalties. Nisei are Americans. They will be loyal to their master, the United States."

"How can you be so sure?"

"I have studied the American system, the way of life. Those Americans who doubt the loyalty of any of its nationalities— now take the German Americans. Some of them have told me how they were treated. But those who doubt show little faith in their American system. Psychologists say that we are shaped in the first six or so years of our lives. Now—"

"Wakatta. Wakatta," Abe said hastily. Hotta's theories and philosophy made his poor brain spin. Next he would expound on his interpretation of Marxism and socialism. Or worse still, because it made him uncomfortable, about Abe himself. Something called psychology and a man named Freud. Then his poor head would ache.

Hotta laughed. "The trouble with you, Abe, you are loyal to what your heart says, not your brain. Now don't spoil Tora."

With only a primary school education Abe, like most Japanese, respected the knowledge and education his friend possessed. Hotta treated him as an equal, even though he came of nobility and was an ex-colonel of the Japanese army. He never put on what Japanese called high-tone airs. One of his faults, as far as Abe was concerned, was that he was too honest, too blunt, often so candid as to hurt the feelings of others. Then Abe, the more sensitive one, would take him to task. Abe's trait of speaking his mind, regardless of whom he was addressing, both amused Hotta and earned his respect.

Abe's transparent, down-to-earth qualities appealed to the more sophisticated Hotta, who had wearied of what he considered the straitjacket of conformity found in Japanese society from the social unit of the family to the halls of the Diet, even to the Emperor himself, no less hidebound by protocol than the veriest peasant.

Hotta's war experiences had broadened his horizon. The third son of Baron Ichiro Hotta, he had risen to the rank of colonel through attrition of superior officers, merit, and linguistic ability. He had learned Russian because of its immediate practical use, and could read German and English.

He spoke English with deliberation, as though he were translating in his mind what he wanted to say. He had learned to pronounce *th*, which is not found in the Japanese alphabet. It was a perennial wonder to him why his friend in Seattle had named his daughter Ethel when it would always come out "Essel." Actually, an American friend of the family, without knowledge of the Japanese language, had recommended the name.

The problem of when to use or not use *the*, ever a dilemma for bilingual Japanese, annoyed the logical processes of his mind. Matching verbs with singular or plural subjects troubled him, and when it came to matching collective nouns with the correct verbal number he would think *wasureta hō ga ii*, better to forget it.

He had one secret ambition he had not disclosed even to Abe, and that was to read the *Encyclopedia Britannica* from *A* to *Z*. He kept his set with Ethel's father in Seattle. He had brought *D* and *E* with him, as he had finished *A*, *B*, and *C*. In the beginning when he had finished *A*, he had started in on the suggested supplemental reading and related subjects, but when he realized that he would be reading half a dozen books at the same time he had thought, "There's a limit. I would be gray-haired before I reached *Z*. I will read what is before me."

Blessed with a retentive memory and an absorbing interest, Hotta had in this fashion been mainly self-taught in what might be called his graduate studies since his years at Imperial University.

It was this thirst for knowledge and new experiences and his preference for a scholastic life that had motivated him to emigrate to the United States. A month after he had parted from Abe on the Yokohama pier, after he had settled his personal affairs with his father and family, he had written Abe to join him.

Abe replied that he did not have the passage money or the "show money" that U.S. Immigration demanded of all immigrants, but that he was saving every yen he could. Maybe in a year he could join Hotta.

Hotta wrote back: "Don't be so stiff-necked. You're just like my father. Pride, pride, pride. Forget it. I told you I would advance you the money. I am not giving it to you. You can pay me back in America. If it will make you feel any better my father tells me that the Japanese Government is giving a four hundred yen bonus to every veteran. You can pay me out of that whenever you receive it. I have booked passage for two. I am waiting."

Hotta remembered the derby hat, no longer black, the ill-fitting brown suit given to him by a missionary, the black button shoes in which Abe had appeared at the pier. He glanced now at Abe as they joined the workers who trooped over the wooden sidewalk built on piles toward the cannery building. His heart went out to Abe, not quite so stiff-necked now and less red-faced. Abe's rages flared like matches and died as quickly.

Hotta's memory skirted the past once more, to the day Abe had repaid his debt. He had been proud to the last cent, which he gave to Hotta with a flourish. "Now we are equal."

"We always were equal."

"A debtor is never equal."

Hotta had given up.

He returned to the present and gave Abe a slap on the back. "You're a good man," he said, and headed toward the Iron Chink.

Abe looked after him and thought, "He always was mad."

Thor's thoughts reverted to the crisis that had lacerated his guts. Why should the United States and Japan fight? They had been allies in the war just past. It was inconceivable that he would ever be put in the kind of situation Hotta had projected. The question of his loyalty had never been raised, much less put so bluntly. There could be no question. He was as American as Gus, George, John and the rest of his friends in Juneau. He was one with them.

Thor was unconscious of his race. A few times he had been made aware of it. He recalled his teacher saying in art class: "The Japanese are such skilled artists they can draw a leaf with one stroke of the brush." Everyone in class turned to look at Thor, or so he felt. The Swedish girl sitting next to him smiled, "Can you do that?"

Thor recalled an incident initiated by Kubota. Thor and George, his Finnish friend, were walking home along Glacier Highway from Salmon Creek. Kubota had taken Thor's family for a ride in his Ford pickup and was driving back to town. He stopped as though he meant to pick up the two boys, so they hopped on. Kubota told George to get off. As the car started up, Thor's mother motioned to him. Thor jumped off and re-joined his friend.

George was walking fast and fighting back his tears. They walked home in silence, bewildered by this show of prejudice they had felt for the first time. When they arrived at Thor's home his mother invited them in for cookies and some Dolly Gray's soda water. At first George refused, but he yielded to her insistence.

"He's a bad man," Thor said, trying to make amends to his friend.

"He was kind enough to give us a ride," Mama said, her gentle voice a bit sharper than normal. "Some white men cheated him of his fishing boat and he's been bitter ever since. It isn't right to hate all white people, but can you blame him?"

"But we're only kids," Thor said.

"Prejudice touches everyone," she said. "Some day it will destroy us all."

As the boys went out to play Thor interpreted what his mother had said.

"You understand Japanese?"

"Sure." Thor added, "Most of it. Well, I get the general idea."

"I never hear you speak it."

"Don't have to. But ohaiyo, like the state, Ohio. That means good morning. Kirai. I use that a lot. It means 'I don't like it.' You should taste this stinky stuff my father likes. It's called ta-kuan. It's pickled radish and the color of piss. It smells worse than skunk cabbage."

Thor was jarred back to reality as the filling machine jammed. Sven Larssen, the mechanic—the superintendent, the foreman, the mechanic, the engineer, and the trap watchmen were all white—was called over to adjust the machine. The Native women went over to the water faucets to wash their gloves. Thor walked around until the circulation of blood removed the prickly feeling from the front of his thighs. He welcomed such respites because they relieved the tedium of his work.

"All right," Larssen said. Suzuki pulled the lever.

For two meals Thor stuck to his resolve not to talk to the others. He rebuffed Abe's advances and acted as if Hotta did not exist. He ate quickly and disappeared from the table.

"His resentment will wear off," Hotta said.

"Don't be so sure," Abe said. "He hates himself more than he hates us."

"You amaze me. A shinri-gaku sensei," Hotta said, "a psychology teacher, could not be more discerning."

As if on cue the *City of Spokane* arrived with the guarantee boys. Among them was a sprinkling of high school and college students. Abe directed two of the newcomers to the room occupied by Thor and Gen, who had the lower bunks. Abe stood smiling expectantly in the doorway. It was good to have young people together. The new arrivals cast disparaging looks around.

"Iya da na!" Sho Asamura said. "Disgusting."

Abe reddened. A vein throbbed at his temple. "Did you expect a hotel room? Baka!"

Saburo Sato laughed at his friend. "He's right. You can't expect a tatami room here. Kawatta koto shitakatta daro," he pointed out. "You wanted to try something different. This is it."

"I should have left some bedbugs for you," Abe said.

"Oi, kozō. I'm thirsty. Get me water."

Thor started to move, then sat back. "Get your own water."

"Good," Abe said. "Now you are learning. You don't have to please a kisei chū, a parasite like this."

To the Japanese foreman who was passing by he spoke crude Japanese of the streets. "Oi, Nagatani. This Asamura. Why don't you put him at the sliming table." It was the dirtiest job he could think of.

Thor was hard pressed to picture the elegant Asamura at the sliming table. He wore a fawn fedora hat, a double-breasted drab corduroy jacket with rollaway wombat collar, and brown corduroy trousers. His oxford shoes were the latest craze in the capitals of Europe.

Although he didn't understand all the Japanese, Thor gathered from the newcomers' conversation that Asamura was the son of an influential and powerful *zaibatsu* (whatever that meant) executive, and was attending the University of Washington in Seattle along with Sato. Aboard the ship he had bought his way into cabin class and eaten at the cabin-class tables.

Thor couldn't understand the respectful attention with which Gen listened to Asamura. To Thor, Asamura was as obnoxious a man as he had ever met. His hair, parted in the middle, was stacombed to his fat head and his sideburns curled forward like fishhooks. His small eyes were almost buried beneath thick folds of eyelids. His pencil mustache was curled upward at the ends above thick lips. His neck was short and fat.

Like most Japanese college students who did not have enough to eat, Sato was built like Gen, lean and wiry, with intelligent eyes set in a bony, almost emaciated face. Even Thor sensed that he was playing a role, that of a lackey to someone who could and would do him favors. It was he who went to get water for Asamura.

Asamura wanted a lower bunk. Thor imagined it would be difficult for the fat man to climb upstairs each night, but he had no choice. Thor wasn't about to give up his lower. First come, first served. He glanced over at Abe, who still lounged in the doorway. He shook his head. He was annoyed when Gen offered his lower bunk, saying he would take the bunk over Thor's. Gen was being subservient like Sato.

Thor was even more mystified when Gen introduced Hotta to Asamura as the son of Baron Hotta, and Asamura in turn became respectful, as to a superior.

"Why?" he asked Abe as they went outside. In his curiosity he forgot that he wasn't talking to Abe.

Abe laughed as if highly pleased at Thor's discernment. "Japan is not as democratic as America," he said. "In old days some at top—Eigo de wa— In English—" He turned to Hotta who had come up behind them. "You tell him."

"You let me speak, eh," Hotta jabbed Abe with his elbow and laughed. "Japan has caste system. Caste mean different classes of people. On top lords and nobles. Next to them samurai. They sword fighters, most of them work for lords, before Meiji period. Below them artisans, peasants, and merchants. Besides these there were outcasts. This is—what is English word—oversimplification. Black and white for a primary mind. But is much more complex that that. They even speak different to each other. This you will learn some day. Okay, Tora-chan?"

"Hotta-san is of nobility," Abe said. "Asamura is merchant class."

"In old days, lowest of the low," Hotta said.

The three walked out on the pier as the sun, a giant orange of fire, sank behind the headland. A huge red scow, waist deep with salmon contained by wooden walls, was being moored to the escalator float.

"Oh, no," Thor said, aghast. "There's millions."

"Not quite," Hotta smiled.

"We run three lines tomorrow," Abe said. "Work late. Better we get some sleep."

As Thor was to learn through bone-tiring hours, this was only the beginning of a flood of salmon that was to be channeled by purse seiners and traps from the ocean into one-pound cans. The harvest seemed inexhaustible. As the salmon catch increased, the workday started at six a.m., sometimes at five, with a half hour for lunch.

Whenever work started at six or earlier the men got a break at nine o'clock, when doughnuts and coffee were served. Thor welcomed this break in the routine. He couldn't very well ask for cocoa, postum, or fresh milk, so it was here at his age that he learned to drink coffee out of an empty salmon can: half coffee and half condensed milk.

The normal working day was from six a.m. to six p.m. Time worked before or after, and the half hour at lunch and at dinner, was considered overtime, for which Thor received twenty-five cents an hour. When the catch was especially heavy the canning lines ran till nine and ten p.m., with half an hour for meals. On such nights the cook, who had to get up early, would leave a huge pot of coffee on the stove, bread or biscuits, rice, and pickled radish. Breakfast was miso soup, rice, salmon, and pickled vegetables.

One morning Thor heard Abe's high-pitched voice raised in anger at the coffee stand. He learned later that Abe was bawling out Asamura for trying to snitch an extra doughnut. At night Abe could be heard saying, "Leave something for the wash can boys."

The workers at the retorts finished their work almost two hours after the last salmon was canned, as they had to bring the last stack out of the boilers, wash the cans, and then clean up. Their work, Thor used to think enviously, was relatively clean as they did not get smelly from touching raw salmon, and they were free to move about, a condition which to Thor was the ultimate in jobs.

In July when the blueberries were ripe, Thor picked six cans full, had Gen seal them, and asked Jose Gomez, the Mexican wash can boy, to put them in a tray with the salmon to cook. He watched Gomez tie a cord around the cans to identify them. When they went to claim the cans they discovered that someone had removed the cord.

"I want my blueberries," Thor said. He had planned to take them home as a treat.

"You going to open every can?" Gomez asked.

The next morning the superintendent came around carrying an open can of blueberries. "Anyone know about this?"

"Somebody had bright idea," Abe said.

"Abe, we're here to can salmon, not blueberries."

Behind the superintendent Gomez was holding his fat sides suppressing a laugh.

When they were alone Abe said to Thor, "Good thing he did not see your face."

Gomez had let go. He was slapping his thigh, laughing with his mouth toward the ceiling and having hysterics in general.

Then and in after years Thor used to visualize a housewife opening a can labeled salmon only to find blueberries inside. He could see her, all indignation, marching off to her grocer to demand why he was selling blueberries when the label plainly said pink salmon. The bewildered grocer would turn to wholesaler and the complaint would go up the chain of supply.

Elsewhere in the world this would be repeated. In darkest Africa. On the banks of the Amazon. Maybe Tibet. The possibilities were endless. It made a good story Thor was fond of retelling, but always lurking in his subconscious was the thought, "What really happened to those blueberries?"

In his boredom Thor envied Gen. One day he became indignant. Why should Gen have the privilege of a job that was hardly a job at all? He watched Gen put down his book, take a stack of lids and place them in the vertical holder. Then he returned to his book to read another three pages. Thor grinned in glee when Nagatani paused near Gen. "Oi, Gen, shikkari seiyo," he said. "Look sharp."

"Hai! Hai!" Gen jumped to his feet. When the foreman was gone he picked up his book again.

Thor waxed more indignant. What kind of foreman was he that he let Gen get away with it?

Thor envied Abe his skill and dexterity, but knew that he had neither the experience nor the strength to do the sorter's work. It must be fun, he thought, to separate the different kinds of fish. He marveled at the split-second speed with which Abe made his selections. At least he had to use his mind.

Abe's job became doubly difficult when night fell and he had to keep his eyes peeled below the weak lights. He was joined by another sorter, a Tlingit who had learned to distinguish between salmon since he was a boy. This man, named Sam, admired Abe's skill.

"You got Tlingit blood in you," he said.

Rarely, very rarely, Tanaka, who lined up the salmon for Hotta, would throw a fish back to the deck. "Oi, we make mistake," Abe would laugh.

"I never make mistake," Sam would say. Then he would laugh so disarmingly that Abe, whose blood pressure was about to jump, could not take offense.

At the start of the season Thor's mind had been alert, sensitive to impressions; he found humor in his human condition. Perhaps this was when he first learned to laugh at himself. As the summer moved on the numbness in his body spread to his brain. For the most part he lived in a dream world. Occasionally he made up a ditty:

> Chunk, chunk, chunk grunts the machine
> Tink, tink, tink come the cans
> Thump, thump, thump go my hands
> Whirr, whirr, whirr hum the belts.

All nonsense. He would laugh silently. He caught Suzuki looking down at him curiously so he composed his features. He looked at Sven Larssen walking by, the Tlingit women chatting at his side. Three racial groups living in circles of their own, circles that intersected at the cannery building. Working together, but strangers. Three circles that would drift apart at season's end, and individuals in each circle would disperse to their own destinies.

As the unceasing flow of salmon continued, Thor could visualize the scenes at the approaches to the streams and rivers from Bristol Bay at the southern reaches of the Bering Sea, down the Alaskan coast to the Columbia River: hordes of silver fish drawn as by magnets from the oceans' secret depths to their birthplaces. Millions running the gauntlet of boats with seine nets, trollers, floating and standing traps, all the accoutrements the ingenuity of man could devise to stop their journey home.

And then the bruising battle upstream, leaping falls passable only to an indomitable will. Thor had watched them running up Salmon Creek so thickly that, as Alaskans were fond of saying, "You can run across the stream by stepping on their backs."

In fresh water their silvery sheen became mottled with ugly red bruises. The humpback salmon turned hideous, flat as flounders, their humps more pronounced as they lost weight. The hooked jaws of dog salmon came to resemble their namesakes. The salmon never ate on their way to the spawning beds where they had been born.

Thor weighed the phenomenon in his mind as it had been taught him. Here was a fight to the death in which there would be no survivors, a death wish that would be realized after the salmon gave birth to life. What insane contradiction was this? It was one of nature's mysteries, as unfathomable as that of the lemmings who trek like armies from the mountains to drown by the thousands in the Atlantic Ocean or in the Gulf of Bothnia off Sweden.

Though each day drained the energies of the men, the quality and quantity of their provisions (except for a surfeit of salmon) hardly improved. Hens that had been brought north in April had been providing eggs that were scrambled into egg fu yung. Occasionally they had fresh food. One Sunday in July a hen and a hog that had been brought along to fatten were slaughtered. The squawking of the chicken and the terrified squealing of the hog drew Thor to the scene. He arrived as the cook chopped the head off the hen and tossed it into a large barrel. The chicken fluttered out of the barrel and ran in bloody circles around the kitchen area. The sight sickened yet fascinated Thor. It seemed to him that he could hear the bird crying above the flapping of its wings. The cook's helper was holding the frantic, struggling hog. With one motion the cook slit its throat. Nauseated, gagging, Thor fled to where he could breathe freely.

He enjoyed the bitter Chinese greens grown near the cookhouse and poured the left-over broth on his bowls of rice, a treat he relished all his life. He also learned to like green tea over rice, eaten with *umeboshi* and *takuan*.

Salmon roe was a free delicacy. The red eggs came from the belly of female salmon, stuck together in one piece about the size and shape of a cucumber. Hotta salvaged the eggs at the request of Abe, who took them back to the bunkhouse. At this time salmon eggs were not saved for commercial caviar. Abe placed them in a baking pan and sprinkled them heavily with rock salt. The next day he washed off excess salt and served the caviar with *shoyu* and the juice of a lemon he bought at the company store. Nothing was more soul-satisfying with hot rice. Caviar not saved floated out with the tide each day.

Salmon was smoked in a small structure the shape of an outhouse but much smaller, about a foot square. Strips of salmon were hung inside and a smoky fire kept burning underneath. These tidbits helped to vary the menu of salmon, served three times a day. But even salmon, considered a delicacy Outside whether fried, baked, broiled, or marinated, is still salmon. Enough is enough, Thor would think. He hungered for the big steaks and thick pork chops that he could have for the asking at the City Cafe. A gleam lit his eyes.

As the season wore on, many of the workers surreptitiously brought back salmon bellies, considered the best part of the fish, and packed them in rock salt. The secret was not to let the pieces touch or they could spoil. They also sliced cheeks from the discarded salmon heads and salted them down. These were packed in nail kegs and boxes lined with discarded oilskins in an attempt to make the containers waterproof.

As the catches of salmon tapered off and the canning lines reduced from three lines to two and finally to one, the men spent their afternoons labeling cans and packing them into cases in the warehouse. The lessening of the tension and pressure was appreciable.

Thor was entranced by Yee Sing's speed and dexterity at labeling. He sat on a salmon case and used another upright with a board on top as a table. He would line up the labels face down with a thin edge showing, make one swipe of a wide paste brush and he was ready. Picking up a bare can with one hand and slapping a label on with the other, he flipped the can over, pressed the pasted edge down and put the can in the case at his feet. The operation was performed in what seemed to Thor one motion. There was a cadence in the movement of Yee Sing's body and rhythm in his hands as beautiful as any musician's.

Thor could see why he was reputed to be faster than a labeling machine. The experimental one that the company had brought north was forever jamming, and Larssen spent many minutes removing torn labels and cleaning off glue. About the only advantage it had was it didn't need opium. Each afternoon Yee Sing would retire to his bunk. Whatever stimulant he used, he would reappear a new man with the speed of ten.

As he did everything else, Thor gave labeling a try, but Yee Sing would be finishing a dozen to his one.

Abe, who was as fast at nailing tops on the cases as Yee Sing was at his specialty, let Thor nail a few tops. Abe kept nails lined up between his lips and lined them up between his thumb and forefinger. *Bang, bang, bang, bang,* and another *bang, bang, bang, bang* on the other end of the top board, and the case was carried away to be stenciled with the company's brand.

Thor liked the hammer Abe used. It had a square head with a ridged face. Instead of a claw it had a small, flat blade with a notch in it to pull out damaged nails. This could be done with a half twist of the wrist. Nobody had ever seen Abe bend a nail.

Thor took advantage of the freedom warehouse work permitted. No more clammy gloves or sweaty, heavy boots. He could almost fly again in his elkskin moccasin shoes, and his dungarees felt light and dry. What a relief!

He was shocked out of his complacency one afternoon when he ran across Asamura taking a snooze behind a pile of cans. Thor was indignant. What privilege did he enjoy that he could loaf on the job while everyone else was working hard? He was of a mind to report him to Nagatani, but boys don't squeal.

Hotta happened by. He strode over to the sleeping man and kicked him on the sole of his shoe. Asamura sprang to his feet in a crouch. When he recognized Hotta he lowered his hands and stood up straight.

"Oi, shikkari seiyo," Hotta said. "Shape up. Now get to work."

"Hai! Hai!" As Asamura passed Thor he muttered, "Kozō."

Hotta grabbed Asamura by the shirt front, half lifted him to his toes. "The boy said nothing. I happened to come by. Wakatta ka?" He shook Asamura. "Understand?" Hotta pushed him away.

"He is spoiled brat. Spoiled like rotten salmon. I wish I had him in the army."

As Hotta walked away Thor thought, "Gee, I wish I was as strong as him."

On the last Sunday before his departure, a melancholy morning when dark clouds were moving in over the mountains threatening rain, Thor was drawn to the pier by the sound of music. The lanky Sven Larssen was sitting with his feet dangling above the gray, troubled waters. He was playing plaintive music on an accordion, his eyes half-closed, a bemused look on his long, lean face. Thor listened silently, his heart drawn by a longing he could not fathom.

Thor was surprised. Throughout the long, eventful summer, Larssen had been a taciturn shadow, moving from one recalcitrant machine to another, plying the magic of a mechanical genius with his hands. Sitting here on the deserted pier he was like a man Thor had never seen.

Larssen, as if he sensed Thor's presence, opened his gray eyes and looked around. "Morning, Thor." He smiled, and it was like sunlight on a rocky mountainside. "Thor," he repeated. "Just can't get over your nickname."

"My friends couldn't pronounce my real name," Thor said soberly.

"It's a proud name. Wear it well." Larssen looked around at the frowning forest where the shadows of the coming rain were lurking. "It was Sunday and I had the mood. The music, I call it my homesick song. Every year, when the season ends, I think of the times when I was a boy just like you. In country like this. Alaska is the only place in the world I know like Norway. Guess that's why so many Norwegians and Swedes come here."

They looked toward the sound of footsteps. The Tlingit

named Sam came around the corner of the fish house.

"Another early bird," Larssen said.

"Your music make me cry," Sam laughed. "Been pulling up stakes, getting ready to fade away like Indian."

"Where you heading?"

"Back to my village. Maybe run a trap line this winter. Same as always. You?"

Larssen shrugged. "Maybe sawmill. Logging camp. Or maybe tuna cannery in California. Maybe I try that this year. Yah!"

Abe and Hotta came strolling up.

"Well, what's this? A gathering of the clan?" Larssen said. "What you doing this winter?"

"I want go sawmill," Abe said. "Hotta want study. So maybe I short order cook in college town."

"Trouble with you," Hotta said, "you don't like to use brain."

"Naruhodo." Abe ducked an imaginary blow from his friend.

The same packet that had brought Thor to Funter Bay returned him home in time for the start of school after Labor Day. Hotta and Abe saw him off at the dock. Abe gave him a small box covered with a gunnysack in which rock salt came. He had washed the salt out of the material, and it was dry and clean to the touch.

"Some salmon bellies and cheeks," Abe said diffidently. "For your family." His eyes were moist and his voice soft with emotion. "You were a good worker. Sayonara." He shook hands as with a man.

"You have good instincts," Hotta said. "Be careful and go well." He shook hands.

As the boat pulled out into the bay, Thor waved at Abe and Hotta, who gradually receded into small specks. He gulped and blinked the tears from his eyes. The boat turned the point and closed a chapter in Thor's life. But his thought remained with his fellow workers. For the first time in his life his conscience had come into day-to-day touch with the lot of the itinerant workers. He felt gratitude to men who had befriended and watched over him. Vaguely, without knowing how or why, he wanted to help men of good heart, such as Abe, or a concerned man like Hotta. The thought remained a seed in a fallow part of his mind.

19

Not the High Road

T HE DAY WAS CUT OUT OF GRAY air but the clouds ran high and luminous above Juneau's mountain peaks as Captain Olaf Johnson turned the breakwater and headed his boat toward City Dock. He blew his whistle five times in a sequence of two-one-two to inform his wife he had returned safely to harbor. It was a ritual he performed each trip. There were times when winter storms delayed him and added gray to her hair. The signal eased her anxiety.

Thor shouldered his blanket roll and leaped from boat to pier. In his eagerness at being home he forgot the box that Abe had so lovingly prepared for him. He made a beeline for the City Cafe. At the entrance he glanced up Front Street. The town seemed to have shrunk, an illusion that was to reoccur whenever he returned to Juneau after any absence.

It was past the lunch rush hour. Ken was behind the counter wiping the silver and putting it away. Thor smiled at the familiar scene. Johnson was cleaning the range top with a gunnysack. Frank Amano was busy banging pots and pans in the two-compartment, iron-sheeted laundry tub that was used as a sink.

Thor swung himself up on the tall, revolving stool without using the brass footrail. He made a couple of revolutions and felt at home again. Ken greeted him with a smile. He nodded toward the kitchen. Thor hopped off and trotted into the kitchen.

"Hi, Mr. Johnson. I'm back. Hi, Mr. Amano."

Johnson's mouth gleamed with gold in a broad grin as he shook hands and felt Thor's biceps. "You've grown so big and strong. How was it? But you must be starved. Oi, Ken, some pie and cocoa."

Eagerly Thor jumped back on the stool. "Make that coffee."

"Coffee?"

"Yep, I like coffee now."

Johnson came up to the end of the counter. He laughed. "It stunt your growth. You learn to drink, too?"

"That moonshine. Ugh."

"What do you want to eat? Salmon steak?"

"Jōdan!" As Thor used the Japanese word for "jest" the men raised their eyebrows. "I thought I would grow fins. I would have this nightmare. I'd come in here and you wouldn't let me have a T-bone steak. Said I was too young. I would wake up sweating."

Johnson tousled his hair and marched toward the range, his pate glistening through his thinning hair.

"Jōdan," Ken said. "You learned Japanese, too."

"Some." Thor was busy smelling the sizzle permeating the air. "Mr. Johnson, could you make it rare. I like the potatoes crisp and crunchy."

Ken was pleased with his brother's overnight development. He had Johnson to thank for making an on-the-spot decision with Tang.

"Shikkari shite kita," Johnson said to Ken as he brought the steak to the counter. "He has become more self-confident."

Thor grunted as he took his first bite. The fat melted in his mouth. And the meat—How could he describe the taste! And the french fries! Um!

As Thor finished he could feel the stretch of his stomach muscles. A great void had been filled. For dessert he sprinkled sugar over the buttered toast. Ken was more tolerant than their mother about eating too much sugar. This was because he had perfect teeth and never gave them a second thought. He was more concerned about the position Thor assumed when reading or when he held a book too close while reading by an inadequate light.

"When you going to ask me how much I made?" Thor asked as he finally pushed away the plate.

"We've been waiting," Ken said.

Thor unbuttoned the breast pocket of his blue flannel shirt. He drew out a folded check and straightened it out on the counter. Ken pushed it toward Johnson so he could look first.

"One hundred and eighty-two dollars and fifty cents," Johnson read.

"Including overtime," Thor said excitedly.

Ken picked up the check. "That's great."

"That's more than I make in a year," Amano, who had come over, said, thinking to please Thor. The implication of what he had said occurred to him. "Jōdan, jōdan," he said to Johnson, but the latter was so pleased at what Thor had achieved that he did not take offense.

"Oh, oh," Thor said. "I forgot the box Mr. Abe gave me."

"You left it on the boat?" Ken said. "Go get it."

Thor was saved the trouble. Captain Johnson entered carrying the box. "You forgot something, young man."

"Gee, thanks, Captain Johnson."

"Give me a cup of coffee," the captain said to Ken. "The old woman will have a big dinner waiting for me."

"Be my guest," Ken said, placing a cup of coffee in front of Johnson.

Thor told the men about the kindnesses Abe had shown him and what Hotta had taught him.

"What good-hearted men," Johnson said. "They should be dropping in on their way south. I would like to thank them."

"I hope so. Be sure to let me know. Oh, and I want to thank you again, Mr. Johnson, for getting me the job. I'm going to put all the money in the bank."

Ken looked at Johnson. Like his father, he tended to procrastinate when it came to breaking bad news. Johnson believed in coming straight to the point. He said to Thor:

"Your father has not been feeling well. We think it best if he returns to Japan for a while so that he can recover his health.

We're trying to find a buyer for his business."

Thor looked from Johnson to Ken, who nodded. "It's not serious," he said, "but we think he needs a good rest."

"You mean we're all going?" Thor felt conflicting emotions. He did not want to part from the family, but he had no desire to go to Japan. The experience at Funter Bay had enlarged his world and enriched his life, but he felt comfortable where he was. The unexpected news stunned him and he groped to sort out his thoughts.

"Are you going, too?" he asked his brother.

Ken shook his head. "I will have to work here and send them money in Japan."

"I don't want to go."

"But there won't be any place for you to stay."

"I don't want to go."

"You are facing big decision," Johnson said. "You must think things over from all sides. Ken-chan may have to borrow money from you."

"No." Thor clutched his check. "This is mine. I earned it." He thought of the summer past. "You don't know how hard I worked."

"I'm sure you did," Ken said. "But think of Papa."

Thor looked at his check. It represented the biggest achievement of his life. Twelve years old and he had made all that money. Now he was being asked to practically give it away, or so it seemed to him. He folded the check and put it in his shirt pocket. "I want to show it to them," he said. He shouldered his bedroll, tucked the box under his arm, and turned to Johnson. "Thank you, Mr. Johnson."

He turned to leave. "And thank you, Captain Johnson."

As the door closed behind him Ken said, "It was difficult."

"He must learn."

"But what am I going to do with him?"

For once the resourceful Johnson had no ready answer. With a thoughtful frown on his face, he returned to the range and burnished its spotless top with clean flour sacking.

Captain Johnson interrupted their thoughts. "You mean

we're going to lose the best barber we ever had? We're going to miss Fuse."

Thor walked reluctantly along the board sidewalk of Front Street toward home. The news had drained the life out of the stories he had rehearsed to tell his family and especially his friends. So they listened with pop-eyed wonder, what did it matter? This was really taking the joy out of life. He returned greetings perfunctorily and absentmindedly. The shopkeepers and others looked after him and wondered what was ailing the normally lively and animated barber's son.

The shades were drawn on the barbershop window. In the living room–kitchen Papa was sitting in his favorite chair, a battered rocker one of his patrons had given him. His handsome face was drawn and his mustache black against his pale skin. He opened his eyes as Thor entered the room.

"Hello, Tora," he smiled. "Yoku kaetta na," he said. "You returned well." He closed his eyes again.

Papa had aged in two months. He looked worse than Thor had imagined. It was frightening. The display of his check in front of his admiring siblings was anticlimactic. He gave the check to his mother.

"Ii musuko," she said. "You are a good boy."

She pressed his hand briefly as she accepted his check. He looked into her small, soft eyes and felt rewarded. He had given her evidence of his manhood and he had to do it graciously.

For dinner she cooked his favorite *osekihan*, what he called *azuki gohan*, consisting of *mochigome*, a glutinous rice cooked with red beans. It was served sprinkled with salt and *goma* (black sesame seeds).

He almost forgot about his hard-won check as he related his summer's adventures. While he talked he observed objectively for the first time in his life his siblings and Mama and Papa. Until now he had accepted them as naturally and freely as the air he breathed. Soon he would part from them, for he had decided definitely not to go with them to Japan.

The family had reached a crossroad. Thor stood on a side road that would lead him on a solitary journey. He looked at them anew under the yellow light.

George, his younger brother, was the quiet one with the beautiful eyes, who made loyal and responsive friends despite his introverted nature. Helen, who was not much taller than Mama, was of a similar temperament, unassertive and even-keeled. She was the bond between family and George when he, as he grew up, lost touch with reality. Helen loved to climb the rock pile above the sawmill—it was her jungle gym—and would follow George. Little Peggy, the lively one who took more after Thor, he remembered as the one who had put her finger on a nailhead just as he brought the hammer down. In his fright and anger he had berated her for being so dumb. Fortunately her finger had not become infected.

Mama had a job putting her to sleep at night, so Papa used to sing to her. Sitting in his rocker and holding Peggy in his lap as she looked up at his face, Papa would sing a *komori uta* or lullaby. Among these were Schubert's "Cradle Song," or "Chihō komori uta" of Shimabara Prefecture, or the popular "Nen nen kororiyo, o-kororiyo."

Thor had never been close to his father. He was someone who stood behind a barber chair, clipped untidy hair and shaved whiskers, whiskers so tough Thor could hear the scrape of honed steel separating beard from skin. Papa worked six days a week, on Saturdays all day on his feet, usually without lunch. After supper he would have his sake and doze off over a week-old Japanese newspaper from Seattle.

He was symbolic of so many immigrant fathers who worked from dawn to dusk and beyond in field, office, and shop to establish roots in an unfavorable soil. Unfamiliar with American sports, he could forge no bond on diamond or gridiron.

Papa did not talk much of his gold prospecting days. He was like a war veteran or former concentration camp inmate who is close-mouthed except when sharing a common bond with others. As he cut a miner's hair his memories threw the light of little joys on the tundras of his mind. They helped to alleviate the dreariness of his routine. He did not regret the course his life had taken or resent the responsibility for bringing up a family. But dull embers of a yearning for something more burned in his breast.

His problem was he had no clearly defined personal goal and thereby no motivation. Nothing could be deadlier to a man's soul. He found surcease in the amber light within a bottle. Liquor had ravaged the body that had withstood the worst that Alaskan elements had brought to battle. He was almost to the point of no return.

Mama was something else again. She had no illusions of *hito hata*, raising the banner of success over the old homestead. She was more interested in knowing where the next silver dollar was coming from and how far she could stretch it for the family welfare.

Perpetual motion was embodied in her small frame. She was up before the seagulls and the last to take a bath at night. She was forever cleaning the two bathtubs for miners who came to wash away rock dust, doing their laundry and that of her children, sewing, tidying up the house, and cooking for six hungry mouths.

Among the children she was a mediator, pacifier, teacher, and diplomat, as well as doctor and nurse. She presided over her domain using insightful native intelligence. Though she had a grade-school education, she hardly ever read the newspaper, depending upon Papa for the news. In Mama's strength the children found security.

Mama was a perfect hostess. In the Japanese way she would apologize for the squalid condition of her home (which was quite spotless), the poor food she had to serve (fit for a gourmet), the honor she was being paid by her visitor. As soon as she had seated her guests she was stoking up the fire to heat water for tea. She never gave guests a chance to *enryo*.

One day Thor had an opportunity to observe this custom in reverse when Mama and he visited his friend's family. Gus's mother asked Mama if she would have some coffee and cake. Mrs. Anna Tolquist made the best Swedish coffee cake in town and Thor, who was famished, had his tastebuds on alert for the first bite. To his dismay Mama said, "No, thank you. We just eat."

Thor was indignant. He tried to catch Mama's eye. What she'd said was a downright lie. They hadn't even had lunch. The ghost of his breakfast was a growl in his stomach.

Mrs. Tolquist was a large woman, with the clear skin, blue eyes, and blond hair of her forebears. She caught the gleam in Thor's eyes. "I just heated up some coffee, and maybe Thor would like some milk."

Thor kicked Mama's leg under the table before she could open her mouth. Mama was no fool and took the hint. "Thank you," she bowed.

"Mrs. Tolquist's coffee cake is better than the baker's," Thor said, a compliment their hostess could hardly ignore.

Mama thought, I will have to talk to Tora about this.

This was Thor's first encounter with *enryo,* a restraint or holding back out of consideration that one may be putting another to an inconvenience. *Enryo* was not so obvious within the young members of the Fuse family, who developed in the American way, but it was still the family custom in relation with others. Mama saw to that. Thor was puzzled for years by this little charade where the hostess insisted on your having tea and you refused, though your tongue might be hanging out from thirst. In the end, out of politeness, you accepted.

Thor was to hear of a Japanese student freshly arrived in this country who practiced *enryo.* His hostess took his first refusal as final. He hadn't eaten for twenty-four hours and barely made it back to his room for a can of beans.

These traditions were part of Thor's legacy from his family, from whom he was soon to part.

"Why don't you want to come with us?" Mama asked.

"I don't want to," he said stubbornly.

"You will be alone. Who will feed you or take care of you when you don't feel well? I will be worried sick."

"You worry too much." Thor spoke curtly, trying to stem her pleas.

They were both close to tears.

Ken, who had come to help them pack, said, "Mama, Tora was away on his own all summer. He has grown up."

"Jūnisai!" Mama said. "Twelve years old!" Her tone implied Thor was still a baby.

Mama looked doubtfully between her two eldest sons, at

the other children looking on solemn-eyed, possibly not quite comprehending. She could trust Kentaro, she thought. Since Papa was sick, it was Kentaro who was taking care of them.

"I will be here to take care of Tora," Ken said. "I still don't understand, but Tora has made up his mind to stay. It is a big decision. You are sure? Last chance."

Thor nodded, gulping and not trusting his voice.

He was torn by doubts and fears, but overriding these emotions was this crazy notion that he did not want to be left behind his class at school. Taken in perspective it was not that important, but at this particular moment in his life it was a governing factor. His competitive spirit was so strong that he would think to himself: I won't let those buggers get ahead of me.

He found a certain amount of security being one of the top students. He enjoyed being liked and admired, and he had especially strong ties with his friends, bonds as strong as his filial ones.

Sadao Suda, who had sold this same shop to Mat five years earlier to go prospecting, had bought it back. Since the death of his friend Frank Dulac aboard the *Princess Sophia* the previous October, he had become a recluse.

"It seems," Mat said, with a spark of his old self, "that our lives are twined together."

Suda nodded, his face lighting up like a reflection of Mat's expression. "From the time I gave you poor advice in that Seattle furo—"

"Please don't say that," Mat held up his hand. "You were telling me what I would be up against. The facts."

Suda said, "You have never been sorry? No regrets?"

Mat shook his head. "Prospecting was the high point in my life. And you?"

"If I drop dead now, my life was what I wanted to do. If I had found gold—"

"The stories of our lives will be richer in the telling," Mat said. "From hino maru bento to sourdough." (*Hino maru bento* is a lunch of rice balls with *umeboshi* centers which are, by stretching the imagination, comparable to the Japanese flag.)

They laughed with their faces to the benign Alaskan sky. It was amusement tinged with irony.

As the family was leaving for the wharf, Mama suddenly hugged Thor. They were alone. It was a gesture she would never do outside in the presence of others, whether they were friends or strangers. Thor was taken aback because showing emotion in such a physical way was not a trait of the Fuse family, nor of most Japanese families. Mostly you bowed and mouthed platitudes even though your heart was breaking. Mother and son, he now taller by inches than she, walked along Ferry Way to the pier. Mama was looking forward to seeing her daughter Miyoshi, whose husband, Tatsuo Kurita, had opened a French dry cleaning shop in Seattle.

By coincidence the ship Ken had booked the family on was the *City of Seattle,* the one that had first brought them north. The cannery crew from Funter Bay was aboard. Thor had a brief, joyous reunion with Abe and Hotta. The latter was in rare high spirits. It seemed that Sho Asamura had tried to buy his way into cabin class, but all the accommodations were taken. The poor man would have to sleep and eat with the peasants.

An agreement in the sale of the barbershop was that Suda was to room Thor and feed him until Ken could work out other arrangements. Ken, knowing prospectors and their ways and the life of a bachelor, had misgivings from the start. Suda was a good-hearted man, but not the type to be a foster father, or mother, for that matter. Thor began to show up regularly at the City Cafe for dinner. As he explained to Ken, "Bacon fried with chopped cabbage tastes okay, but not five times a week." Sometimes Suda joined him.

Ken's worst fear had taken root. Further, he gathered from Suda that the roomers he had taken in weren't exactly fit company for a boy. "I can't be choosy," he said, almost apologetically, remembering the conditions of the sale.

Ken confided in Johnson. "That miner in room seven is going Outside to get married," Johnson said. "Tora can move in there."

"Your offer is considerate. Thank you very much. You have been so kind." Ken turned to the practical aspects of the suggested arrangement. "It means board and room. I will pay for him. I owe him that much." He thought of the check Tora had given Mama.

"Maybe he can find part-time jobs. As I think about it, he could type out the daily menu. I will pay him for that."

Harry Nakamura, the oldest Japanese in the town, who had come in for his weekly New England clam chowder and salmon steak, had overheard the latter part of their conversation. He moved from a table to the last seat at the counter to be near them.

"Mr. Valentine," he said, "is looking for an errand boy to help him after school. And Thor can help me on Saturdays at the saloon."

The three men shared a Cheshire cat grin. Thor walked through the front door into a *fait accompli*.

Nakamura was unique. He had bushy eyebrows over large eyes that sloped down at the outer corners, the opposite of the slant-eyed stereotype of Asians. His nose was almost aquiline and had a Roman hook. With his light skin and in spite of his small stature he could have passed for white, possibly with a touch of Comanche.

Nakamura was a veteran of service in the United States Navy, he told Thor. Like those trying to blot out terrible memories, he was reticent about his experiences. It seemed that he had survived the explosion that sank the U.S. *Maine* in Havana harbor on February 15, 1898. Six of his Japanese messmates were among the 260 men who were killed. Their names, for whatever immortality, were inscribed among those carved into the marble walls of the memorial that was erected at the southwest entrance to Central Park in New York City.

The gold rush of '98 lured him to Seattle and then to Skagway. When he viewed the madness that infected normal human beings he withdrew with the tide. Like a piece of flotsam he cast ashore at Juneau. For lack of any skills he became a town porter and made a comfortable living. By this time America was in his heart. Mount Jumbo became his Fujiyama and the tides of Gastineau Channel were enough of the sea that he loved. He never returned to his native land. His only concession to civilization was a vacation Outside.

Soon after school opened Nakamura introduced Thor to Emery Valentine, a jeweler and several times mayor of Juneau.

One Saturday, Thor helped Harry Nakamura clean the Mecca, a restaurant and bar next to Valentine's jewelry store. He listened with his hands on his hips while his mentor instructed him on the art of sweeping and mopping up the floor, cleaning out the spittoons, and polishing the brass rail.

Nakamura frowned at him. "A worker never stands with his hands on his hips," he said. "You are not the boss, are you?"

Thor was surprised. Disrespect had never entered his mind. "No, sir," he said.

He had finished polishing the brass rail that ran in front of the bar when Nakamura came over with a mirror and flashlight. He held the mirror under the rail and turned on the flashlight.

"You polished the top beautifully, but the underside is not as clean as the top."

"But nobody can see underneath," Thor said.

"When you do something you do it one hundred percent," Nakamura said. Thor was rebellious. He didn't see what difference it made. When he had finished, Nakamura pointed to the brass spittoons. "Now those."

Thor looked with distaste at the cuspidors. What a mess, he thought. Dried spittle, chewing tobacco stains, cigarette and cigar butts, nicotine-stained water.

Thor caught Nakamura looking at him with his eagle eyes. Recalling Hotta, Thor realized he was being put to the test.

"You can use gloves," Nakamura said, "but it is easier to wash your hands afterwards.

As Thor went about his chores, he thought of the older boys and wondered why they would want to roll dried horse manure in cigarette paper to smoke, or why they bought cubebs at the drugstore to circumvent the ban on smoking by minors. How disgusting, he thought.

His resentment turned toward Nakamura. "He's making me do all the dirty work."

When they had finished the cleaning Nakamura went to the bar. He made Thor a sarsaparilla ice cream soda and drew himself a draft of beer. As they sat at a wrought-iron table, Nakamura looked quizzically at Thor.

"Would you want to do this all your life?"

Thor finished a sip of soda and thoughtfully punched the ice cream soft with his straw. "I would hate my life," he said. "You do this every day?"

"Every day except Sunday, for more years than I can remember. Like your father, your brother, like most of us Japanese immigrants. You know what Issei are? No? It means first generation. We are the ones who came first from Japan. I came before 1900.

"We did not know English, so we worked on the farms, the logging camps and sawmills, the railroads, the canneries. In the cities we were bellhops, waiters, janitors, short-order cooks. A few of us started our own businesses to serve our countrymen. Or the Americans, like Johnson, the Fukuyamas, the Makinos."

"I worked in the cannery," Thor said.

"Would you want to do that all your life?"

Thor shook his head. He began to realize that Nakamura was teaching him the most important lesson in his life.

Nakamura laughed. "You speak English. You are getting a good education. Use it. Now, I will introduce you to Mr. Valentine. He is a good man. He needs an errand boy."

Valentine left the work bench where he was repairing a watch and came out in front of the showcase. He was not a tall man but was sturdily built. He held his heavy chin in, and though he walked with a cane his back was as straight as a ramrod. He had a military bearing. Like Hotta, Thor thought. He had white hair and a full mustache, and black eyebrows above level, direct eyes.

"Glad to know you, young man. Mr. Nakamura has told me a lot about you. I understand you are bright and industrious. I've seen you around town, always doing something. I could use you to do some delivering, maybe an hour or two after school, a few hours on Saturday. Pocket money."

Thor liked him on the spot. On clear days Thor was accustomed to seeing him sitting in front of his shop sunning himself "for his rheumatism," and smoking his big black cigars. On certain days—for instance, the Emperor's birthday—he would fly the Japanese flag from the flagpole on his Valentine Building. He was a Japanophile and according to some of the Japanese who had visited him his rooms were filled with Japanese memorabilia.

Valentine opened his jewelry shop in 1888. Early on he interested himself in the development of the fire department at a time when the fire truck was no more than a wagon with rubber buckets hanging from its sides. By importing coal from Nanaimo (known to the Japanese as Nana-imo or Seven Potatoes) on Vancouver Island, he helped to break the monopoly on coal that the Pacific Coast Coal Company had on the town. During one of his terms as mayor he was called a czar for what the town council regarded as high-handed methods.

Thor was more impressed as on the way home Nakamura elaborated on ways in which Valentine had helped the Japanese.

In 1910, Nakamura said, a Japanese fishing boat, the *Tokai Maru,* approached within the twelve-mile limit and was intercepted by a Coast Guard ship. An international incident was averted when Valentine and his lawyer reached an agreement with officials whereby it was understood that the ship was seeking food and water when it entered forbidden waters. The ship and crew were then released.

In another case a Japanese was convicted of killing a Mexican in a gambling argument and sentenced to death, the first Japanese in the Territory to receive the death penalty. Through Valentine's efforts the sentence was reduced to life imprisonment. He was released from a federal penitentiary for good behavior after twenty years and sent back to Japan.

(On December 14, 1922, after Thor left Juneau to continue his high school education in Seattle, Valentine was awarded the Fourth Class Order of the Rising Sun and appointed Honorary Consul of Japan for Alaska.)

"It is such good Americans who give me faith in the United

States," Nakamura said. "But there are hundreds more like those who drove the Chinese out of Alaska who will try to drive the Japanese from the United States."

Thor was unaware that an oracle had spoken.

20

The Landslide

MOUNT ROBERTS, WHICH ROSE almost straight as an evergreen-studded wall above the town, was usually a benign, bear-shaped colossus. It was Thor's personal playground. He had explored almost every yard of its slope above Juneau.

He measured the immensity of the mountain by the sweating exertion it took to pull himself up from root to root. On occasion he climbed the zigzag trail through the timberline with a BB gun in search of grouse. The accident in which Gus almost lost his life revealed the fact that the bear had claws.

The mountain gave of its yellow treasure to maintain the economic life of the community. Occasionally, though, it exacted its toll, and Thor would hear the ambulance screaming down Front Street to the office below the stamp mill. The siren was a heart-stopping sound to every wife of a miner. The dead or injured miner would be brought from the bulldozing chamber, where falling rock had crushed him, to the office for transfer to St. Ann's hospital.

The people of the town also learned to live with the danger of a landslide. When Juneau was founded in 1880, its entire area was covered with giant spruce, hemlock, and fir down to water's edge, just like the mountain-islands and sea coast of Southeastern Alaska. As the land was cleared away the network of roots that held the steep slopes of Mount Roberts together was exposed to the erosion of rain and running water. To the concerned citizens the leakage from the flume that carried water from the mine down to the channel added to the danger. But as usual nothing was done about it.

On January 2, 1920, a Friday morning, at 11:30 a.m., a prolonged roar of heavy-throated thunder reverberated across the town for every soul to hear. In the void of silence that followed, alarming screams of ambulances and firetrucks brought the townspeople running through the rain to the heart of the business district.

Thor was studying in his cubbyhole over the City Cafe. Friday, sandwiched between New Year's Day and the weekend, had been a holiday from school. Thor raced up Front Street past the crowd gathered near Goldstein's store, up the flight of steps that led past his former home. He reached the edge of the avalanche and gasped.

From the chaotic mass of broken lumber, partially demolished walls, and household furniture, intermixed with mud, tree trunks, and bushes, he heard cries for help and the moans of the injured. Some men were frantically tearing away the debris to rescue victims. Thor looked several hundred yards up the mountain at the deep wound that marked the path of the landslide.

Days of continuous rain had caused the worst disaster in the forty-year history of Juneau. Undermined by water, the earth had slid down the steep slope, swept across Gastineau Avenue, and carried with it six homes that had piled up beside Goldstein's store. Miraculously, only the edge of the tons of wreckage had scraped alongside the building.

In the first hour ten victims were pulled from the wreckage and rushed off to the hospital. A hasty head count revealed that one, possibly two persons were missing. Who had been in the Larson house, who in the Peterson home?

As usual after disaster, there was the grim jest about one survivor who had been taking a bath and had ridden to safety in his makeshift boat. Or the ironic touch that one of the missing had moved in only a few weeks before from the safety of a home on the tideflats.

Thor was torn between the desire to watch in fascination

and to spread the news. He yielded to the latter and dashed off to the City Cafe, which then became an information center for all the fishermen and whores in the neighborhood.

All excited, Thor raced back to the scene of the disaster. As the short Alaskan day crawled to a close, searchlights were improvised and lights extended from the closest stores and shops. After they pulled aside the larger pieces of debris, the searchers decided that the only way to remove the rest of the mess was to sluice away the earth and mud around the Goldstein building, across Front Street and into the channel waters. Fire hoses were hooked up and men dressed in slickers and hip boots, looking like the devil's own legions in the eerie light, carried on their grim quest.

Ken, when he came off work at midnight, found Thor still engrossed at the scene of the disaster.

"That slide could have wiped out our family," he pointed out to Thor, "if they had still been here and the slide had come down this way a hundred feet."

Thor, more absorbed in actual events than fitting them into perspective, still understood the point his brother was making. In a thoughtful mood they walked back to their rooms over the City Cafe. Residents of houses and businesses located along Front Street, the whole length of which lay under the threat of future slides, retired with a shadow of uneasiness at their backs.

The bodies of two men who had either been smothered to death or killed by timbers were found the next day. In a community of thirty-five hundred, where almost everyone knew everyone else, a pervading sadness touched all.

When the fall term opened, Thor was surprised to see that two Tlingit girls had enrolled in his class. As the teacher introduced them to the class she said they were from the Taku tribe just south of Juneau. Both were shy and inclined to titter to hide their embarrassment. The class learned later that one of them died of tuberculosis, and the second never returned. Thor left Juneau before he learned whether this was a breakthrough in Sheldon Jackson's dual school system.

During the following year of 1921, the Japanese newspaper from Seattle reported the rising demand for excluding Japanese immigrants from the United States. Ken read the accounts with growing concern. What he and Nakamura had feared was taking center stage. The rhetoric of politicians and the vilification of the newspapers were punctuated by the gunfire of night riders.

Nakamura, who had dropped in for his customary chowder and salmon steak, and Johnson leaned over the counter as Ken read a news item on the forcible removal of Japanese farm workers from bunkhouses in the Turlock, California, area.

"Without workers, how can the farmers survive?" Johnson asked.

"From what I have been reading the situation is much more serious. Anti-alien land laws are aimed at driving them off their lands. But I am more concerned about my family. That comes first. Sore wa ichi ban."

"Would you have them return to this?" Nakamura waved his hand over the newspapers.

"The children are American citizens." Ken said firmly. "Their lot, come what may, is here. This is their country."

"You are right," Johnson said, in his positive way. "You must send for them before they pass this exclusion act they are talking about. If you need money—"

"If I can be of help," Nakamura said.

"Thank you," Ken said. "I can manage. Besides, I understand Father has recovered enough to do some work. I have written them to return and have already sent them passage money."

Toward the end of the school term in 1922, Ken learned in a letter from Yonezawa that the family had booked passage for Seattle and would arrive in June. Ken wasted no time and booked Thor on the next ship south after school's end. He felt Thor's future lay Outside.

Like the severing of ties to the past the heavy hawsers splashed into the gray waters of the channel. The S.S. *Alaska*'s propellor churned in protest. Sadness possessed Thor's soul as he waved at Gus and George and John who had come to see him off. They had been his friends and classmates since the first grade.

Six years. And Ken was there. He had given Thor fifty dollars and an envelope from Johnson Tanaka that contained another fifty. He was leaving behind his sense of belonging, of his identity with thirty-five hundred souls among whom he had grown up. He was leaving security.

He looked up at the mountains wreathed in clouds. The thought occurred to him: They could be ramparts against a hostile world. Or, they could be prison walls. It seemed strange that his mind entertained this concept. He felt Mr. Nakamura's comforting hand on his shoulder. He was not quite alone.

The temperature began to fall and giant raindrops bounced on the moving deck. A cold front was passing through, engaging in battle with warm, black, and ugly clouds that threatened the ship's course. Nakamura guided him to the protection of the salon. They watched lightning split the clouds that thundered and reverberated across the islands of the Inside Passage. Though he was not cold Thor shivered. Was this a portent of his future?

Nakamura said, "Good weather will follow this cold front. But you must be prepared for future storms. Just as our older generation suffered and fought through them. You are armed with youth and good English.

"If I wore a sword," he jested, "I would pass it on to you."